GETTING BACK 2 HAPPY

GETTING BACK 2 HAPPY

THE CHRONICLES OF TABBY

JAYLONNA STEVETTE

ISBN: 978-1-950719-42-6 (Paperback)
ISBN: 978-1-950719-43-3 (eBook)

Library of Congress Control Number:

Any references to historical events, real people, or real places are used fictitiously. Names, characters, and places are products of the author's imagination.

SECOND printing edition 2020.

J Merrill Publishing, Inc.
434 Hillpine Drive
Columbus, OH 43207

www.JMerrillPublishingInc.com

CONTENTS

My Deepest Thoughts   vii

1. The Swirl   1
2. Puritan Paul - The Beginning of Happy?   9
3. The Honeymoon is Over   31
4. Present Day Misery   57
5. The Proverbial Straw   85
6. Livin' it up in L.A.   133
7. Part 1: The Destruction   153
8. Part 2: The Aftermath   185
9. Getting Back to Happy   213

About the Author   245

MY DEEPEST THOUGHTS

As I thought about who I wanted to thank for writing this book, way too many people came to mind. For there were those, who molded and shaped me into who I am and where I am headed. There have been many family and friends who have supported me, in one way or another, along this incredible journey. And you all know who you are, and my heart is full of joy.

I first want to thank God, who has always kept me. Whether you acknowledge our Source as God, Universe, Spirit, or any other name, I know that I have always been kept. Source has seen me through the toughest times in my life. I am rising like the phoenix out of the ashes. I am getting back to happy. May I continue to be the best that I can be, in goodness, appreciation, spreading love, and doing my life's work.

To my Mom Deanna Billingsley and my Sister Tracie Fields, you two were and always will be the leading ladies in my life. I love you both for always being my biggest cheerleaders, as I watched you both put your dreams on hold to make sure that others strive to live theirs. I know you are both looking down from above and saying well done. I love you, and may you rest in heaven.

To my children Aaron, Eric, and Erica. Thank you for being the greatest gifts that God has ever given me. I have watched each of you grow into beautiful, amazing adults, and I love all the life lessons that each of you have taught me. You all are beautiful, and each has made my life so much more worth living. Thank you for teaching me how to love unconditionally, but most of all, thank you for believing in me.

Lastly, to Jayvon Woodfolk. It was my greatest desire to write this book with ease, and you provided that in the midst of many storms. Thank you for standing by me in one of the most tumultuous times in my life, and thank you for believing in me also. You were my biggest supporter during this time, and even the mirror to help me self-reflect. I will never forget the tough lessons you taught me to help me grow.

To all of my readers. May you find joy and happiness as you read this book. May Tabby's adventures be just the escape you need to take you back to that special place, Back 2 Happy.

I love you all,

JAYLONNA STEVETTE

THE SWIRL

They say all bad things happen in threes. But what about four, five and six? That's the way my life seemed to be going, a long senseless swirl. It's like being in a tornado, trying to figure out what's the best spot for safety, when in the end the reality is, you're still in the tornado. Every aspect of my life was falling completely apart, and I couldn't seem to get a handle on any of the things in life that were supposed to be important to me.

Here I am, at 45, and my marriage of 10 years, career, and life all seemed to be up in the air. I finally dared to walk away from my controlling husband, but at the same time, my new career that had just taken off was ending just like that. I received a promotion on my job only to receive an "Atta girl" and to train my successor over the next six months effectively. Sure, they don't come right out and say it in Corporate America, but certain things are implied. While dealing with my own personal tragedy, I was delivered a devastating blow by way of my best friend. Cancer in her abdomen had come back, and she needed aggressive treatment and very quickly. All this had me feeling as if I had to be too much to too many people, and I felt broken. And to make matters worse, the role of madam "save the world" had taken a toll on me physically spiritually, and emotionally. The walls were closing in around me, and I didn't even realize it at the time. I had no more energy, and nothing left to give.

As I got up and prepared to get dressed for work, I took a long look in the mirror and began to sigh. I thought about everything that I didn't like staring back at me. My hair is too short, I have too much belly fat. I'm starting to develop bags under my eyes. Not only am I ugly, but my life sucks, so I am bad at adulting. I stopped. I tried to tell myself to snap out of it, but I just couldn't help the thoughts that crept in. Then I looked at myself again and frowned. I thought to myself, you will NEVER be happy. I looked again. I asked myself, "Tabby, will you ever be happy"? Then I said to myself, because yes, I have deep conversations with myself. "Tabby, how can you get back to happy"?

To be honest, that was a question in which I did not have an answer. I had no clue what happiness truly was. I reflected on a time when I thought I was happy. Sure, on paper, everything looked legit. I had a great husband, with a good job he was retired from, one kid in college, and one graduating that year. I also had an amazing career that seemed to be well on its way to taking off. All those things together appeared to be a divine recipe for happiness. But why was I not happy?

Then I remembered part of it. A few years back, James and I hit a serious bump in the road. Since I had just gotten promoted, James decided it was the perfect time for him to retire, although we still had one child who still needed to finish high school. Or should I say, I had a child, my baby girl, Vanessa. My children were not his children, and James had no problem expressing this fact through his words and actions. James had a son, who he really didn't have much of a relationship with. Oh, his son Christopher was present, but the relationship was strained, and you'll see why later on. He even said on one occasion because he couldn't be a father to his own son that he didn't feel comfortable being a father to my kids. Of course, he didn't mention this tidbit of information until after we were married.

So, as he was basking in the glow of retirement, I was working harder, not smarter. You would think that because he was more available, that he would help with the slack that I could not get to. Don't get me wrong, I worked hard and held it down at the house too. For the most part. But with the promotion came extensive travel that I wasn't accustomed to. This left a void in my presence at Vanessa's extracurricular school activities. So, I asked James if he had the time to take Vanessa back and forth to volleyball practice. He made a big deal about some business venture he was stepping into that was getting ready to take up most of his time. We argued:

Tabby: So, you mean to tell me you can't give your step-daughter a ride to practice?

James: I told you I have stuff to do. She's 16. She needs to get her license.

Tabby: Understood. But in the meantime...

James: Listen, YOU need to work this out. This is YOUR daughter. You should've thought about that before you took this glorious promotion of yours.

Tabby: Oh, so we're going back to this? James, we discussed my travel BEFORE I TOOK THE PROMOTION.

James: And you knew what kind of job you were taking. So, it's up to you to make arrangements for her

Tabby: you know what James

James: ok, ok...damn. Can't have shit to myself

Tabby: Fuck it! FINE

And that's how the whole year went. Conversations like that which had left me exhausted. My travel had picked up to about 60% of the time. The little time I had left was spent trying to go to Vanessa's games, college tours, which James refused to go to, and helping support Vincent, my son, who was finishing up his junior year. And to make matters worse, James was true to his word and spent his retirement doing him. He engrossed himself in his food truck venture, which went from part-time to full time. To be honest, James was bringing in more money with that than when he did when he worked. But again, what was mine was ours, and what was his. What was truly left for me?

Our relationship, which had already been deteriorating, turned into short choppy conversations about bills and things around the house. The romance was far, and few between and our sex life was nonexistent. This caused extraordinarily frustrating and lonely nights, which forced me to take matters into my own hands, literally. Our limited sex life had become a series of quickies, where James managed to compose himself for all of four minutes in which I had to attempt to get my penis pleasure. Those four minutes were foreplay to ejaculation with no intimacy, just caveman like lust. Damn, that was frustrating! But what were my options?

1. I could cheat and have a big black beautiful penis inside me, pounding me as hard as the day is long.

2. I could continue to nag James about my sexual frustration while it continued to fall on deaf ears

3. I can take matters into my own hands by self-pleasure

At the time, the best course of action was option 3. James left me no choice. I decided to take matters into my own hands by purchasing some male companionship that I eventually named "Johnson." Johnson was a chocolate bullet about 4 inches long with a curvy tip and 12 speeds. Johnson could take you from pleasure to intense erotica in 0.5 seconds. Johnson became my stress reliever, and Johnson knew exactly what to do to take me to my happy place.

My relationship with Johnson was slow and gradual. I met Johnson at a Pure Romance party, and the way the hostess was working his magic, I knew he had to go home with me! Johnson was short and thick, with a silky dark brown curvy tip. As I watched the hostess give him a whirl, I noticed the movement of the tip could be isolated in circular motions at 6 different speeds. At the same time, the remaining portion of the bullet performed its own action. I was mesmerized and intrigued at the same time. The hostess also said he was the perfect enhancement to couple action. I thought it would be nice for James and me to step out of our comfort zone. At first, my purchase was to try the couple's action, although I knew in my heart that James would not be down.

James had always been prudish in the bedroom. Anything outside of his penis, hands, and sporadic tongue was totally off-limits in our love nest. James felt that HE was all he needed to get the job done, and anything or one that was extra bought feelings of intimidation with him. In times past, I would try to spice things up in the way of massage oils and sexy lingerie. James always had a reserved side, so introducing small items as such was a gradual way to get him open to other things. But of course, I was always shut down. James would make excuses like the fabric I was wearing felt funny, or the smell of the massage oils and perfumes would irritate his allergies. After a while, I felt defeated and stopped making attempts at putting the spice in our bedroom. Even approaching James with "Johnson" would be a leap of faith and far-fetched. I knew if I was going to purchase Johnson that I had an executive decision to make. Hell, I made executive decisions in the boardroom all the time! I knew if I approached the subject of introducing Johnson to our bedroom that it would be, yet another argument ensued. So, I decided that Johnson would be my best-kept secret.

As I recalled my first experience with Johnson, my insides began to tingle. I had just gotten home from the Pure Romance party and had already had a few drinks. Vanessa was at a sleepover, and James had a rib festival to attend in Georgia. So, there it was me, all by my lonesome.

I took Johnson out of the package. I stared at him. I then took my fingers and stroked him up and down, pretended he was a penis. I imagined myself taking a man into my mouth. That was something I really enjoyed. My lower parts began to pulsate at the thought of giving another man pleasure. I took a deep breath and took Johnson in my mouth and thought about who I could fantasize about. I wanted to pleasure someone completely different from James. Who could my lover be? He could be an Italian stallion from the rough side of the tracks, or he could be an African straight from the Zulu tribes in Africa. Either way, he was getting his dick sucked. When I put that penis in my mouth, I take special care to make love to the dick. Giving head gave me so much pleasure, I could orgasm while pleasing my partner. James, however, wasn't so big on oral sex. He gave sporadically, and he had a hard time receiving. Every time I tried to dive deep, he would stop me and turn his attention elsewhere. If I didn't already know what I was working with, I would have felt some kind of way about my head game. But I already knew what my mouth could do. In all these years of marriage, I felt incredibly deprived of doing what I really loved. Giving amazing head was something I happened to be gifted with. I could suck a man's soul out of his body! Unfortunately, because I was married to "Prudish Paul," anything out of his comfort zone was a "no-no." And, I never got to show him what I could really do.

Now that I had Johnson out of the package, I focused for a moment. Thought about my lover. How I would take him in my mouth over and over again. I would play with his penis and tease the tip with every single lick. I took Johnson in my mouth slowly. I pulled him in and out of my mouth as I thought about my lover. He was standing over me, dominating me. I was on my knees and at his mercy, yet he was also at mine. I took him in my mouth slowly. He gasped. I took him deeper and deeper until I couldn't take anymore. I devoured his dick slowly with every single lick as I pushed my mouth deeper and deeper onto his shaft. He grabbed hold of my hair and yelled: "fuck"! I smiled, turned on my Johnson, and turned off the lights.

I opened my massage oil and poured it on Boo Boo Kitty. I rubbed it in and immediately felt the heat on my inner parts. I wanted to explore. And since I was alone, I knew I had all night. I thought about my lover again. Now he was between my legs exploring my love cave. I imagined him stroking my pussy with his hands and licking the wetness off of his fingers. He was delighted with what he tasted and decided he wanted much more. I took Johnson and began to rub him slowly across the lips of my vagina. The vibration against my lips caused my clitoris to stand at attention. My clit began to flicker with anticipation of being erect. I started to stroke myself with the assistance of Johnson and thought about my lover again.

His tongue was amazing, just as good as my mouth. As Johnson vibrated on my lips and my clitoris, I imagined my lover licking me with masterful perfection. He took his time with me. He opened my lips wide. His tongue stroked the inside of my lips and then edged closer and closer to my clitoris. I began to shake. I took Johnson and applied him on top of my clitoris. I changed speeds. Johnson pulsated faster as I took his curved tip and dug him deeper and deeper into my walls. I changed speeds again and thought about my lover. He took my clitoris into his mouth and sucked it like candy. He took it out and licked. Took it back in and sucked. I put Johnson back on my clitoris, and it began and tingle. My legs quivered. I took short small breaths as I stroked Johnson harder and harder against me. My love cave exploded from the inside out, and I felt my release. My lover had done what he set out to do, give me brief pleasure, take me back to happy.

It was times like those in reflection that made me think about the pleasure and pain of happiness. Happiness was Pleasure because the things that you find the most joy in, like sex, can be genuinely ecstatic. Happiness could also be Pain. If you're going through the motions of life, not knowing what you truly want. So even in a lonely existence, one can find happiness if they truly tap into their pleasure zones. And for me, it started with my relationship with Johnson. Good sex, although with myself, was a constant stress reliever in a world where everything else seemed to be falling apart. Johnson was the pleasurable part of the pain of finding happiness.

Now to be clear, to understand what being happy is, I guess you have to know what makes you happy. Outside of my so-called relationship with Johnson, I had gotten away from thinking about the things that made me truly happy. I snapped back to reality, and I looked at myself again and frowned slightly. I looked away, looked again, and tried to smile. I finally did smile. It looked and felt uncomfortable and ugly. I asked myself, are you ugly? Then, I thought to myself, "why would you say that"? And then I thought about the constant battle I had in my mind repeatedly that had to stop. I snapped back to reality and focused on the task at hand, getting ready for work. I guess my happiness would-be put-on hold for yet another time and place. But at least we did the dance.

PURITAN PAUL - THE BEGINNING OF HAPPY?

My relationship with James was an interesting one. When I met him, I was at a place in my life where I felt that I was lost, and since he is a rescuer by nature, he had no problem stepping in. I had just left a relationship with Travis, my children's father. Travis had decided after 6 years of us living together that he didn't know if he was ready to make a commitment. Then 6 months later, he marries some chick he had been working with at his job. AIN'T THAT SOME BULL SHIT! I guess 2 children that he fathered and a whole ass 6-year relationship was not commitment enough.

So, when I met James, I was looking for someone who was the exact opposite of Travis. Travis, by nature, was a strong-willed, take-charge kind of guy. Travis did things on his own terms and in his own time, hence the hesitance of walking down the aisle with me. I learned the hard way that "nagging" is the most ineffective tool a sista can have in her arsenal. Put it away, ladies. After year 5 of being together, I put on the pressure, and it pushed Travis running in the other direction.

Don't get me wrong, I felt justified in my actions. We had been together for 5 years. More like 7 if you count the first 2 years that "technically" didn't count. We started off as a one-night stand. That one-night stand resulted in a surprise pregnancy. When Travis found out, he was excited because he had no children up to then, and like all men his age, he fantasized about his first child being a boy. Travis was excited about the child, but not necessarily excited about the possibility of being in a relationship with me. I think his intention was to hit it and quit it as well. He also told me I was not his "typical type" of woman he dealt with, whatever that meant. We were both on the same page. To be honest, I really didn't want to be with Travis, either. As a matter of fact, I didn't really care for his personality after we fucked. He was borderline abrasive at times and seemed to have jealous tendencies. He spoke what was on his mind without caring how it affected the other person. He also appeared to be paranoid about me being approached by other men or having opportunities to meet other men. His reasoning was he didn't want any other men raising his child. So, it's safe to say our relationship was getting off to a fucked-up start.

Travis would come over and spend the night while I was pregnant. Although we technically were not a couple, we slept together as a mutual arrangement. Hell, we both had needs, and I was carrying his child after all. And the sex, by the way, was amazing. Travis had skills in the bedroom that I had not encountered up to that point. I had a few interesting partners, but sex with Travis was always exciting, eventful, and intimate. With Travis, there were no rules, and he was willing to explore every erogenous zone. I was not that experienced, and to be honest, I was not ready to go to a lot of places that he wanted to go sexually. But Travis knew that and would take it slow and introduce me to only what he thought I was ready for. And so, it went with our relationship; bomb ass sex and no substance. This foolishness went on beyond the birth of our firstborn Vincent. Travis kept the sex exciting, and he didn't care when or where.

One night, Travis just had to make love to me during game night. Even the thought of the memory now makes me laugh. We were all gathered at my girlfriend's house in the burbs. Not the suburbs. The Burbs was a low-income apartment complex that had been newly remodeled, so they looked better than all the others, hence the Burbs. Our game night consisted of video and board games, along with spades and dominos, added to the mix. That night I was wearing a little black baby doll dress with the cutest pair of sandals, and of course, my nails and feet were slayed. Game night was a big thing for us in the hood, and we even had rules for hosting, food, and drinks. We took game night very seriously in the hood, and all violators would not be invited back.

Well, that evening, Travis was drinking a bit more than usual. He was a man who favored dark liquor, which I never had a taste for. Travis was in good spirits and was a little more flirtatious than usual. The more he drank, the more "hands-on" he became. Travis began rubbing my back and arms while trying to lead his to hands to other places. The other couples' thought it was so cute until he kept drinking, then they became concerned that he was going to be sick. So was I. Travis took one last shot that had him running into the bathroom, slamming the door. Travis yelled, "Babe, I need you," and I ran in the bathroom after him. When I got into the bathroom, Travis closed the door and turned off the lights. He whispered in my ear, "Babe, can I taste your pussy right now?' I tried to push him away and said, "stop it, you're drunk."

Travis: Nah baby, I ain't drunk

Tabby: Yes, you are...Stop

Travis: (whispers in her ear) When have you known me to get sick, baby. That liquor makes me one thing..horny. so you gonna let me taste that pussy or what.

I tried to get out of his grip, but it was useless. He held me real close and started saying sexy shit in my ear about how good my pussy tasted. Then he whispered, "Now tell me to stop." I whispered, "stop." He then took one hand and moved it under my dress to slightly feel my wetness. I gasped, then said, "stop." He whispered in my ear, "I feel this wet pussy, and I already know what it's gonna taste like. Sweet, sweet, chocolate. That's my Boo Boo Kitty. Let me taste her." Now let me pause right here for a second. I know when I mentioned my escapade with Johnson earlier, I referred to my lady love as Boo Boo Kitty. Well, she was coined, "Boo Boo Kitty" because of her milk chocolate color with her sweet strawberry tasting center. Hey, those are Travis's words, not mine. He said she reminded him of a pretty, black kitty with a pink bow. Travis and I would do this thing where he would call Boo Boo Kitty, and he definitely expected her to answer! That man made me feel like my pussy was special. Klondike Bar special. But Boo Boo Kitty became her name, and she was always at his beck and call.

As he stroked my pussy and continued to whisper in my ear, begging to taste my pussy, I let out one last moan and said, " Sto... oh baby, please don't stop." Travis pulled my panties off and hiked up my dress. He sat on the edge of the bathtub and pulled me towards him. He laid me on the floor in front of him and pulled my legs up in a quick sweeping motion until my pussy was right in his face. Travis began to lick my lips until I was almost about to cum. He then began to suck on my clitoris, taking it in his mouth and rotated between licking and sucking. My legs began to tremble. At that moment, I forgot where I was, and I began to moan loudly. Travis begged me to cum in his mouth as he licked my clitoris and sucked her wetness. I didn't disappoint. Travis then picked me off the ground and sat me right on his dick. Damn, it felt like heaven as I bounced slowly up and down on his shaft. As I bounced, he pulled me in slowly. I could feel every inch of his dick going in and out of me. I gasped as he dug deep in my pussy. Travis began to pick up the pace. I matched him. He dug deeper, and I moaned. My clitoris began to flicker. I moaned loudly. He said, "cum all over this dick, baby." I gasped louder. He dug deeper in me, deeper than he had ever before. I felt the pleasure and the pain, and I yelled, "Yes, Daddy, you all up in this pussy!" I felt his dick pulsate. I knew he was about to cum. I started saying, "I feel that daddy, yes. Come for me, baby" his dick throbbed again, I knew he was on the edge. I moved my hips in a swirl type motion. He yelled, "Oh shit!" I felt his intense pulsating as he dug deeper and deeper in my walls. I yelled, "Oh God, I'm Cumming!" Travis let out a roar and exploded inside me.

Travis turned on the lights, and we looked at each other and laughed. I couldn't believe what we had just done, and I was trying to figure out a way to conceal what happened. We both took a hoe bath and washed our private parts. I got myself together and straitened up as best I could. Travis then looked at me and told me to leave the bathroom first. AIN'T THAT A BITCH! So, we immediately got into what we thought was a whispered argument. I found out quickly that when you're drunk, you don't do anything in silence. As we are "whispering" about who should come out of the bathroom first to not make it look so suspicious, my girlfriend says, "How bout yall both come out! We can hear ya, you know." The rest of the crew started laughing, and we both came out of the bathroom, embarrassed slightly. At least I was. All the men seemed to have a smirk on their faces. Of course, impressed with Travis and his conquest with their beating their chest asses. What could I do from there but apologize to my hood hostess and continue with the night? That's exactly what I did. Some of the women laughed it off, while others looked at me like I was a hoe. But oh well, I mentioned earlier there was protocol to this game night shit. Needless to say, we were mysteriously left off the guestlist for the next few months. I guess it didn't really matter because I discovered I was pregnant. Again…

The second pregnancy happened within a year of Vincent. By then, it was apparent to both of us that we would be together for a while. Unfortunately for us, sex was the only thing we seemed to get right in the relationship. Travis was spontaneous and full of sexual energy. Still, he didn't understand that a relationship took place most of the time outside of the bedroom. So, after having two kids with what felt like little emotional help, my requests turned into nagging. His desire to fulfill my requests turned into resentment. And in the end, it was toxic for both of us. Despite our one-sided relationship, I really loved Travis. But he totally fucked my world up when he quickly married someone else after our split. I was furious. So furious that I was on some petty shit and continued fucking him for the first two years, he was married. That accomplished nothing for me but a wet ass and more anger issues. I needed some time to myself after that to regroup. One thing was certain; however, I knew when I was ready to get back in the game, my new man would be NOTHING like Travis. That was a promise I intended to keep. And that is how I met James.

James was a General Manager at a warehouse who was up for another promotion when I met him. As a GM, he had over 50 direct reports that were in our office and located in California as well. They were making him a Regional Manager, which would increase not only his direct report total and responsibility but his paycheck significantly. That really impressed me because he was a go-getter. I was a customer service phone operator at the same place. Although we worked in the same building, our lives would typically never cross paths because warehouse workers, managers, and customer service were all from completely different worlds. I happened to meet James for the very first time in a semi damsel in distress scenario. James had the pleasure of saving me for the first of many times, at the vending machine.

I was on my afternoon break and decided to take a quick walk. I wanted to break up the monotony of what the current day had presented. Calls were coming in back to back that day, and it felt like I couldn't breathe. In addition to that, it just happened to be the anniversary of the day, Travis, and I hooked up for the first time. That was the icing on the cake. The last thing I wanted to do was be at work answering over 100 phone calls from whining customers demanding discounts on their orders. I wanted to be in a bar having a drink, or in a ball curled up somewhere eating a gallon of ice cream and feeling sorry for myself. Nah, I did that yesterday. The bottom line was that I had moped about Travis way too long, and he had moved on. So, where was love for me? Wasn't karma supposed to be a real thing? Then how come I get done dirty, and he rides off into the sunset. Fuck me hard. As I let my thoughts wander about the reality of my present situation, my legs ended up taking me to a part of the warehouse that goes less ventured, the vending machine. I decided at that moment, it was the perfect time to get some chips to take back to my work area. I usually didn't indulge in junk food. Still, I had forgone my lunch because of "business needs," according to my "supervisor." I was starving and grateful we were in a factory. Otherwise, folks would have been able to hear my stomach growl. I looked in the machine and did a quick scan for something semi-healthy. Nothing but some old peanut and trail mix. I moved to plan B; potato chips. Potato chips were my constant companion, and today I needed them to get through the rest of the day. And besides, those sour cream and onion potato chips were screaming my name, and who was I to ignore them? After I put my money in the machine and made my selection, my chips got stuck midway. Son of a bitch. I hit the machine as hard as I could. Nothing. I shook the machine violently and let out the sound of a battle cry as the snacks in the machine moved from side to side. Still nothing. I sighed loudly and turned to walk away and ran right into James.

Tabby: Oh, I'm sorry

James: Don't worry about it. You need some help?

Tabby: Nah, I'm good. I gotta get back to work.

James: Are you sure? So, I have to assume that you were banging and shaking the vending machine violently for no reason?

Tabby: Ok, ok you got me

James: I see that you have something stuck in this machine. According to the policy here, you have two options-shake the hell out of the machine, hoping your item falls, put more money in the machine; or, do the appropriate thing and report this to management.

Tabby: That's three options

James: ok. You have three options. But since I'm management, I think option three is the best one. My name is James, by the way.

Tabby: I'm Tabitha. But my friends call me Tabby. Wait, you look familiar. Are you James Taylor from the pictures in the main hallway? Oops! Hi! I'm Tabby. Tabby Monroe. I really gotta go. My break is almost over.

James: Ok, Tabby. Nice to meet you. But stay here. Don't worry about your break. Let's get this taken care of for you.

And the rest was history. James spent the next 6 months, calling in favors at the job and making my life easier. It started off with getting me time off the phones to do special projects. My name started getting out there as a subject matter expert on calls, and I even got a promotion to the Customer Service Supervisor. Meeting James had turned out to be a good thing. I did notice, however, that although James was happy for me, he reminded me that a man is ultimately the provider. He also wanted to take credit for all the good things happening in my life. And because I know a man needs his ego stroked, I fed into it along with him.

James was confident in who he was and what he wanted, which was a wife and family. He was forthright about it and made his intentions clear from the beginning. I can recall him having a candid one-sided conversation with me that went something like this: "I'm at a place in my life where it's time to settle down. I am getting older, and I am a businessman. I don't want my time wasted. I just got promoted again, and I have an awesome career ahead of me where I can provide for a beautiful woman and her children if that's the direction this goes. That beautiful woman must decide if she is willing to live a life with me. I feel like because I have created this amazing life and career that I deserve every blessing coming my way. I know my worth." As I look back on it now, I can see the arrogance in that whole conversation. But when you're hungry for attention and respect after being hurt and someone throws you a bone, it can be easily mistaken for meat.

I'm not gonna lie though. His confidence was on ten. He wasn't the best thing to look at, but he knew how to wine and dine me, and he had no problems taking care of my household either. I mentioned he was a rescuer. His logic was that he understood the plight of the single mother, after all he had a baby mama. He also managed to brag and complain simultaneously about the amount of child support he paid. It was very arrogant yet impressive at the same time. When Travis moved out, it left me with additional bills that I never had to budget for and didn't have a clue how to make ends meet. But when I met James that changed. With my promotion came a raise that went a long way. I didn't have to use that money on bills because James said as his woman it was his responsibility to take care of my rent. Again, he understood what single mothers endured so it was his way of giving back. In the beginning I refused because my pride wouldn't let me. But James told me the help would only be temporary until I got to a place where I was comfortable. As I look back on the situation, I can't help but wonder if a part of me looked at him as a long-term solution to a temporary problem. As I watched my savings account grow, I kept my mouth shut and began to ignore all the little red flags I started to see.

James was really into me. Although my feelings were not as strong as his, I felt a sense of obligation to the relationship because of his financial contributions. In my mind it wouldn't be right to break off the relationship when he had put so much into it financially. So, when James wanted to make us exclusive, the answer was an easy one. We celebrated our exclusivity with a romantic night out, in which he gave me my first official Tiffany box. He assured me there would be more where that came from, and I was very pleased that I decided to take our relationship to the next level. I mean, how bad could it have been. He cared for me, provided for me, and now wanted to make me his.

This new level in our relationship also meant taking our sex life to the next level. Although we had been seeing each other for six months James tried his best to be a gentleman. He said he wanted to show me something different because I was a lady and he wanted to treat me as such. At this point in our relationship, James and I had only made out mostly. We did a lot of heavy kissing, while his hands roamed my body but that was it for the most part. That left me horny as hell. If I had a pair of balls, they certainly would have been blue. Seeing someone for months with limited sexual contact can be extremely frustrating and leaving you wanting more. Now don't get me wrong, when done right one can experience an orgasm through their clothing. And it was an encounter like this with James that had me longing to see exactly "what that dick do."

I let my mind wander back to the night that we made it official. We were out at an exclusive jazz club where some of the hottest locals were showcasing their talents. It was a private member only club where the "Who's Who" of the business community held memberships. James promotion gave him access to this club as a perk. James liked to take me to places like that because in his mind he was showing me the finer things in life. As the musicians played their melodic tunes the soulful singers bellowed beautiful lyrics that grabbed the heart and soul of the listeners. The atmosphere was amazing. The place was decorated with white angelic fabric that billowed as the wind blew. Couples all over the room were gazing in each other's eyes or holding each other close on the dance floor. James order champagne with dinner. We drank the whole bottle and talked and laughed and danced. Every couple was in their own world and although it was a jazz club it felt very intimate. It felt like a new beginning. Wow, it felt like happy. Happy yes. I think I was happy.

After an amazing night of dinner, dancing, and jazz music we had come back to my place for a night cap. I poured two shots of Patron Platinum, his glass had a little bit more liquor than mine. I was trying to spice things up and that Patron was for special occa-sions. Hell, it was $185 a bottle. And tonight, there would be two special occasions;

1. I was officially his woman, and

2. Tonight, we were doing the damn dang

We were having great conversation and I laughed at his corny ass money jokes he liked to tell. But this time I was not laughing to get through the night. I tried to really listen and to see where he was coming from. This was a money man. And if he wanted to tell corny as money jokes while taking care of me and mine, I was all for it. James switched gears and reached out and kissed my hand. He began showering my arm with kisses until he reached my shoulder. His kisses were slow and sensual. He then nibbled on my neck. My neck tingled and so did my Boo Boo Kitty. He nibbled and licked my neck and all the hairs on my body stood to atten-tion. My pretty Kitty was so aroused by what James had to offer and tingles began to intensify. Nah that bitch didn't tingle, that bitch throbbed. After all it had been a while and all that build up from six months of "making out" had me thinking tonight would finally be the night. We had an such an amazing time earlier and we both had a little more to drink than we should have so it was definitely on!

The neck nibbles turned into passionate bites and sucks. My body was beginning to heat up. He then planted his lips to mine, and our lips parted lightly as our tongues desired to do a slow methodical dance. I loved to kiss. We did that for about ten minutes straight without coming for air. James was an amazing kisser. As he kissed my mouth, his hands began to explore my body. He took his hands and begin to caress my nipples in a circular motion, then up and down. I got hotter. I took my hands and begin to stroke his manhood through his slacks. I could feel him growing bigger and bigger. I was pleased by what I saw and felt. As I stroked him, he released soft moans of pleasure. I began to slow down my strokes, and he slowed down caressing my nipples at the same time. Our hand movements were in sync.

The energy we felt between each stroke was electrifying. He then moved down to my stomach, then to my thighs. My juices began to flow. Now I didn't want to be a thot, but he was turning me on. I decided to help him out a bit by opening my legs to reveal my red panties underneath my dress. As I kissed his mouth and stroked his shaft he slowly edged down to my thighs. James made his way to my love box and took his fingers and stroked her so sensually. He brushed his fingers lightly first against Boo Boo Kitty. Lightly and slowly until my juices began to build. I begged him for more. He stroked some more, but lightly brushing and barely touching this love box that was screaming for his attention. My breathing intensified. I looked at him with an expression of pleasure and pain at the same time. He looked back at me. Lightly brushing Boo Boo Kitty. Still. I could feel his energy and I wanted him in that moment.

His strokes intensified. He was stroking my pussy without parting my lips. I was on the edge of exploding. He looked at me intensely and moved his hands back to my nipples. Played with them through my blouse. I wanted his mouth on my twins, and he could tell. He obliged but didn't take them out. His hands traveled back to Boo Boo kitty. He stroked her though my soaked wet panties. James then did something that surprised me and took me to a place of climax. By now my legs were wide open ready to receive. James grabbed my panties and began rubbing them against my lips. I began to cream. He took a portion and rubbed on my clitoris. She began to swell. I begged for the dick. He whispered in my ear not yet, I just want to please you. He tongued my ear and rubbed my clit with my panties at the same time. I felt his breathing. I stroked him some more. His breathing increased. Mine accelerated too. He looked at me intensely. We stroked each other. His eyes narrowed, and his shaft began to pulsate. His stroke intensity increased. I closed my eyes and my clit flickered. I opened my eyes and looked into his. We both had decided to come together, without speaking a word into the universe. We stroked faster, together. I moved my hips into his fingers and imagined just the tip of his penis rubbing up against my soaked vagina. As I had this pleasurable thought, we looked into each other's eyes, and we both exploded at the same time. James kissed me passionately and then immediately became embarrassed. I was confused. He jumped up quickly and excused himself from my house, dick still in hand. When he got home, he apologized for allowing himself to lose control. What the hell? that was weird.

When we spoke the next morning, I reassured James that it was ok, but James said he didn't want to show me any disrespect in any way. My first thought was about how romantic that it was that James had respect for me. That was a stark difference from Vanessa and Vincent's dad. Travis was never outwardly disrespectful. But the shotgun marriage was the ultimate sign of disrespect. The simple fact that he was able to marry another whole ass woman after 6 months was an indicator that he obviously had something else going on. We were supposed to be a one-night stand. There's no respect in that. A woman knows what respect looks like, and when I looked back, I saw all the signs. I also saw the early signs with James, but because he treated me so well, I thought it was worth seeing the direction in which our relationship would take.

James loved spending time with me. He would take me to all kinds of fancy restaurants, shopping sprees, and the best shows that would come to town. And true to his word, he kept his hands to himself. Outside of a passionate kiss goodnight, he was always on his best behavior. I found it kind of romantic, yet a bit frustrating at the same time. I was also still a woman who was very much alive and had needs that were going unfulfilled. My relationship with Travis had been may things, but sexually unfulfilling was not one of them. As a matter of fact, it was Travis's skills in the bedroom that kept me in the relationship. Sex was the glue that kept us together. He was quite an accomplished lover, who didn't mind trying new things. Travis was the master teacher, and showed me how to truly learn, explore, and appreciate my body. And to go from feast to extreme famine was not on my agenda. I NEEDED to be pleased. However, for the sake of monogamy I decided to curve those needs until James and I had OUR night together. After all, I wanted to be respectful of what we were building. But let's just say there were many lonely nights.

Nine months into the relationship, James decided he wanted to have "the talk." As you can tell James was always direct in communicating what he wanted when he wanted it. Oh, there was no mystery with this that I had to uncover, he made it very obvious in his conversation:

James: Tabby, baby it's time we had "the talk"

Tabby: The talk?

James: You know, THE TALK.

Tabby: James, can you be a little more clear

James: Ok. We've been seeing each other for a little over nine months. And I really like you. A whole lot. Enough to make you my wife.

Tabby: James, what are you really…

James: I know it's only been nine months, but I know where my life is going and what I want. Tabby, I love you. I love the way you allow me to take care of you, and spoil you, and I want to do that all the time. As a matter of fact, that's what you deserve. So, What I'm asking is… (pulls out a Tiffany box and looks at it). Here we are box number two. I'm a little disappointed in myself. I promised to show you the finer things in life, and I haven't really had the chance to do that. If you agree to be my wife, I'll spend the rest of my life living up to that promise. Tabby, will you be my wife?

Tabby: James, I really don't know what to say..

And in that moment, I didn't, but I allowed that shit to go down. I got caught up in the moment and said yes. I said yes! Why not, I was happy wasn't I? My yes was a yes for a few reasons, and here's what I thought about in that moment. It was quick, a matter of about 3.5 seconds. Oh, you can't leave an answer to that question in the air for too long. Here is why I got caught up and said yes:

1. Vincent and Vanessa were two of them. In essence 1 and 2. Vincent and Vanessa were my pride and joy. I was looking at showing them that they can have a life greater than we already had.

2. I also fell in love with the idea of being in love and being married. James was so good to me and I knew he really cared about me. But was it love? I really didn't know. He was nice to me so maybe in his mind he really did love me. I started having a conversation with myself, (Yes, I did that even back then).

Tabby: Tabby, what are you gonna do..he's nice, generous, loves you provides for you. You can grow to love him…Wait what? Hold up…grow to love him, that's not enough is it? Yea, you can grow to love him. And girl…He already hinted in the past about a honeymoon out of the country, Paris or Italy or something. That sounds so romantic….just do it. Do it girl do it!

Let's keep it real, I LOVED being financially provided for. James had already proven to be a financial asset to my household by supplying money for rent and utilities. All my money was going straight to the bank and taking care of the kids. They were living really good these days! James also loved taking me out and sparing no expense when he did. Damn that felt good. It felt like a whirlwind. And this man was promising a lifetime of this. Why not sign up for it?

James: Tabby…

Tabby: Yes, James..The answer is Yes! I WILL BE YOUR WIFE!

And that's how that shit all went down…

Shortly after the proposal, James decided he did not want to have a long engagement. He had talked it over with his pastor who was in complete "agreement." His pastor? "Agreement"? Wait a minute, he never mentioned this before. Well, that might explain a few things. The resistance to have sex, and the guilt of "almost" having sex all made sense now. However, I can't believe I had spent nine months with this man, and he had never mentioned he went to church or that he even practiced religion. How can that even be possible? Now, I was all for a short engagement, but I had a few ideas for the wedding of my own that I didn't want to be deprived of. But first, we had to have a talk about him being a man of God and never bringing it up before now. Maybe he thought I would judge him. Don't get me wrong I had nothing against Christian men. I just never considered dating one. I often wonder though if I would have known upfront would I still have taken this path? I thought about this all day and I needed answers. So, I asked James over to talk about the engagement. In typical fashion, James pulls up in my apartment complex in his BMW 325i. He loved to show off the BMW to my neighbors, so they could see that I was coming up in the world. I opened the door and he greeted me with a kiss.

Tabby: Hey baby, have a seat

James: My beautiful fiancé! (He kisses me on the lips) typical woman! Wanna get right to the wedding planning!

Tabby: (Smiles) James, I wanna talk about the wedding yes, but let's talk about your religion first.

James: You mean my relationship with Christ?

Tabby: Yes, that.

James: Well 3 years ago when I had a break up with my kid's mother…

Tabby: Your kids' mother? Wait a minute, back up

James: Yes, I you know I have a son, Christopher. He's 12 now. The one I'm paying all that damn child support for.

Tabby: I am very aware of the significant amount of child support you pay.

James: Then why do you sound surprised by that? Well anyway, our break-up was bad, me and Keisha. She wouldn't let me see Christopher. She felt like if we weren't going to be together then I didn't need to be around my son. So, I prayed about that whole situation. I wasn't a praying man at the time, but I was hurting. It was in my sadness that I felt like God wanted me away from the situation. I moved to another city to heal. And that's when I found Christ. And that's when that vindictive woman went after me for child support.

The conversation became so loaded in my mind at that time. My Spidey senses were starting to tingle. Concealing his religion bothered me, but I was also picking up a vibe when he talked about his ex. I thought to myself, "think fast." I needed to address both concerns before we could move forward, but I didn't know what, if anything, I was addressing with his ex. This was just a feeling, I couldn't bring that up, could I?

James: Earth to Tabby...You still with me?

Tabby: Ok. So, James, don't you think your religion was worth disclosing to someone you say you want to share your life with? I don't understand the secrecy.

James: You mean, my relationship with Christ? And that's why I'm sharing it now. Pastor said I needed to tell you because we are building a life together.

Tabby: Pastor said? Ok, this might be an issue.

James: The Bible says to let your light shine before men, so they see your good works and glorify your Father, who is in heaven. Has my light not shined before you? Do I have to run around yelling, "I'm a Christian" from the top of my lungs? I'm a good man. My works alone should have told you I'm a man of God. And God has been good to me!

Tabby: So, you're saying that I should have just figured this out after spending time with you for nine months? Ok, gotcha. What else don't I know? Should we even be getting married right now? I'm so serious.

James: Baby, there is nothing else to know, I promise. In our ministry, we live by the teaching of doing good works. Letting our actions speak for our connection to God. That is why I don't run around carrying a Bible. Although I do live by the word of God.

Pause here. This is the same man that I told you was drunk earlier. We drank all the time together. Isn't religion against that? Some of what he was saying was a little different than what I was used to seeing in churches and religion. I decided since I had already agreed to marry James, I could at least hear him out on the conversation about his God and his church.

James: I think you would like it! And as a matter of fact, I want you to meet Pastor Doug. He's really down to earth. He's more like a teacher and not a preacher. Jesus was a teacher, you know.

And that was the end of the conversation. As I look back on it, I find the insanity of it all astounding. My fiancé had withheld another side of his life from me for nine months. But the most absurd part of this twisted tale is that I was going along with it, and he had convinced me to meet Pastor Doug in his chambers. When we arrived at the church, Pastor Doug's chambers were exactly that.... a chamber.

Pastor Doug's office was the size of an average home in our local area. I'll repeat that his OFFICE was the size of a home. It was like having a house inside of a church that I had never seen before. The foyer area to the office had a purple marble floor with two gigantic pillars that sat on each end of the entrance. Two lions sat at the entrance on top of the pillars, and above the foyer area hung an angel with the scripture, Matthew 7:14: "But small is the gate and narrow is the road that leads to life, and only a few find it." His office had a front room area that was decorated with plush oversized couches and eclectic furniture that looked odd but seemed to all go together. I could tell this man had all the finer things in life. He had expensive-looking art on his walls and around his workspace. There were also pictures of him with celebrities, preachers, and celebrity preachers.

I was amazed at the beauty of everything I was taking in but uncertain as well. Everything in this house-sized chambers smelled of fortune and money, and it made me question everything I knew about religion.

Pastor Doug was just as James had mentioned, very personable. He came into a room and commanded your attention with his looks and aura. Pastor Doug was wearing crisp grey Gucci slacks with a red sweater. The Gucci logo on the sweater matched the grey in the slacks. This man definitely had swag. He was young, energetic, and had a personality that instantly drew you in. It also didn't hurt that he was easy on the eyes to look at. Pastor Doug had charisma, but he seemed genuinely passionate about how he made a living. Pastor Doug shared his own personal life stories. Although they seemed purer, he shared them in a way that you could relate to spiritually. Pastor Doug didn't have the sex, drugs, and Hip-Hop story the rest of my peers had, but tied the experiences he shared to how they applied in his life spiritually. He prided himself on being a man that found Christ fairly early in life. He also talked about how finding Christ early has helped him avoid many pitfalls in life. Pastor Doug was incredibly proud of himself for saving his first romantic encounter for his wedding night. He mentioned being tempted many times while single, but following God's law, and saving himself for his wife, was the best thing he ever did for himself and for his wife. And for that alone, I was impressed. Pastor Doug at that moment, went and retrieved a picture of his wife. She was STUNNING! She was a beautiful light-skinned petite woman with supermodel features. She looked like a real-life light-skinned barbie. But what impressed me most was how much love and adoration he had for his wife. I thought to myself if this man loves his wife like this, and James is in his church, it could only be a good thing, right? So, in just a few short hours, Pastor Doug had won me over.

Before we left his chambers, Pastor Doug decided to pray over our upcoming union. As he prayed and "spoke in tongues," Pastor Doug said he heard the Spirit of the Lord say that he wanted our union to be quick. He said God had amazing things to do through us as a couple, and he didn't want his work delayed. Pastor Doug started Rocking back and forth and speaking in tongues again.

Pastor Doug: HONDA LA HONDA LA HONDA LA!!! I feel the spirit of God saying..HMM... God is saying 3 months, yes children, 3 months is all the time you need to get your affairs in order and to become as one.

Wait? Was he supposed to be God, right now? I was getting confused. Even his voice changed up a bit. Pastor Doug continued to lift his hands in the air and continued to speak in tongues.

Pastor Doug: HONDA LA OHHH BABABABA! The Spirit of God is saying the number 3 represents the Father, the Son, and Holy Spirit. Do you know how blessed you are? The fact that you have been together for nine months is prophetic. The number nine is an exponent of three…OH, GLORY!

James: Hallelujah! THANK YOU, JESUS!

What was I experiencing? More of this went on for about 15 minutes or so. I observed as Pastor Doug and James begin to shout in unison about all the wonderful things that God had planned for us. After the "Holy Ghost" party ended, Pastor Doug suggested that James and I get married based on the number 3. He also reminded us of how God wanted us to do this quickly. Pastor Doug asked us to search our hearts to determine when to get married. He also suggested 3 weeks or 3 months. Pastor Doug felt anything beyond that was outside of the will of God.

Pastor Doug looked at both of us. "Have you searched your hearts?" he asked. I was thinking to myself, damn! Yes, even in the house of God, damn. I felt like this Pastor, who had just won me, was putting pressure on me. He must have sensed my uneasiness because he reached out with a reassuring hand on my shoulder. Pastor Doug started talking about moving quickly when the spirit moves, and when the spirit is speaking. He said the uneasiness I felt was normal because I was not used to moving with the spirit. He told me to trust my instinct with the number 3 and decide in the spirit. I had no idea what that meant, but I decided to play this little game. James wanted to get married in 3 weeks. He said he wanted to be obedient to God and move quickly. I opted for 3 months. They both looked surprised, but I wanted to slow this train down, at least, a little bit. Pastor Doug suggested we take some personal time to talk it out and come to a decision before the day was out. We both agreed.

In the end, after another discussion later that day with Pastor Doug, we decided on 3 weeks. The reasoning behind it was that, according to James and God, I was entering a new season with marriage that requires submission. This first act of submission in surrendering my proposed wedding date was pleasing unto the Lord, and I would set a fantastic precedence for my marriage. Plus, submitting to my husband would create an atmosphere for God to come in and do miraculous things. After all, it was in the holy scriptures. That was their logic with this; James and Pastor Doug, that is. In my mind, it went a little something like this; after James and I left the Pastor's office, James decided we could not move forward in our day without coming into agreement. He felt like this was our first test as a couple, and he wanted us to pass with flying colors. "Let's give the devil a black eye," he said. The funny thing is I had never heard him talk about God this much in the whole nine months we were together. James was more religious than I had thought. However, when he spoke to me in the manner that I grew to know and be happy with was when I gave in. James asked me to trust him. He asked me to trust everything that I already knew about him. He said he loved me and would take care of me, and it didn't matter if we got married in 3 weeks, months, or years. He had me at just trust me. I trusted James, and we decided to take this journey of compromise together.

I took a leave of absence from work and put together the most amazing wedding I could muster in 3 weeks. Oddly enough, things fell right into place. Our wedding was elegant, and the guest list was small, but we had the most important people in our life there. For me, it was my kids and my best friend. James had his best friend and a few close colleagues from work. After the reception, James told me how much he appreciated how I put the wedding together so quickly. He knew I made a huge sacrifice, and he had a surprise for me. When we were wedding planning, we had discussed getting married and situated and then taking a honeymoon later. I was kind of disappointed, but again, I was starting a new chapter of compromise. Well, in James fashion, he made everything right. I looked up to see we were going in the direction of the airport.

Tabby: James, where are we going? Are we really going on a honeymoon?

James: Yep, sure are. SURPRISE!

Tabby: Wow, Baby! I had no idea.

James: Yea, while you were busy planning the wedding, I was up to this.

Tabby: Where are we going?

James: Our itinerary is in the glove box

I opened the glove box. There was nothing there but a medium-sized Tiffany Box.

Tabby: What the…. Oh, James, it's BEAUTIFUL!

And it was. It was the most beautiful tennis bracelet I had ever seen. It had emeralds and diamonds beaded together, and the name "Tabby" was engraved in gold. Oh, James had definitely won me over with the Tiffany bracelet. He knew that I loved receiving beautiful gifts. But it wasn't the gift that won me over. It was the sincerity and appreciation he felt for me. And at that moment, I was truly happy. I didn't find out where we were going until we got to the airport, and I think James planned it that way. James had also made it up to me by taking me to Italy on our honeymoon. As we set sail to happy, we were off to the best start ever.

THE HONEYMOON IS OVER

The honeymoon phase of a relationship usually deals with the beginning of the relationship, where all facets operate on all its best cylinders. The communication, love, and sex are generally at their peaks because the couple is still putting their best foot forward in the form of their "representative." The representative is the symbol of all things perfect in your life. This alter-ego of a person is all you want yourself to be. Your representative is usually 50 times nicer than you are and will usually tolerate 100 times more of the BS in the beginning for the sake of harmony and trying to keep up appearances. Nine times out of ten, your representative shows up in the honeymoon phase, and that's who your partner falls in love with. Since our whirlwind romance only began 9 months prior, I would say both of our representatives were front and center. Just like the honeymoon phase has an ending, so does the appearance of the representative. Unfortunately, when our honeymoon ended, so did the phase.

We touched down from Italy on a brisk Sunday morning. I was still basking in the glow from our honeymoon. Italy was just as romantic as I imagined. We stayed in Rome, but also visited Venice and Tuscany. There was fine dining, plenty of romantic tourist spots, and most of all, we did couple's spa activities. While in Venice, James paid for a romantic boat ride on the Grand Canal. The Grand Canal was nothing short of beautiful. As our boat rowed through the 2 miles of river, we took in all the fantastic scenery. We got some unbelievable photos along the way. Couples in love were in boats along the canal and posted in several spots on land in restaurants and shopping centers. The whole atmosphere was truly breathtaking. James spared no expense for me. So, imagine my surprise when I looked over at him to realize he had a somber expression on his face all the way from the airport. I asked him what he was thinking. He told me he had such a great time that he didn't want it to end. I shared that sentiment.

We got unpacked and settled in for what was supposed to be our last night of "freedom" before Vincent and Vanessa would return. My sister agreed to keep the kids while we went on our honeymoon. James lit the outside fireplace, and I poured the wine. We nibbled on light snacks and were settled in and relaxed. As we snuggled on the patio, James' cell phone rang.

James: Hello….Uh yea uhm Keisha?

Hold up? Keisha? The baby Mama? The only mention he has ever made of her is about child support. Why would she be calling him? James looked at me and kissed me on the hand and walked from the patio back in the house. Five minutes later, he returned with the same somber look as when we touched down. I asked him if everything was ok. He said, "not really." James paced a few times and took a long deep breath. He sat down and asked me to sit next to him.

Tabby: James, what's the matter?

James: You're not gonna believe this (grabs his head in his hands), man, oh man.

Tabby: What's wrong? Is it Christopher? Is he ok?

James: It's everything, man, I'm being tested right now. Why God? Man, I need to talk to Pastor Doug.

Tabby: James, if you don't tell me what's going on…

James: Keisha and Christopher just landed at the airport. She's moving here with my son.

Tabby: Excuse me? What do you mean she's *moving here* with your son?

James: She called me and said she and Christopher needed a ride to the hotel

Tabby: Are you kidding me? James, I'm confused. Did you know she was moving here?

James: I'll figure all of this out later. I'm gonna pick them up and then talk to Pastor Doug when I'm done. We'll pray and figure this thing out.

He grabbed his keys off the counter and kissed me on the lips lightly. He rushed towards the door and said he'd be back soon. I walked over to the fire pit and put the fire out in the fireplace. So much for our last day together. I sat with my head in the clouds trying to figure this shit out. Why would the woman that refused to allow him to see his son suddenly move to the same city that he resided in? I thought their relationship was strained. It didn't make sense. I couldn't wait for James to return so I could get some answers.

A few hours later, when James returned, he said he had a chance to get a face to face conversation with Pastor Doug after he dropped Keisha off at her hotel. He seemed to be in better spirits. James explained that Keisha was working for a manufacturing company that was experiencing layoffs. Her assembly line was relocated here, so to keep her job she moved here. That made sense to me. And I told him that I believed there were no accidents. James smiled, and said Pastor Doug said the exact same thing. James assured me God had a plan and we had to trust that this would all work out. That night we had a romantic candlelight dinner, and we spent the evening making love.

At about 2am, James cell phone began to ring. I opened my eyes. He answered and started talking in a low tone. James left the bedroom and took the call. I stayed awake for a while. About 35 minutes later, I began to be angry and concerned. I already knew in my heart and mind who he was talking to; Keisha. As I thought about what she could possibly want at that hour I tried to give her the benefit of the doubt. My eyes began to get heavy and I dozed back off. When I woke up in the morning, James had already gotten up and left to get his day started. I showered and prepared to pick up the kids. The phone rang, and it was James. He said good morning and told me how beautiful I looked sleeping so soundly that he didn't want to wake me. I smiled. Then he apologized for the interruption from last night, and when the phone rang, he took the call in another room. I asked him who was calling so late. He explained that it was Keisha. BINGO! Did I call a spade a spade or WHAT? I tried to be diplomatic. I said, "I pray everything is ok with her and Christopher. I know the move must be hard on them." He said, "Yea, they will be fine. But the conversation was interesting. She started off by asking me how the honeymoon was in Italy."

Excuse me? Why the fuck was she asking about my honeymoon. He continued. "Man, I swear I didn't even want to have this conversation with her. But the Holy Spirit told me to talk to her." WHAT! This was getting insane, already. My husband took a call at 2am from his baby mama that just literally moved into the same city we reside in because the Holy Spirit told him so? Bullshit. Continue James, continue. He said, "then she began to cry. Keisha said to me she couldn't believe I really got married. Man, I wanted to hang up the phone, but the Holy Spirit told me not to." At this point, I was completely done. I wanted to cuss his ass out. I was angry and hurt at the same time. James had life completely twisted. How could God put us together and then tell James to do something that would be hurtful to me, his wife? James continued.

"Keisha was saying that reality hit her when some of the family came back with photos from the wedding. That's also how she found out we went to Italy. I forgot when we were together that she said she always wanted to go there." My eyes started to burn on the other end of the phone as I tried to hold back the tears. Heat began to rise from the hand that held the receiver all the way up to my head. He said, "she just kept going on and on, and I wanted to hang up so bad." I said, "but let me guess, the "Holy Spirit." I couldn't stop myself. The crazy thing was that he couldn't even hear me because he was so engrossed in what he was saying. So, to summarize, she still had feelings for him, and thought somewhere in the back of her mind if he didn't actually go through with the wedding, she still had a chance. Why was James telling me all of this? The more he went on, the more furious I became. The conversation lasted for about ten minutes, then Pastor Doug called in, so he wanted to share this with him. I was curious as to what his thoughts would be as our Spiritual Father. As I waited to see what the next drama of what had suddenly become my life unfolded, I went to get the kids from my sister and wondered if I should share any of this with her. I decided to keep it to myself. Although it made for good gossip, I wanted to see if we could overt this crisis first.

After picking up the children, I began to prepare our new surroundings for what would look like our new normal. After all, our romance and marriage were a complete whirlwind. For my kids, James had to mentally switch from "Uncle" to Stepdad. James had already decided on the sleeping arrangements, and the goal was to purchase a home in which there was room for all of us. In the meantime, Vincent would take the finished basement since he was the oldest. Right now, it was James' "Man-Cave," and he had no issue talking about the sacrifice he was making for the good of the family and how his sacrifice was "pleasing to God." At least that's what Pastor Doug said. It seemed he used that line a lot. As handsome and charismatic as Pastor Doug seemed to be, I felt like there was something off about him. For one, why was he the final authority on what God was saying? It seemed like James had to check our every move to the Pastor. Was he like this before we got married and I just didn't know it? And secondly, Pastor Doug seemed overly concerned about a woman submitting to her husband. I thought back to the pressure I felt from him 3 weeks earlier. It all still left me feeling uneasy. It was the personal investigator in me that wanted to get to the bottom of things if there was something to uncover. Hell, I was just nosy and wanted to know what was REALLY going on with this man.

James returned early afternoon and greeted me with a kiss. He immediately began helping me get the kids situated and I was grateful for the help. I wanted to dive right into the conversation, but I also didn't want to seem like a nag at the same time. I wanted him to bring it up. But he wasn't. Here we were together alone, and he acted as if nothing had happened earlier. James worked diligently getting the man-cave transformed into a third bedroom for Vincent. All the while assuring me this was a completely temporary situation. I decided that perhaps this was not the right time to bring up his discussion with Pastor Doug. I knew all this was hard on James. I reflected on everything that had transpired and wondered how he was holding up. I knew I was still in a state of shock, so I could only imagine how he was feeling. I decided not to add any additional pressure about how I felt about the phone call at that time. I didn't want to add to the already stressful situation. Even though I felt that whole thing left a bad taste in my mouth. I went over to his side of the basement to check on his progress. James pulled me in for a long hug. I told him I loved him. He drew a big breath in and out. He then told me again it would be ok. I looked again around at the transformation and said, "Yes, baby, it will be."

Later that evening, we had dinner as a family at the dining room table. James had his chef, Maria prepares us an amazing meal. James told a lot of kid-friendly corny jokes trying to impress the children, who pretended to laugh. I thought right at that moment that this was going to be an interesting journey. Later that evening, we decided to allow the kids to have some time to get adjusted to the new house. While the kids had their alone time, we had ours. James decided we needed a do-over, and he re-lit the fireplace on the deck. We sat and had cocktails and reminisced about our time in Italy. We both agreed that the Grand Canal was the most romantic spot we both had seen thus far in our lives. At that moment, I felt a sense of gratitude for the man that I had married. I laid my head on his chest and kissed it softly. James looked at me and leaned in for a kiss. James released his kiss and told me there would be plenty of trips like that in our future. I got excited! He also mentioned that he wanted to take a family trip to Disneyworld. I knew Vincent and Vanessa would love that. I thought about something briefly. What about Christopher? Would he be joining us? He was his son, after all. I decided to not make mention of it and allow James to paint his own picture of what our family should look like.

After our cocktails, I laid in his arms as we watched one of his favorite shows, "Bondage in America." Bondage in America was about couples across the US that were into secret sexual fetishes. He watched intensely as a woman was in a cage, and the man fed her dog food. I looked over and said, "Are you really watching this? You gotta be kidding right"? he waved for me to be quiet. I sat and watched it with him. Although interesting, I often wondered how a man of God found it acceptable to engage in such crude material. Wasn't there something in the Bible against this? I could feel it in my bones. Well, I suppose everyone had their vices. At least he was respectful enough to make sure the kids were asleep first.

James leaned in for a kiss. The woman in the cage must have turned him on because his hands made their way to aggressively to my shirt. He then massaged my breasts, and I moaned as we kissed. He stopped and looked at me. We switched positions. I hiked up my dress around my waist and mounted him. I kissed his mouth passionately. James began to move his waist in a circular motion. I started to grind my body into his. I could feel his erection begin to rise through his pants. I moved faster as I continued to kiss his mouth. James removed my blouse and began to stroke my breasts. He looked at them as he placed them in his hands. He took both nipples in his mouth and began to suck. I moaned. My Boo Boo Kitty began to get wet. The erection through his pants began to pulsate, and I rubbed his hard cock from inside his pants. I began to stroke him. He let out a deep gasp. I unbuckled his pants and stroked him through his zipper, pulled him out. I took my wet box and began to rub it against his penis. I placed his penis between my lips; played with it. Rubbed him between my lips as I listened to the sound of my own wetness. This time he moaned. Said he could not take it anymore. That he wanted me right at that moment. I slid down on his manhood slowly as I grinded in a circular motion. He yelled, "damn Baby." He was a perfect fit. He grabbed my breasts with both hands and sucked them as I slowly grinded Boo Boo Kitty into his penis. I moved slowly back and forth, feeling all the intensity of his shaft as it moved in and out of me.

Every stroke was an intense pleasure and excruciating pain all in one. As I rocked back and forth, James continued to dig deeper into my love walls while giving my breasts the attention they needed at the same time. The feeling was so intense. This time I let out a sigh. He took turns, pleasuring my nipples with his tongue and his fingers. I increased my pace to match the intensity of his strokes. As he moved deeper, I moved faster, and the cadence of our bodies made an amazing symphony. I grabbed his face and planted a deep wet kiss on his mouth as our bodies continued to create beautiful music. He gently squeezed my nipples. I gasped as he dug deeper into Boo Boo Kitty until her cave let out her waterfall of juices on his erect shaft. His shaft began to pulsate. James let out a roar as he came inside me, and we both collapsed on each other. James stroked my hair and pulled it behind my ear. He looked deep into my eyes and said, "Baby, I love you so much. I promise to spend the rest of our lives just showing you how much.

As I laid in James's arms, he fell into a deep sleep. I played with the hairs on his chest and thought about what lied ahead for us and smiled. I thought to myself, "I could really be happy with this man." Then I thought about what we never got around to talking about. Keisha, and what Pastor Doug had to say about the situation. I immediately felt a little somber on the inside. I honestly didn't know if I could deal with a lifetime of what had happened right after our honeymoon. Just like that, the honeymoon was over. Where does that happen at? Most couples get a good solid year before the shit hits the fan. And yet, here we were. As I was deep in thought, I hadn't realized that James' cell phone had been ringing. James' cell phone rang 6 times to be exact, and he didn't awake. What the fuck and who in the fuck. Immediately my blood began to boil. The phone rang again, and I looked at the number and noted it was Keisha. No, this bitch did not! I decided to introduce myself and answered the phone.

Tabby: Hello?

Keisha: Yes, I'm sorry. I must have the wrong number, I was trying to reach James.

Tabby: Keisha, you have the right number. This is Tabby, his wife. Nice to meet you.

Keisha: Oh, hey, Tabby. His wife, ok. I guess congratulations are in order?

Tabby: Excuse..(breathes deeply). Kesha, James is unavailable right now is there something that I can help you with?

Keisha: Well, I called to talk to James, but perhaps you can help me with this, considering I called his phone. I expected him to answer. Help me out here, why is it that you feel you can answer his phone?

Tabby: You know Keisha, I really didn't want to get into this with you, especially since this is our very first encounter, but I must let you know that it's the vows that he took before God that gives me the right to answer his phone whenever I choose to. So, I ask again, is there anything I can help you with?

Keisha: Thank you for your little introduction and your monologue as to why you have privileges. However, James and I will ALWAYS have business, we have a son. So, in essence, your little vows before God mean nothing to me when it comes to our son. So, yea Tabby, you can help me by kindly putting James on the phone. He and I have business to discuss.

Tabby: I believe I already told you that James was busy.

Keisha: Oh, I'm sure he'll make himself unbusy for me

At that very moment, James began to stir.

Tabby: Oh, is that a fact

James opened his eyes and asked me two things;

1. Who was on the phone, and

2. WHY was I answering his phone in the first place?

I swear I could hear Keisha snickering through the other end of the phone. Ain't this some bullshit? James jumped up, grabbed the phone, and realized it was Keisha and walked out of the room. Not only did he leave the room, but the sound of arguing could be heard in the faint distance. This not only infuriated me but also left me wondering what the hell I had gotten myself and my children into. One thing was for certain, and two things were for sure; this was NOT what I had signed up for.

Fifteen minutes later, James re-entered the room with a look I had never seen before; agitation. I opened my mouth to speak, but no words came out. He looked at me irritated and said, "What did you say to that woman, and why did you even answer my phone, to begin with? Forget it, I don't even want to know. Look, it's late, and I really don't wanna get into this tonight. Let's go to bed." I took a long look at James. I really wanted to get into it with him, but I knew as angry as I was, it would be a knockdown drag-out kind of fight. The only thing I could formulate my mouth to say was "fine," but on the inside, I was secretly seething. I knew he could tell. The crazy thing is he looked angrier than me. He dared to be angry with ME in this whole situation. I had just been disrespected by his ex, and there was no discussion just barking orders. We went back to bed, and no cuddling or affection was residual from earlier that night. We slept on opposite sides of the king-sized bed, which seemed extremely larger than life, and for the rest of the night, I slept on and off feeling lonely and wondering what the next morning would bring.

When I awoke the next morning, James had already left the house for work. Since I was still on a leave of absence, I got the kids up and ready for school and began my day. I began doing more unpacking. Trying to figure out where to put what. I wanted our new home and life together to have a touch of our new family; my family. I was also trying to figure out what that dynamic was going to look like now that Keisha and Christopher turned up in our city. There were so many thoughts swirling around. I sat down on the chair in the living room to gather my thoughts.

While sitting there, I had just come to the realization that in the last 30 days, this moment was the first time I actually had a chance to think. Everything up to this point had not only happened so fast, but I hadn't really had a chance to think about anything except the wedding and transitioning my life. Sure, I thought about the to-do list items, but I didn't have a chance to emotionally process what was going on. Now seemed to be a good time to do that. At least I thought. Unfortunately, the more I thought about everything, the more my head started hurting. I came to the realization that everything about James that I knew to be true may not be. There seemed to be so many red flags, and although we just got married, I felt the need to see how this would all play out.

The first red flag was the whole religion piece. How can a man be faithful to the church and not share that with the people around him? Especially someone who he wants to spend his life with. I also felt a sense of pressure in the timing for us to get married. Why so soon? I would have preferred to be married about 6 months after the engagement just for the sake of proper planning.

Hell, even 3 months out, but 3 weeks? That was a bit ridiculous. But the gigantic red flag for me was this weirdness that James had going with his baby mama. That dynamic was one I was unsure of how to deal with. They seemed to have this love-hate thing going, and I couldn't tell if there was true resolution in their previous relationship. James mentioned that he moved to get away, had he really had closure?

But I also had time to think about the positives. Every relationship had them, right? James was an honest man, for the most part. He was a financial provider, and he always made sure I was taken care of. James had religion, which means his life had structure. It also meant that he was not afraid to follow the lead of someone else. Perhaps that's why he was so successful. Did I mention he was a strong financial provider? I'm sure I did. Being with James meant that my children and I would want for nothing. In the end, that outweighed all the bad that had happened in less than 48 hours. At that moment, I knew this would be for better or for worse. I decided that I would call my husband and fix this situation with the phone so we could move on quickly. I called James. His assistant told me he would be in meetings all day. I thought maybe that was for the best. Perhaps we both needed some time to cool off.

Later that evening, when James arrived home, I greeted him with a kiss. He looked at me with a half-smile and walked right into the living room to sit down. He took off his shoes and sat back with his eyes closed. "how was your day," I asked. He looked over at me again and shook his head, and said, "don't ask." All of a sudden, the room seemed a little colder than usual, and I didn't know what to say to break the ice. I didn't want to ask about his day because it was obvious. But I also didn't think it was a good time to bring up the phone situation either. All I could think of to say was, "Maria, prepared a nice meal for us tonight. I was doing some things around the house. He looked up at me and said, "that's fine. I'm exhausted. Can you give me a minute"?

He had no objections from me there. As I exited the living room, James' cell phone rang. Can you take a wild guess who it was?

I guess James had a sudden burst of energy, because just like that, after his 10-minute conversation with Keisha, he had changed and run out the door without even a goodbye. What kind of shit was that? I called him. He didn't answer. I called again. The phone went to voicemail. Instantly a text comes through that says, "Can't talk right now, I'll call you later." Was that a canned response? I refused to believe it. So now he wasn't taking my calls. The only thing I could do was wait for him to come home and I was seething on the inside. But I refused to let this ruin my evening, I had 2 kids to think about and I would not allow them to see us start our new life like this. If he wasn't going to be here neither was I. I decided we needed a change of scenery, so we took a visit to my best friend Ebony.

Ebony was five years older than me and was single with a son that was grown. We grew up in the same neighborhood, and she always served as a big sister to me. I would go to her house for slumber parties, with her little sister Katrina. From elementary to high school Katrina was my partner in crime. Anything and everything we would try to get into Ebony was front and center. Katrina was the "fun, crazy daughter," while Ebony was the responsible one. Although Katrina and I were the best of childhood friends, as we became adults Ebony and I developed a closer bond throughout the years. Ebony has seen me at my best and my worse and vice versa. Although she lived by herself, she had learned to live a full life. She was a world traveler, and would always say, "You only live once in this body. Let's celebrate!." It was Ebony's goal to complete everything on her bucket list before she reached the age of fifty. Three years ago, she was diagnosed with Stage 3 cancer in the abdomen. It was a trying time, but she was able to beat it. If you have never seen a loved one battle with cancer, I pray that you never do. But Ebony was always in good spirits through it all and there was never a day that she didn't laugh although she wanted to cry. That was my friend Ebony.

As we hit the door of her home, Ebony instantly knew something was not right. She said, "Yep, Spirit says there is tension that needs to be RELEASED." She set the kids up in the playroom with a light dinner, and we sat down for a chat.

Ebony: Now, girl, you know I've been knowing you longer than anybody, you know. So, what's up?

Tabby: Girl, the shit has hit the fan already. His baby momma has moved here…..

By the end of the conversation, Ebony was left speechless. But for only a few moments. She looked at me and said, "Tabby, what are you gonna do about all this? Baby girl, it's all up to you how you handle this situation. And there are only two outcomes; misery and happiness. The good thing is you get to choose." And just like that, I felt ok. I was in the situation, and I needed to resolve it and be happy, whatever that meant. And I had to choose. I made a rash decision to marry this man. Did I want to make a rash decision and get out? In my mind, that was too easy. I decided I had to work through this with my husband for the good of everyone involved. At least for now.

We arrived home a few hours later, and there was still no sight of James. The kids began to question his whereabouts, and I just brushed it off and prepared them for bed. An hour later, James arrived home with the smell of alcohol on his breath. He looked at me and chuckled. At that moment, I could no longer contain myself. We were going to have a chat, and he was going to get it out no matter how ugly it would become.

Tabby: So, we're chuckling now? Why don't you let me in on what you think is so funny?

James: (laughs again) Funny, I'll tell you what's funny; the fact that you answered my phone and had not only a conversation with my ex but an argument.

Tabby: Yea, that's real funny, James. That's EXACTLY what I

wanted to be doing, arguing with your baby mama, who was way disrespectful. And the crazy thing is that you're upset that I answered your phone.

James: You're damn right, I'm upset. What were you thinking? You don't even know Keisha and what she's capable of. You put yourself in the middle of something that you have no idea about, and who is left fixing this situation? Me, that's who!

Tabby: Well, I thought, as your wife...

James: Well, you thought wrong! This issue with Keisha is delicate, and I need to handle this my way.

Tabby: It sounds like you're not handling the situation at all if you ask me

James: That's the issue, Tabby. Nobody asked you. We just got back from the honeymoon, and I have a huge mess to clean up. You have no idea.

Tabby: Well, why won't you tell me, James?

James: I will. In my time and my way. And you need to let me handle this. But right now, to be honest, I don't want to talk about this, and I prefer not to talk to you. That's how upset I am. I need you to give me my space. For now, I think I need to sleep on the couch.

And just like that, James gathered a pillow and blanket and left me standing puzzled. Damn! I didn't see that argument ending that way. I thought I would light his ass up, he would apologize, and we would go to bed. Not so.

Later that morning, James came into the bedroom to shower and get dressed. I looked up from in the bed and said, "good morning," and he looked at me and nodded. James got dressed, approached the bed, and sat down. He said, "listen, a lot has happened since we returned, and I don't want to be upset with the situation or you. I need you to give me some time to think this through without you pressuring me." I said, "how have I applied pressure James? All I did was try to talk about the situation." "Again, Tabby, I told you I was not ready to talk, and you need to respect that." "Well, when will you be ready to talk, James?" I asked. He then said, "all the unnecessary pressure you're putting on is not helping Tabby. I have asked for my space. Your response is when, when, when. I asked you to be respectful of my wishes, and since you obviously can't, I think I need to sleep on the couch for a couple more days." James got off the bed and exited the room. I was left sitting there with all kinds of thoughts swirling in my head. How could that conversation have gone differently? Maybe I shouldn't have asked when he would be ready to talk. But in my mind, I thought the key to marriage was communication, so I was confused as to why he didn't want to talk to me, his wife, about the situation. But I also knew at this point, if I pushed the issue, it would make matters worse. I decided that I would respect his wishes and be there when he was ready to talk. When James came home that night, he was true to his word. He barely spoke to me that evening and headed straight for the couch. That went on for about a week.

At about the ten-day mark, James began speaking to me about the basics of the household, and the next steps in our process of becoming one. That was spiritual talk for being a family. On day eleven, he even mustered a good morning before he left for the office. I spoke back and felt there was finally hope in us fixing the situation. But why did it take so long for him to talk to me? Was this his way? This was definitely a deal-breaker. I would, however, wait until the right time (when we were talking) to address this concern with him. Perhaps even Pastor Doug could weigh in and give us some advice. Oh no. Was I becoming one of "them" already?

Later that evening, James came home with a bouquet of flowers and greeted me with a kiss at the door. The first kiss was a short peck then followed by a slow, passionate, drawn-out kiss that took my breath away. I guess just like that, we were on good terms.

Tabby: Well, good evening

James: Hey, baby, I've missed you, where've you been?

Tabby: Oh, I've been here and there. I think some crazy woman possessed my body over the last week or so.

James: Is that so? I think I was missing in action myself.

James drew me in for another kiss. He said.

James: Baby, I wanna say I'm sorry and thank you at the same time. I'm sorry for how I dealt with this situation with Keisha and the phone. The truth is I was madder a Keisha then at you. She came out of nowhere and has caused a disruption to my life, just like she always tries to do. To be honest, I just don't know how to deal with it. But I also wanna thank you, baby, for allowing me the time I needed to think about this and try to figure out how to fix it.

Tabby: Baby, I'm sorry too. I shouldn't have pressured you into talking. But I'm a talker by nature, and I like to fix things quickly. I will try my best not to pressure you going forward. But honey, we're a team, and I really want to help you with this.

James: I know, dear. But the pressure to talk about the situation only adds more stress to me. I need to do things in my time and in my way. Let me handle this situation with Keisha. I know there will be times that Chris will be with us, but I don't want you dealing with Keisha. That bitch is CRAZY!

Tabby: Yea, Keisha might be crazy, but did you not forget I came from the hood? That's where you met me, baby!

James: I know, but you're a lady now; classy in every way, and you're my wife. I don't want you to have to deal with this yet. So, let me handle this.

And just like that, I conceded. Although that "lady now" line threw me off for a second. "Nigga, I ALWAYS been a lady," I thought to myself. But in the whole scheme of things, it was not necessary. I decided having peace in my home was more important than us creating a war zone, especially so early in our marriage. And for what, a woman who was a non-factor in the end? I was determined to make the rest of our evening as memorable as possible. I looked at James and asked, "So what do you wanna do this evening? Maria had the day off, so…" he said, "don't worry, I already have plans, but let's take a quick ride first."

I got the kids ready, and we headed out for a drive. We ended up in Clareville Estates, which housed the upper echelon of the city. As we entered into the estates, we stopped at the gate where we were allowed entrance. I thought to myself, perhaps, we were taking a visit to Pastor Doug. But I didn't recall if he resided in that development. Maybe he had more than one house, that could be plausible. Vincent asked, "Mr. James, where are we going"? James said, "Patience, son, you'll see." We drove past all of the big beautiful homes until we came to a big empty lot. James parked alongside the curb and stopped the car and removed the keys. "c'mon, get out," he said. We all obeyed, and the children ran straight to the top of the mound of dirt in the center of the lot. James grabbed my hand, and we strolled to meet up with the children. James had something to say.

James: Guys, when I bought my beautiful condo, I was a single man with no plans for a family in my future. But I met your beautiful mom here, and she changed my life. I wanna give you and her the world. How would you feel if we moved out here in a big beautiful house with your own bedrooms, your own bathroom, game room?

Vincent: AND SWIMMING POOL!

James: Yes, we can have that too...

Kids: YAY!

James: (looks at me) Baby, welcome to your new home!

Tabby: Wait a minute! James, are you serious?

James: Of course, I'm serious. You know I don't play games with my purchases. Yes, baby. For the last few days, I've been thinking. What do we need to at least begin to make a statement about what you and our marriage mean to me? This home is our fresh start. I know I should have said something, but I wanted to surprise you, all of you. Baby, you deserve this, especially all you've put up with already…with Keisha. THAT BITCH..anyway, I'm not gonna let her cloud this moment.

James walked away to gather his thoughts. As he got farther in the distance, I noticed something fall out of his jacket. I yelled, "James, you dropped something on the ground"! he said, "Can you bring it to me"? I walked towards the object that fell from his jacket. As I got closer, I noticed that it had a light teal color. This was interesting. The closer I got to the object, the more recognition sparked in my mind; on the ground before me was a small Tiffany box. What was this man of mine up to? I open the box. There in the box was the most beautiful Ruby earrings that I had ever laid my eyes on. The Ruby earrings were Blue Nile with diamond starbursts centered in platinum. I knew those had cost a pretty penny, $15,000, to be exact. The Blue Nile Ruby is one that never loses value but only appreciates. I took a deep breath in at the beauty I beheld before me. I looked up, and James was standing there. He tilted my head upward, said, I love you, and gave me a passionate kiss. He took my breath away. We stood there and held each other as we watched Vincent and Vanessa playing on the mound of dirt for a while, and then we all headed back home.

The rest of the evening was business as usual, and it was as if we didn't miss a beat. After we visited the grounds for our new home, James took us to dinner to celebrate. This time we didn't partake in a fancy restaurant, but Pizza Palace, which was the ultimate fun zone for kids. I watched my kids playing laser tag, bowling, and even hitting the trampolines. They ate and played until they were exhausted. We then headed home to prepare for bed. As I got the kids showered and tucked in, James lit the outside fireplace. He poured two glasses of Chardonnay and a shot of whiskey for himself. We toasted to our brand-new home, then he took his shot of whiskey. We talked about our new place, and what it would look like as we drank wine and he took a few more shots. Man, my head was spinning a little. Not just from the wine, but from the amazing way that things had turned around for us in an instant. At this moment I was happy. I giggled a little, a drunk giggle. James smiled at me. He reached in for a passionate kiss, and I remembered how much I missed him intimately.

James' tongue felt like pure pleasure in my mouth. Our tongues did an intimate dance as they played together, and our senses began to heighten. James moved his tongue from my mouth, to my ear and then down the back of my neck. Boo Boo Kitty began to become aware. It had been almost two weeks and she was craving some attention. James then began to rub my back. His hands stroked my back up and down until he took one finger and stroked the spine of my back which gave me instant chills. I let out a soft moan. James stood up and so did I. As my back was facing him, James slowly began to massage my breasts as he unbuttoned my shirt. My nipples became erect. My shirt dropped to the ground and my bra instantly followed. James sucked my neck as he massaged my nipples. I immediately felt his pleasure and I began to rub my ass against his shaft. I took my hand and reached back for his manhood. James sighed. I took my hand and stroked slowly until I felt a little release from his tip. James moved his hands from my breasts to my belly, and then to my love box. She was already wet and ready to go. James took his fingers and brushed lightly against Boo Boo Kitty. Her tongue flickered in anticipation. James knew this and played the game with her of slowly stroking her tongue, her lips, and her opening until she could no longer contain herself. Boo Boo Kitty released her juices.

James undressed. We were standing naked on our patio by the fireplace taking in the moment. James had an intense look in his eyes, one I had never seen before. Her was determined in that moment to accomplish whatever he desired, and I was going to let him. He said, "Turn around." I obeyed. James bent me over the luxury patio chair and stroked my backside. He took his hands and massaged my back as his hands centered on my spine. He then stroked my ass. Damn, this felt good. James then began to give my bottom soft wet kisses. James kisses led lower and lower until he spread my cheeks completely, and his tongue began to kiss my inner parts. I gasped. My juices began to flow from Boo Boo Kitty in amazement, as his tongue played in and out of my anus. James then lifted my ass, and his tongue hit my clitoris. I screamed. James began to suck and lick and bite in a frenzy. Boo Boo Kitty exploded again, and James entered me from behind. I forgot how good his long black dick felt inside me. James stroked slowly first. He dug into my walls until I came all over him. James began to pound faster. I moaned as James grabbed me by my waist and pounded faster. James then grabbed me by my neck and pounded faster. He then began to choke lightly as he pounded harder. It felt like heaven. He choked harder and pounded harder. I began to gasp in pleasure. James pounded hard and fast as his grip got tighter. I gasped for air, but my Boo Boo Kitty was so heightened that I didn't want him to stop. James yelled, "Is this what you want, Huh?" and he began to choke harder. James pounded hard and put every inch of his penis inside me. He stroked harder. Faster. I gasped for air as Boo Kitty's tongue flickered back and forth. I was turned on. He said, "you will learn to submit to me, that's God's plan, you feel me"? I began to stroke my nipples as he pounded away. I yelped as I came all over his dick, and James released inside me and removed the grasp from my neck. I fell to the ground and gasped for air. James laid down next to me. We looked at each other and laughed and held each other for the rest of the night. At that moment, as we laughed, I knew what happy felt like.

For the next two weeks, I experienced more of the same; happy. It was like the events from the honeymoon never even existed. We went to church and worshipped as a family. I was surprised that there were plenty of activities for the kids who seemed to enjoy themselves. I even picked up a brochure on the Greeting Ministry, and Pastor Doug seemed pleased that I was diving right in. He even began to give us counseling for marriage, and James was getting individual counseling to deal with the "Keisha" situation. Pastor Doug wanted to have a man to man conversations with James. He did this twice a week, once in person and the other via phone conference. I must say that I couldn't complain, considering we had bliss in our home, and Keisha was not a touchy subject. Sure, James had to have contact with Keisha, and Christopher had even been to visit a couple of times, and he and Vincent hit it off. But he was true to his word and was handling the situation. Keisha called his phone at respectable hours, and from what I could tell, the conversation was limited to their son. I felt like I could do this; be happy with James. And no matter what, it appeared, we would get through anything together.

But the old saying is that all good things come to an end. The shit unexpectedly hit the fan six months later. James and I were plugging away at happy, then instantly out of nowhere, he would have attitudes and mood swings. He would always make mention of how, when he went to pick up Christopher that Keisha was entertaining company. I also overheard him asking Christopher on several occasions about who the guy was and how often he was over there. Why was that any of his business, especially since they were not together? When I asked him about it, he got upset. Why would Keisha's entertaining company make a married man upset? His reasoning was he had no clue who the man was that she was entertaining, and therefore her recklessness could put his son in danger. I sensed something different, though. I flat out asked James if he still had feelings for Keisha. His response, "HELL NO, I HATE THAT BITCH"! I offered suggestions to James, but he refused and said he would continue to counsel with Pastor Doug. I agreed because, for the most part, things were going great.

At the same time, I had just got a promotion on the job as Supervisor of call center operations. With the promotion came a hefty pay increase, which came at the right time, since it seemed James was becoming a little more frugal with the finances. He was never one to be cautious about spending, but these days he wasn't as extravagant as normal. His reasoning was that we were saving for our future. I rolled with that because I wanted to leave something behind for my children as well. So, with my promotion income, I found myself spending more money on the needs of the kids. The great thing was I had a huge nest egg from when James was taking care of me while we were dating.

I also knew there was the expense of the house coming up. James was obvious, he wanted to spare no expense there, so he said he was also putting money back for that. I understood and even got excited about the limitless possibilities of decorating. I thought about my excitement, as I slowly began to pack up our things one lazy Saturday afternoon. James was preparing to play a round of golf, and the kids were going through their clothes and shoes to see what we could take, pitch, and throw away. A sense of excitement was in the air as we prepared for what lied ahead. James, in typical fashion, grabbed me from behind around the waist and kissed me on the neck. I smiled. He said, "Baby, don't wait up." I kissed him and smiled as he headed out the door. I thought about our life and what lied ahead. James seemed to really be putting in the effort and us having a spiritual grounding made a difference in our lives. Although I couldn't fully buy into it all or understand it, organized religion seemed to bring order and peace to our home. I guess I would never understand everything about God and religion, but as the fanatics have been saying at my church, "I'll understand it in the by and by." Whatever that means.

As I mulled over all these thoughts, the phone rang. I didn't recognize the number, but I answered anyway.

Tabby: Hello?

Keisha: Tabitha. You are just the woman I wanted to talk to.

Tabby: I'm sorry, I don't recognize this number, who's calling?

Keisha: Well, don't you sound the part of the Stepford Wife. Shameful

I immediately knew who this was, Keisha. But why in the hell was she calling the house phone? And how did she get this number anyway? All I could think of was what in the hell she wanted and why she wanted to talk to me.

Tabby: Keisha, how can I help you?

Keisha: Oh, so now you know who this is?

Tabby: Keisha, I'm not for these games. What is it that you want?

Keisha: There she is, that Ghetto chick that has always been there. I told James a long time ago about you that he definitely couldn't turn a hoe into a housewife

Tabby: you know what...

Keisha: No, you know what! Sweet Tabby, you have no clue. He's putting you up in that big beautiful fancy house, and you don't realize you're just the side chick. Shaking my head.

Tabby: Excuse me? Side chick? Honey, that is something I could NEVER be. First of all, don't try to play bougie..your name is Keisha. There is no polish on any chick that I have ever met named Keisha. Stop it I say! And as far as the side chick goes, that's apparently you. As a matter of fact, I'm the one rockin' the 10K ring on my finger Boo Boo

Keisha: Ten K, is all he could afford for you? I thought as wifey, he would have done right by you. I got one of those myself in the dating phase. You need to step your game up.

Excuse me? What the fuck was this bitch getting at? I could only entertain this BS for so long without losing it. I had to remember that James and I were in a good place, and the last time this chick and I had a conversation, things went south quickly.

Tabby: Keisha, can you get to the point and tell me what the fuck it is that you want? I think we've gone way beyond the pleasantries here.

Keisha: Sweet, Sweet Tabby I just called to give you a reality check. You may be preparing for your role as the main chick, but you have no idea the kind of power that I hold. I can snap my fingers, and James will come running, don't you forget that. Everything that glitters definitely isn't gold, kind of like the fake jewelry you used to wear, and James is a creature that does not change. You need to watch your so-called position as wifey very, very closely.

Tabby: Is that a threat? Because if it is, I have no worries. I got this when it comes to my man

Keisha: Famous last words sweetheart, trust, and believe. You know, James was always big on being competitive and vindictive at the same time, that was kind of his way. So, it didn't surprise me that he purchased you this big beautiful home after he made the purchase on my luxurious condo.

Pause. What did this bitch just say? Did she say that my man, my HUSBAND bought her a condo? Oh, HELL TO THE NAW! Ok, Tabby, keep it cool…pull it together

Keisha: Boo Boo Kitty? Cat got your tongue?

Oh, hell, no? Does she know about Boo Boo Kitty? Is this motherfucker talking to her about our sex life? Nah this is just coincidental, I'm paranoid. One thing is for sure, I cannot let this bitch know that she's getting to me. I need to handle her and deal with James later. I was seething on the inside but composed on the outside.

Tabby: So, Keisha, you calling me to tell me about your condo and James' purchase of it proves what? I mean, you are the mother of his child. And we both know the caliber of man that James is. So, if that's all you needed, Keisha, I really think you wasted your time here today. Is there something else I can help you with?

Keisha: Actually, yes. You can tell your HUSBAND that he can stop popping by every evening before he comes home to you. I have a man now, and he needs to respect that. And you can also tell your HUSBAND to stop getting an attitude when my man is here. I mean, I know he bought this condo for me and all, but he's your man now.

Tabby: Keisha, I'd be more than happy to relay the message to

MY HUSBAND. I'll make sure to tell him tonight after we make love. Any other advice you'd like to pass on?

Click. Just like that, Keisha had ended the conversation. I was on the other end of the receiver, still fuming with the phone in my hand. The bomb that Keisha dropped on me was atomic, and I could not wait to confront my husband.

PRESENT DAY MISERY

*M*isery is the opposite of happiness and can be defined as a feeling of significant discomfort or stress in the mind and body. Although both are present in our minds, misery, and happiness cannot dwell in the same space about any given subject. Misery and happiness are like the Hatfields and McCoys; they serve as constant arch enemies that do battle in our minds about who we are and how we feel. When one is present, the other is lurking in the shadows, waiting to seize the opportunity to be in control. Although we get to choose misery or happiness, sometimes we allow the trials of life to shape who has power. My present reality had me buddied up with misery as a constant companion.

As I pulled up to that glorious place that I currently had employment, I sighed and took a deep breath. I didn't want to go to that damn building. For what? My time was winding down there, and to be honest, I was tired of all the corporate games being played in and out of meetings. I was even told to "choose a side" when dealing with those on my level, versus those that worked below our pay grade. I knew then that shit was going to get real. You see, in Corporate America, it is a dog-eat-dog kind of world, and if you are not a shark-minded individual, you can and will get devoured. If I was frank with myself, I would say that because of everything going on, I no longer had the stomach for the corporate shenanigans. Coming to work was more like a chore instead of this glorious positioned that I had once fantasized about.

I sat for a moment in my thoughts. The phone rang; it was James. I didn't answer. He called again. And again. And A-FUCK-ING-GAIN. Immediately, the text messages started coming through my phone back to back. This mother fucker was insane. Why couldn't he leave me alone, that fucking control freak! I had moved out over six months ago, and he was acting like a mad man ever since. My decision to leave James was an easy one. Long story short, I was tired of his bullshit. He wanted to be in control of everything that was my life while having his own freedoms. That mother fucker had life twisted. All that drama with Keisha and the church began to be too much for me. We had been through too much, and when I moved out, I knew I was never turning back. James knew that my high-powered job was stressful. He also knew that they were fucking with me here yet, and still, he was calling and texting all day every day, BEGGING me to come back because the Bible said so. I had had enough!

I turned on my meditation music. My best friend, Ebony, had turned me on to that. Since cancer had come back, she began to focus her energies more on positive things like meditation, prayer, and wholistic living. I can hear her voice now yelling at me in my mind saying, "RELAX! TUNE INTO YOUR SPIRIT AND HEAR"! That is her way. And now, even as she is fighting for her life, she is acting like my life guide. Wow! Who does that? It comes as no surprise, though. Ebony has always been the oldest and the strongest. In some ways, she has always taken care of her sister Katrina and me. She was still the one who would make sure we met curfew, and that we didn't sneak into any parties, we weren't supposed to. I couldn't stand her ass for that. But she was also the one who encouraged us to get our shit together and think beyond what life was like in our neighborhood. Katrina took her advice almost immediately and went off to college and got her degree, got married, and started a family. As for me, well, you see that a hard head makes a soft ass.

I took a few breaths in and out. I tried to focus on the good of the day. Sad to say, however, other thoughts kept creeping in as I was listening to this "positive" music. Oh yea, it was really positive. I thought about the demise of my marriage, my crumbling career, and my dying best friend since childhood. I immediately got sad. What the fuck was this meditation supposed to do anyway? I decided that I needed to switch gears. I knew I had a meeting in thirty minutes with my Director to discuss the transition with the new merger, and I had to bring my A-game. To do that, I needed to relax my way; the only way I knew how-Trap Music.

Now don't get me wrong, I was very professional in the office. But you must remember I came straight from the hood. Today I was in a fighting mood and decided I was not gonna let these corporate suits and ties just take my position from me without a fight. Oh, I'd leave because the writing was on the wall. However, these crackers must think because I am black and from the hood that I am stupid. Black women are the most educated group of Americans in the United States today. So please, Mr. Corporate, don't piss on me and try to tell me it's raining. I thought about that madness and put on Cardi B, "Get up 10," and decided to "shit on those niggas" before I got out of the car.

As I stepped foot in the building, I felt an uneasy heaviness. Every step that led closer to the elevator felt like the kiss of death. My phone vibrated again, and I knew who it was. I immediately picked up the phone and put it on vibrate. I did not need this shit right now from James. I looked at my phone and saw a flurry of text messages begin to appear. "call me," "answer your phone," "I love you Tabby, I'm sorry please call me, and I won't bother you,"

"Tabby, call me, Pastor Doug wants to talk to us." I picked up the pace as the phone kept vibrating as I made my way to my work aisle. I wanted to throw my damn phone against the wall of my desk. I was already pissed, and as soon as I put my belongings on my desk, Becky popped her head up over the wall.

Becky: Good morning, Tabby. Do you have that presentation deck ready that we need to present to the client? It was due yesterday.

Let's pause for a second. Becky is the biggest bitch in the office, and I have the unfortunate pleasure of working directly with her. She is the Executive on the account, and I am the Manager. The relationship is a side by side one; however, she seems to think she is my boss, which all white people tend to do from time to time. Just an observation. Anywho, Becky has done nothing but make my life miserable since the day I got promoted. Becky is also a real Becky in every sense of the word; blond, blue-eyed, petite, and was intimidated by anyone who appeared to have a backbone or was pretty. Don't get me wrong, Becky was a smart girl. But she tried to play on her beauty to get others to do the work she knows she should be doing. And it doesn't help that our actual boss, the director Marissa thinks she's the greatest thing since sliced bread. So, every word that comes out of Becky's mouth is the gospel as far as Marissa is concerned.

Becky: Tabby? Hello, let's start again…Good Morning…

Tabby: Good Morning Becky, apparently you haven't gotten caught up on your emails. I reached out to the VP of Operations to let them know they would receive the presentation deck first thing this morning. As you can recall, I have been traveling for the last 8 days.

Becky: PERFECT! (she smiles)

Five minutes later, I receive an email with Marissa on copy thanking me for the update regarding the presentation deck that was due yesterday. Now ain't that some slick shit! She then immediately got up and took a walk with Amber, the twenty-three-year-old I was secretly training as my replacement. It was supposed to be a secret to me, that is. I don't know why I was surprised at her grimy behavior, this had become my life at least twice a week since I got this job. Becky was pleasant enough during our interview. I also had to spend some extended time with her right before transitioning to this role. She seemed friendly enough. However, she has been nothing but a bitch since I came on, and I can't place my finger on exactly why. The email notification popped up on my computer to alert me that I had five minutes until my meeting Marissa. I began to gather my notes and prepare.

As I stepped into Marissa's office, I felt an instant chill in the air. After being in this position for two years, her office was still intimidating. Marissa was the Director of Sales and Service. She had a team of fifty-plus Account Managers and Account Executives that she was responsible for. She reported directly to the VP of Sales, Stanley Bickens, who was also a smug white executive whose demeanor came across as if he was better than anyone that sat in our location. Stanley popped in occasionally to sit in on the close of important deals, update his top management team on important decisions and to deliver bad news. I wouldn't be surprised if he was lingering somewhere in the building today.

Marissa came across as a woman with a lot of class. She was a short petite redhead with the "I fuck black men" bob haircut. She wore nothing but designer labels, and her red-bottom shoes seemed to go with anything she wore to the office. She came in at eight and left at seven most nights, so if she placed demands on our work, we had nothing to refute it. Marissa was also looked at as a fair Manager. From hearing other's dealings with her, she dealt with everyone on an individual and reasonable basis. And even in this transition out, I would have liked to think that I could give this woman the benefit of the doubt, but my experience with her had shown me otherwise.

That experience was a major "fuck over" in my book. As I mentioned earlier, Marissa was a polished, fair kind of person, but even she had her flaws and made mistakes. Early on in my position I qualified for a prorated bonus. I entered the job one month into the second quarter. When bonuses were distributed in mid-November, I noticed I didn't get one. When I inquired she said she didn't understand why. She also said she would "look into it" and call me back.

A few hours later, Marissa informed me that my licensures were not approved until October which knocked me out of the bonus pool. I told her that all my licensing information was completed prior to July and asked her if she submitted it then. Her reply was no. When I asked her why not, she said she assumed since I had been with the company for over ten years that I was already licensed and bonded by the company. It wasn't until they reached out to her that she realized I was not bonded and submitted the paperwork. Then she followed up with a simple "I'm so sorry, there is nothing I can do." I missed out on over 10,000 dollars due to her negligence. So, if there is some mistrust on my end, I would say it was warranted.

When I took the role, I assumed my one on one time with my Director would be to discuss the account and ways to be consultative to assist our client effectively. We had one dedicated client that had bought in billions for our company. I was promoted into this position because of my previous experience with the company and the fact that I was able to secure my degree and other licensures while dealing with all the other bull shit in my life. This role was supposed to be the beginning of my life taking off. A new happy. Unfortunately, although I did everything I thought I could in this role to bring me happiness, it was bringing me nothing but misery.

In a Director-Manager relationship, I also expected some sort of mentoring and guidance for career development. That was my intention. I even bought the subject up early on in my time in the role. It was then dismissed because this was a key client, and there was too much to do. For the most part, we did discuss the client and the account. Still, I also spent the last two years having to explain so-called rumors about things that I said in meetings and my actions with the client and emails that they deemed not up to their expectations. So after almost two years (approx. 3 months ago), Becky and Marissa decided that I needed to be mentored.

Say what? Oh, I was getting mentoring, alright. It felt more like grade school. It appeared that the expectation was that my emails should be a carbon copy of what Becky would say. After all, Marissa was her mentor at one time, and she coached Becky. So, in her eyes, if my emails were not up to Becky's standards, then they were not up to hers, which was complete bullshit.

As I shut the door to the office, Marissa looked up and took off her glasses. She said a pleasant "hello" as she grabbed her big file of papers that was supposed to be mine. I felt like I had died and gone to heaven to prepare for my judgment to hell. We went into the pleasantries for about two minutes about life, family, and kids, and then Marissa dived right in.

Marissa: So, Tabby. You know this merger will go, though, in a few short months, and I wanted you to be aware of what is happening. But let me address something before we get into that. Let me ask you this question Tabby, how do you think that you are performing?

Tabby: Well, considering I just received the regional award two months ago, I would say that I am meeting and exceeding my performance standards.

Marissa: Is that a fact? Well, let me bring up a scenario and paint a picture for you. That email that I received this morning is an indicator that you are having trouble communicating and meeting your deadlines...

Tabby: Excuse me? I communicated promptly, Becky apparently is a little behind on her emails. Poor thing...

Marissa: In addition to this email, we were at a client meeting last week while you were out in the field. The President of Sales was present along with Becky and Amber, and we got a disturbing report on your communication with the claims data report…

Tabby: Well, this is very interesting, because this is the first that I got wind of this miscommunication with the client. May I ask what Amber was doing there? Shouldn't I have been there and her out in the field? Especially a key meeting in which something I am accountable for is being discussed.

Marissa: What difference does it make why Amber was there? The bottom line is the client is not happy, and something needs to be done.

Marissa pulls out a piece of paper.

Marissa: oh, I'm sure you've seen this before

Tabby: I'm sorry, what is that

Marissa: Unfortunately, I must put you on a performance review. And to be honest, this doesn't look good in the middle of the merger. You can lose out on the potential of your quarterly bonus AND the merger sign-on bonus, not to mention if your performance doesn't turn around, you could lose your job.

Tabby: Let's discuss this further, shall we?

Marissa: My decision is made Tabby

Tabby: Well, let's discuss this anyway. First, why would you assume that I knew what a performance plan was? I have been with this company for over ten years, and I have never been on a performance action; I came in through the call center and have worked my way up to this position. I have acquired the skills and education to be here. I believe my work ethic speaks for itself.

Marissa: Tabby, there is no denying that you have achieved great things with this company. However, your performance in this role is not up to the level that we need for this role. The performance plan is designed to get you there if YOU so choose to be. Perhaps it's just that this role is not a good fit for you.

Tabby: Since when Marissa? I have been getting awards and kudos since I started. I even was invited to the President's Circle this year for my work on this account.

Marissa: And I acknowledge all that Tabby. But as of late, your performance has been way less than desirable. Your work has become sloppy, and Becky has been sending me emails that I would like to go over…

What the fuck? Are you so serious? Emails? This bitch Becky had lost her ever-loving mind. I was officially done.

Marissa: Why the look? See, this is what I am getting at. Tabby, you appear to be distracted and stressed out as of late, is it your personal life? What's going on with the separation? How are you handling it?

Tabby: If you don't mind, I would really appreciate it if we kept this conversation focused on my job and not my personal life.

Marissa: (raises her hands in surrender) Ok, Ok. I was only trying to help you see what may be going on here. Now the business at hand is this; over the next two months, you will have an opportunity to bring your work up to the level we think it should be, Becky and me. If the work does not show improvement, unfortunately, we will have to let you go.

Tabby: Well it sounds like to me that you have already decided what is going to happen

Marissa: Tabby, are you kidding me? I like you. I even hired you.

Tabby: If that is the case, then why is Amber doing the functions that I should be doing?

Marissa: Amber is doing a great job, and she has a fresh set of eyes. This conversation is not about her. You need to take ownership of your performance, not hers.

Tabby: You know what Marissa, to be honest, this is a dead-end conversation. The bottom line is I am on a performance action plan, and my job is in jeopardy, does that summarize things?

Marissa: Yes, it does. And we can do this hard-nosed if you like, but I really don't want to do that. So here are the rules of engagement; we will meet every week once a week to go over your performance. I am pulling your travel schedule, and you will report to the office every day for the next two months. Amber will handle all on-site meetings with the client and will take the lead on the key projects. You will operate in a consultative role for Amber.

Tabby: Wow, ok. So, it has come to this, I see. Basically, I am training Amber to replace me. Marissa, must we continue this dance?

Marissa: Well, Tabby, yes, let's be honest, if you don't perform more than likely she will transition into that role if she chooses. You're a very smart girl, perhaps you should fight for what's yours. I believe you have it in you. Just focus and work really hard. In the meantime, I know that this conversation was a very heavy one, so I want you to go to your desk, acknowledge this conversation, and take the rest of the day off. Tabby, you have a lot to think about.

I took Marissa's advice and did just that. I decided to take a visit to my friend Ebony.

When I walked through the door, I could hear meditation music, and the smell of sage hit my nostrils. That smell was glorious and gave me an immediate sense of peace. I burst into tears, but I was so glad that I had come. I needed this, I needed to talk to my very best friend. Ebony had just finished meditating, and she seemed to be in a state of peace.

Ebony: Hey, little Sis! Shouldn't you be working right now?

Tabby: I took the rest of the day off..more like I was given the rest of the day off.

Ebony: Ok. Have a seat girl, because I sure need a good distraction…

Tabby: Sis, I am going through so much right now. James has been pretty much stalking me, and now I'm about to lose my job. That's the real reason I've been "given" the day off.

Ebony: Is that all? This is nothing but contrast, girl. I told you before that contrast comes to help you decide what you want and who you are. Why do YOU think all this is happening?

Tabby: I don't know! Shit, maybe I'm just failing at life.

Ebony: LIES! Tabby, you're still here, right? Are you among the living?

Tabby: Well, clearly!

Ebony: So then, as long as you have breath in your body, you can change the course of your life girl.

Tabby: I'm gonna be honest with you, all this positive shit is not helping right now. I'm about to lose my FUCKING job, and I am putting not 1 but 2 kids through college! And this damn negro has been stalking me since I moved out. So, you tell me what's positive in all that.

Ebony: First of all, you might be grown, but you ain't THAT grown to be addressing me your BEST friend in that manner. Secondly, we grew up in the same neighborhood, and I was YOUR big sister, so you WILL do as I say! Tabby. Look at me! You are more than that job and that pretense of a marriage that you are shedding. Everything happens for a reason. Embrace what is happening and find your way to happiness. Tabby, are you happy right now?

Tabby: Is this a trick question?

Ebony: No, seriously, are you happy? Yes, you have this amazing new career, and the money is good, but every time I see you, you are stressed out. When is the last time you talked to me about how the kids were doing in college, or when you have gone out and had some fun? Think about that girl.

I paused and thought about it for a moment. Maybe she was right. Hell, I didn't know anymore. But what I did know was that I was not happy, and I had no clue how to bring that back in my life. At that moment, Ebony showed me a breathing exercise and talked to me about the power of meditation. I know she has gone over this before, but this time I decided to truly listen. It was like she was reading my thoughts. But, not only did she want to teach me about meditation, but she challenged me to put it into practice at that very moment. Ebony put on some soft music and begin to talk.

Ebony: When you first begin to quiet your mind, all kinds of thoughts will start to flood your mind, some of them about your life, your daily routine, etc. Don't be alarmed by this. But the more you practice, the longer you'll be able to quiet your mind and focus. I'm going to set the timer for fifteen minutes and give you some privacy.

Ebony left the room. As I sat in silence with my eyes closed, I thought about everything that had happened today. I took a deep breath in and out. I focused on how I wanted to cuss James out for calling me to the point where I had to block his number. I thought about all the different scenarios that would play out in my head when I finally spoke to his ass. I became angry. I then thought about my meeting with Marissa, and how irritating just Becky's presence alone was, and I got even more upset. Then, I started thinking about how this meditation shit was not working and seemed to be just as much as a gimmick that the church, James, and I were going to. Why was I thinking about all the negative shit in my life?

Then I took three deep breaths, as Ebony suggested. I thought about life and how to be happy. I also thought about the last time I was able to really breathe deeply in and out. As I tried to jar my memory, I came across one that dated at least fifteen years back. It made me think. Have I not been able to slow down and take a deep breath in and out over the last fifteen years? I thought about every-thing that had happened, and thought to myself, "yes, it has defi-nitely been that long." I also thought about how I could change that. I imagined having more moments to pause and take a deep breath. Just the thought itself felt terrific, and I wanted more of those happy moments.

Then I started thinking about acceptance. I must accept all the things that were happening to me no matter what and allow them because they were for my good. I immediately felt warm and fuzzy on the inside, as I begin to think about what it was that I truly wanted and what would make me happy. I heard a voice say,

"Tabby, get back to happy. She's waiting for you." Wait. What was that? Was that me? Or was that God, or my inner voice? Whatever it was it sure felt good. Amazing is a better description. As I was fully engaged in warm and fuzzy, the timer went off.

After my meditation session, I joined Ebony in her study where she was sitting quietly. She looked to be deep in thought, almost like she was meditating too. I was almost afraid to enter. She looked at me and smiled. I said, "man, I haven't felt that peaceful in a long time. It must be something about being in your home, Ebony." She smiled again and motioned me to sit down next to her.

Ebony: Peace can be created anywhere, Baby Girl. Peace is what you choose to have during the most confusing situations.

Tabby: You definitely have that here. This house is so peaceful. I need to learn to create this kind of environment in my own home, hell in my whole jacked up life.

Ebony: Well, you can start with this; watch what you say. Your life only looks jacked up because that's what you see. Instead of focusing on what you see, concentrate on what you want to see.

Tabby: Ok, ok. You don't have to get too deep with me, girl. Now you said YOU needed a distraction earlier, and now you're in deep meditation. Again. What are you not telling me? And don't say nothing because I know better.

Ebony: Yea, you know I can never keep anything from you, you're my best friend and my sister. So, I'll come right out and say it; I only have six more months to live….

Two hours later, after a lot of drinking, crying, and trying to accept the news that Ebony gave me, I ended up home. "The luxurious condo that James was financing," I thought. It made me think back to the conversation I had with Keisha ten plus years ago, and the series of conversations after that. I immediately became angry. That man had let that so-called baby mama disrespect me a million times during our marriage. Then he dared to say he wanted me back. That mother fucker was crazy. Then I thought about my current situation and now how I had literally only six months left to spend time with Ebony. Why was everything in my life a shit storm, and how was I gonna make all this better?

I turned my phone back on. Seventeen missed calls and twelve text messages from James. I was getting so weary of this. I wish he would just leave me alone. I knew though that I couldn't avoid him forever. I looked down at the text messages and saw the same old cycle repeat itself, just like in our marriage. Most of the messages were scriptures about marriage and how God hates divorce. Then he would switch up and talk about how much he hated me and how big of a bitch I was. Then the last few texts ended with his apology for his rash behavior and how he didn't know what got into him. He then begged me to call him. As I sat in my car and looked at the text messages, I took a deep breath in and out. The phone rang again. It was James. I knew he would keep calling. He would not let up, and I was not in the mood. As much as I wanted to be civil, I knew this conversation would not be pleasant. I looked at the phone with disbelief as it stopped and rang again immediately. I answered the phone.

Tabby: James, what the fuck is so important that you feel you have to call my phone night and day.

James: Tabby, I know that there is no hope for our relationship, but I just wanna talk.

Tabby: James, to be honest now is not a good time. I just found out...

James: WHEN IS IT EVER A GOOD TIME TABBY!! I JUST WANNA TALK TO YOU! I call, you never answer. I text you don't respond. So, you tell me when the time will ever be right. Look, I'm not trying to get you to move back with me or anything, I just wanna have a conversation

Tabby: Will you stop fucking repeating yourself! That shit is irritating. James, I am trying to be civil, but I have had an awful day. I found out today that Ebony is dying.

James: Tabby, I'm so sorry. Are you ok? Do you want to talk about it? I'm here for you, you know that.

Tabby: James, I appreciate that, but I need some time to myself.

James: Tabby, I understand. All I was gonna say about us was...

Tabby: James, are you really doing this right now after I told you my friend was DYING!

James: I'm Sorry, I didn't mean to. It's just that I never get to talk to you. You're right, it was very insensitive of me. Tabby, we don't have to talk tonight. Can we meet somewhere neutral after you get off work? I'll even come near you.

Tabby: Fine, James. Where do you want to meet?

James: At the Luxford Mall. It's outside in public with people around. We can walk and talk. That way, you don't feel like there will be any pressure on you. Is that cool?

Tabby: I don't know, James.

James: Come on, Tabby. I promise I'll be on my best behavior. Listen, I know you're ready to move on. Let's just have one discussion to go over some things.

Tabby: ok James. Yes, James, that's fine. I'll see you around six tomorrow.

I woke up the next morning in a buzz from all the events of the day prior. My head was spinning, not only from the bad news but the excessive wine coupled with the crying and screaming I did before I blacked out. I hated it when I got like this. I looked around the room, which was in complete chaos. There were clothes sprawled everywhere, and an empty wine bottle on top of the nightstand. I focused hard on piecing together the details from the day before. I remembered that my friend was dying. I vaguely remembered having a conversation with James that appeared kind of sketchy. I also remembered that I had to a meeting early this morning at 8am. I decided since it was only six, that I would get there early to finally talk to Marissa about everything that was going on. After I contacted HR, that is to see what my options were now that I was on performance. And to be honest, I still didn't trust that bitch.

Then the details of my conversation with James started coming back to me suddenly; I agreed to meet him at the Luxford mall. FUCK, what was I thinking? The last thing I needed was to deal with him this evening, especially if things went south at work. I thought to myself, "Well, it should be ok if we're in a public place. Perhaps he won't make a big scene." I decided to go ahead and face this situation head-on no matter what. After all, how bad could it be?

I got showered and dressed quickly. I decided to go casual with a pair of designer jeans, a fitted top, blazer, and heels. I looked casually cute if I must say so myself. I realized that no matter how bad things go in your life if you look better, it does something for your image. I was going to step into that office with confidence, although I felt like my life was crumbling, and I was miserable. My best friend was dying, and I only had six months to be with her and take care of her. What would that be like? What would her quality of life be? How would I manage to juggle this along with managing this transition on performance review?

The job was already stressful enough without the pressure of thinking about my best friend. I took a deep breath in and out. I told myself that it would be ok and that everything would work out the way it was supposed to. I looked at myself in the mirror and smiled. I put on my signature berry lipstick. I looked at how sensual and professional my full lips looked at the same time. I smiled again. Despite everything, I decided today that I would choose to be happy. I got in the car and turned on some meditation music as I headed to the office.

When I got to my desk, imagine my surprise when I saw that Marissa, Becky, and Amber were already in a meeting in Marissa's office. An early meeting before any of the other associates arrived. That was interesting. My initial thought was what I have suspected all along, that they wanted my position taken from me. My second response was that in the whole scheme of the current events that her having this position really didn't matter much to me. However, I was not going out like a punk ass bitch either. I went right to Marissa's office and knocked on the door.

As I entered, I saw Becky's face turn a shade of red I had never seen before. She looked embarrassed and guilty at the same time. Why was I not surprised? I decided to take the high road and apologize for the interruption and asked for some of Marissa's time for an extremely urgent matter. Amber and Becky gathered their things without looking at me and scattered like the corporate roaches they were. Marissa pointed to the chairs in front of her desk to have a seat. She removed her glasses and twirled them in her hands, then looked at me with a sincere look of concern and asked what was on my mind. I began to pour out my heart concerning my friend Ebony, and I could tell that she was genuinely concerned.

As I finished my monologue, there was silence for about 2 minutes. That silence seemed like forever. She finally spoke.

Marissa: Tabby, let me first say how sorry I am that you are going through this, especially with all the turbulence that seems to be happening here at work. So, tell me, what do you think your options are? Although this situation is troubling, I must follow protocol, too. You also know that I am a person that can help create solutions, but you first must bring options to the table.

Tabby: I first want to thank you, Marissa, for taking time with me this morning. And yes, I have talked to HR and can provide the solutions that they have bought forth.

I began to explain what my options were,

1. I could take a leave of absence without pay

2. I could exhaust all my PTO and then take a family leave as a primary caregiver

3. I could be terminated since I am on a performance review, or I can voluntarily terminate. Quit.

In my mind, option two seemed to be the most viable. Still,

being with the company as long as I had, I knew that taking leave would cause unspoken repercussions. In corporate America, when an employee takes an extended leave for any reason, be it health or otherwise, the employer's perception of the employee changes slightly. Although FMLA is a federal benefit afforded to anyone who has worked with their company over a year, some employers look at the employee as taking advantage of their system. They then begin to have secret internal eyes on the employee looking for marks in their performance, attendance, and violation of policies. I have seen many good employees mysteriously terminated at least a year after they had to take family leave. I did not want to choose option two, but I knew Marissa would ask me what I thought was fair. And I decided to put my big girl panties on and speak my mind when asked.

Marissa: Well, those options seem straight forward, what are your thoughts?

Tabby: To be honest, Marissa, none of those options work for me. Taking unpaid leave is not realistic, and we all know how FMLA works around here. I also have put in too much time and achievement to just walk away and quit. So, I will tell you what I want. The fact that I am on a performance review speaks volumes to me about my current position here. I love this company and the work that I do. However, given the current circumstances, I realize that life is very precious, and my friend has to take precedence. I want to be able to walk away from this company with the dignity that I came with. Because we have the merger going, I would like to be bought out of my contract early with no stipulations.

Marissa: Tabby, I want to thank you for coming to me as a professional with this situation, and I know it has been hard given the level of stress associated with this position. As I stated before, I am by the book, but I am also a fair woman contrary to what you may believe. I don't think any of those options would be a good solution for you either. Because I have Manager's discretion, I can override those options. Tabby, I really like you, and I hired you because I believe that you could do the job. Perhaps the stress of your personal life and all that has been occurring has, in some way, affected the level of mastery that I expect with this position. Nonetheless, your reputation here at the company has been flawless. That being said, I am going to grant your request and submit this to HR today. We can have this business wrapped up by the end of the week. Does that sound fair?

Tabby: Marissa, that is perfect. And I want to thank you.

Marissa: No Tabby, thank you

Tabby: Thank me? For what

Marissa: During this conversation, I saw the woman I originally hired. That confident, professional woman who is not afraid to demand what she wants because she knows her worth. If you had selected from one of the options provided, I would have gone with it. But you had the courage to stand up for yourself. Way to go. I know if you ever want to come back to this company, you would do well in any other position here. The only stipulation of your contract would be upon leaving that if you return, you could not return to this position.

Tabby: Marissa, it's obvious something is telling me my time here is over. I'm going to take this time and start over.

Marissa: I agree, perhaps it's time for a fresh new start. Take this time to enjoy your life and figure out what you really want to do. Don't worry about this company or this client. We will make things work here. Tabby, take care of yourself.

And just like that, as quickly as my journey began with this company, it had ended. Marissa and I hammered out a few more details, and we agreed that today would be my last day in the office. I gathered my personal belongings from my desk. I turned in the keys to my corporate car, my corporate credit card and laptop and other equipment. I agreed to have my remaining things shipped to my home, and Marissa saw me out the door and took my badge one last time. As I headed to my car, I thought about all the friendships I had made throughout the years in the various departments.

Throughout the years, I had developed work besties, husbands, and confidants that carried me through some of the darkest times. They say the people you work with oftentimes have the greatest insight to you, and in that moment, I felt that. I had mixed feelings about leaving. A little sad, because I had dedicated a big chunk of my life and career there and it was a place that was familiar, like family. I also felt a little scared because I had no clue what was next. I immediately felt insecure.

Although I had obtained my bachelor's degree while working, I had no formal training outside of this place, and I had worked my way up in this company. Would I have to start over? Was I ready? I turned and looked at the building one last time. I remembered the tale of Lot's wife that Pastor Doug preached about. I said to myself, "don't look back." I turned around, took a deep breath, and continued to head to my car. I called Ebony and gave her the events of the morning.

After I wrapped up my conversation with Ebony, I returned home to be alone with my thoughts. What was next? I honestly did not know. A part of me wanted to take a mini-vacation before I tackled what would look like my new normal. But since I had no clue what that was, the time away would be good, I thought. I wanted to be away from everyone and everything to really process my life. But where would I go? I wanted to go somewhere warm, but not too exotic. I also didn't want to be out of the country. Just in case something were to happen with Ebony or the kids.

I thought, "I have never been to Los Angeles, maybe I should go there." Los Angeles sounded really good right now. Beautiful beaches, and a good massage would be just what the doctor ordered. Plus, my girl Sam was there, and I know she knew how to have a good time. I hadn't gotten to see her since she left, and now would be the perfect time to getaway. I decided to give her a call:

Tabby: Hey Foxy

Samantha: Hey Sexy Mama, what's crackin' girl!

Tabby: A whole lot Foxy. I miss you, girl! You know James and I split right, and he has been harassing me ever since girl. Plus, I just need to get away for a while. I don't know for how long, but I just need some space.

Samantha: Mama, you know that goes without saying! You can come crash with me! Meet some new friends and friends with benefits!!

Tabby: There you go with sex on your mind Foxy, as always. It has been a while, though, to be honest.

Samantha: Oh shit! How long, mama? Don't lie!

Tabby: You mean with a real man

Samantha: Or woman haha

Tabby: What the fuck you mean, woman?

Samantha: Don't knock it until you try it, Sexy Mama! So anyway, we'll talk about that when you get here. How long have you let the cobwebs grow on Boo Boo Kitty? (She chuckled)

Tabby: I see you got jokes, girl. To be honest, it has been almost a year since I had a penis. Not counting the few times I slept with James since we separated. Big mistake! That man has become crazy ever since.

Samantha: Aye, Aye, Aye! Girl, you really need to get away, like NOW! Come down here. You can crash with me but book your hotel if you want some solitude too. You are going through a lot Sexy Mama! Come down here, let's have some fun! You wouldn't believe who I'm a personal assistant to!

Tabby: Who Foxy?

Samantha: You'll see when you get here, mama! I can't wait to see you! Smooches!

And I did just that, decided to go let my hair down some. I contacted the airline to see what flights they had available leaving for LA. The flight attendant said that they had a flight leaving at 10PM this evening. I listened to my instinct and told them I wanted a seat. I booked an open-ended flight and couldn't wait to see my second best-bestie. It had been so long, and I couldn't wait to find out what she was into.

Whatever it was, I was going to relax in the moments and allow myself to feel happy, even if for a moment. There was a reason I had never been to LA but had the opportunity to go now. There was something in LA right now, and I was going to see what it was. Perhaps it's just to knock the cobwebs off Boo Boo Kitty. Even if so, what's so wrong with that? It has been so long since Kitty has been stroked by fingers other than mine. She not only needed fingers stroking her, but she needed to be licked and sucked.

My pussy began to throb at that very moment. I wanted to take my hands and take care of Boo Boo Kitty right then and there. Damn, she was begging me to. I thought about the amount of time I had to pack and finish things before leaving. I thought about Boo Boo Kitty, who was screaming at me. I got up and took Johnson out of the package. I immediately stared at him. Although he looked good, I knew our time would be brief, and a quickie was not something I was looking for. I looked at Johnson with disgust. He made me feel like a cheap whore. "DAMN YOU JOHNSON!" I yelled as I threw him across the room. Unfortunately, this time I needed more. I needed to be held and touched by a human. I sat on the bed and sighed, and continued to make my arrangements.

As I planned my travel, I contacted my sister and Ebony to give them the details. I also let them know I didn't want to be disturbed unless it was an extreme emergency. I would tackle the affairs of life when I returned. Whenever that was. I began to pack my bag for a week and got distracted with my thoughts on what was left to do before I left town today. I remembered that I was supposed to meet James at the mall. Damn. Although I really didn't want to deal with him today, I knew if I didn't, he would only harass me the whole time I was gone. But I also decided not to tell him what happened at work today. We were no longer together, and the last thing I needed was for him to extend his so-called sympathy while extending an offer to have me back into his life. Thanks, but no thanks. I grabbed my keys and headed to the mall.

James and I met in front of Dave and Busters, a family-friendly fun place with video games, food, and adult entertainment. Today they had my favorite local live band "Spice" who blended a mix of R&B and NeoSoul to bring beautiful melodies to the ear of the listener. James asked if I wanted to go in, and I declined. He said, "suit yourself," and we decided to take a walk. As we walked and talked, James continually extended an apology for his part in the end of our marriage. He realized that as a result in his actions that there was no turning back from this. He also indicated he wanted our divorce to be as clean and as private as possible. I agreed. As I looked up, I realized that we were standing in front of Tiffany's.

James asked me to join him one last time inside. I don't know why, but I agreed. As we entered, the clerk said to me that they were closed, and then when she saw James, she said, "My apologies, Mr. Taylor, I didn't realize that she was your guest." I have to admit the fact that this man had this kind of power was still a turn on, although he was an asshole. "Mr. Taylor, you and your guest feel free to look around and make any selections. The space is available exclusively to you for the next two hours." Are you kidding me? I could not believe this. James, in like fashion, had rented out the space in Tiffany's just for me. Although I should feel flattered, I was not, and planned to nip this little plan of his in the bud quickly. James interrupted my thoughts.

James: So, Tabby, I thought that we could spend one last time in your favorite place.

Tabby: Don't you mean YOUR favorite place, James.

James: I don't get that. Every woman loves Tiffany's.

Tabby: James, you can't be serious by bringing me here.

James: Tabby, you know I love you, right? I really don't want this to end, and I know this is all my fault. Listening to other people like Pastor Doug and that bitch Keisha, but I would do anything to get our family back together and do it the Godly way. All of Pastor Doug's teachings weren't crazy, you know.

Tabby: Are you FUCKING KIDDING ME RIGHT NOW?!

James: Tabby, hear me out please, baby

Tabby: (laughs insanely) You must be out of your FUCKING MIND to do this RIGHT NOW!

James: Tabby, please. Look around. I bought you here because Tiffany's has the finest of the finest. And that's what I realize that I have always had in you. Baby, I'm sorry. For everything. Can you find it in your heart to forgive me? The bible says...

Tabby: James….my patience is REALLY running thin with you

James: Ok, ok. I won't bring the Lord into this. Even though we both need him in our lives, and I truly believe we both lost sight of what is important, what God put together. (Sighs deeply) I know, I'm going on and on, just wishful thinking, I guess. Listen, Tabby, I know it's over. I just wanted one more chance to make things right by you, so I bought you here. Look around at all this stuff. Baby, you can have anything in this room you want. There is over $500,000 worth of merchandise here, and I'm willing to give it ALL to you.

Was this motherfucker serious? He still didn't get it. Throughout the years, he always seemed to think that getting me a little trinket from Tiffany's would make everything ok. But this level of insanity was astounding. The whole damn store? Get the fuck out of here! For a brief moment, I had a good mind to go back to the old "Petty Tabby" and have all of my girlfriend's come up and have him ball out on each and every one of us and then leave his ass high and dry in this store. Especially for all the shit he put me through. But no, I decided to let Karma take care of him instead and give him exactly what he deserved. That didn't mean that I wouldn't play his game for a little while. I strolled through the store and looked through the glass at some of the more expensive pieces.

I set my eyes upon a cushion-cut platinum bracelet. The center cut sapphire was purple and was about 15 carats. The surrounding sapphires were a mix of purple and blue with hints of platinum that peeked through in all the right places. It was beautiful! "would you like to try this piece on?" the attendant asked. As I was caught in the trance of the beauty of the bracelet, I imagined it on my wrist and immediately said yes. The attendant took the bracelet out of the locked break-proof glass and put it on my wrist straight away. I admired her beauty as the attendant talked about the cut and quality of the sapphires on this piece.

She then began to tell me that the stones that surrounded the center were 14 carats, and the center was fifteen. "How much for this piece?" James asked. "The Lady Blue Sapphire Bracelet is a steal at $210,000 today." A steal? Yea, ok. I snapped back to reality just as I heard James say, "We'll take it"!

Tabby: No, we certainly will not!

James: But baby...

Tabby: Don't, but Baby, me, James! You must think I'm CRAZY to fall for this Tiffany's crap again. You know, one thing Keisha said about you was right; You ARE a creature of habit. But to offer me a half a million dollars' worth of jewelry in exchange for remaining your wife is the biggest joke of all James.

James: That's how much I love you, Tabby, I'm willing to spend ANYTHING on you. No price is too much Tabby, what do you want a million dollars? Claire, up my tab to one million dollars.

As we had this conversation, I watched the attendant look back and forth at us in a kind of awkwardness. I could tell she was feeling James' every emotion, as he tended to have that fake effect on people. When this man said he would do anything and to up the ante to one million dollars, her mouth opened on an "awe-like" fashion.

Tabby: James, we are not gonna play this game here in this store of all places. So, to be respectful about the situation, I'm going to decline this bracelet and get out of this store. Have a nice evening, James.

As I began to head out of the store, James began to speak. And this time just like clockwork, his "other" person showed up. Oh, so let me break this down for you. The charming, understanding, begging man in Tiffany's is the representative that James sends to impress me and the others around him. This man is wealthy, charming, pleasant, and confident. What person wouldn't like this man on the surface? But the other side of James is quite the opposite. Dark, angry, and into weird fetishes. And because I lived with him for almost ten years, unfortunately, the dark side could only be hidden for so long. James was a controller. And since this situation didn't turn out the way he thought it should, he tried to take control by becoming angry.

James: Tabby…(he yells) Tabby! Don't you walk away from me! If you leave this marriage, you'll get nothing!

I stopped.

Tabby: Excuse me?

James: That's right! You heard me! We signed a prenuptial agreement, and because you gave me no children, you will get NOTHING!

I chuckled.

Tabby: So…during our quickie marriage, you managed to weasel in a prenuptial agreement, which entitles me to nothing if I leave because I didn't give you kids? Did I hear you correctly?

James: I didn't weasel that in Tabby, it was part of our marriage ceremony, Pastor Doug said it was standard.

Tabby: Oh, HELL, NO!

James: I know how you feel about Pastor Doug, but if you leave this marriage, he was right about you. You are Hagar, you're not the promise...

Tabby: Muthafucker, I'm about to get real ghetto up in this bitch.

The attendant gasped, and I regained my composure.

Tabby: You know what James, I told you no. No to everything, the marriage, the money, the bracelet, and this so-called shopping spree, I will be ok. So, if you will excuse me, I have to get packed for my trip.

James: Trip? Where are you going?

Tabby: None of your dam business!

James: It must be work. That's why you're so stressed out.

Tabby: Bye, James...

James: Tabby, wait!

James watched as I headed to the door. As I got closer to the door, I heard James say something to the attendant who giggled. I shook my head in disgust and kept walking. I got into my car and went home to finish up for my trip. A week in LA was just what I needed right now. I just wanted to laugh for once and be happy. As I sat on the edge of my bed, I thought about that; laughter and happiness. I took a deep breath in. I thought again about the last time I was able to do that in silence without the pressures of life pouring in. Wow the realization that it had been years really hit me this time. I thought about the fact that it had been way too long. I then thought about the sadness of that thought.

I also thought about everything my life had become. It was like God, or the Universe was playing some dirty trick on me. I took another deep breath in. Then I heard a voice from within me say, "so what are you gonna do about it Tabby." I said out loud, "Well, I sure as hell ain't gonna have a pity party about this shit. I need to figure out what happiness is." I looked at myself in the mirror. For the first time in a long time, I said to myself, "You're kind of cute. Sexy even." Then I laughed out loud and admired what was becoming my new body. The curves from over 10 years ago were beginning to resurface. I wasn't where I wanted to be, but I damn sure wasn't where I used to be! I then looked at myself and said, "Tabby, you deserve to be happy. Figure out your life, and what that means for you. You are smart, you are beautiful, and you are talented. Make your life count."

Just then there was a knock at the door. I knew I wasn't expecting company, so I peeped through the peephole of my condo door. There was an armored man with a badge. My first thought was, did James actually get petty and send the police over here? Nah, even HE wouldn't stoop to that level. I opened the door.

Guard: Yes, I am looking for Tabitha Taylor

Tabby: This is she. Who is asking?

Guard: Mrs. Taylor, I have a package for you that requires a signature

I signed for the package. Instantly two armed men exited the truck and approached the condo. One of the guards handed me a box inside of a beautiful light teal gift bag, Tiffany's. I tried to make him take the package back. He declined. The guard informed me that upon my signature that the property now belonged to me with no return or exchange. I bubbled just a little on the inside. I took the gift bag from the guard and gave them a pleasant good-bye. I closed my door and looked at the gift bag. I knew exactly what the fuck it was, James' way of having the last word, a control measure. But I wasn't going to concern myself with his bullshit right now because I had a flight to catch. I threw that gift bag on the couch, packed the rest of my things, and headed out to find happy.

THE PROVERBIAL STRAW

In life, we often come across moments that get us to our wit's end, "The Straw that Broke the Camel's Back," if you will. The idiom, the straw that broke the camel's back, alludes to the proverb, "it is the last straw that breaks the camel's back," that describes the seemingly minor or routine actions that occur in life that causes an unpredictably large and sudden reaction, to the cumulative effect of those small actions that occur over time. But in marriage, those actions are never small, they are likened to mini atomic bombs being dropped over Hiroshima. At least in my marriage, it was like that. So, to understand why I left that false happy, I must give you all the straws that led to the proverbial:

1. The purchase of the condo for Keisha
2. Lack of sex, but PLENTY of Tiffany boxes
3. Blatant disrespect from Keisha
4. The Proverbial Straw- Pastor Doug's "Hagar Teaching"

Now, as you recall earlier that I was fuming and could not wait to confront James about this secret that he had kept from me. Well, being from the hood, I learned a long time ago to be methodical and not emotional. That's what separates the female from the lady, and these days I had been practicing the latter. When you go to confront your significant other, you sure better bring something other than your emotions; you need receipts. So, I thought to myself, how can I go about getting proof? I could play cat and mouse with Keisha via text, but I would never stoop so low, I'm the "Wifey" as she so eloquently pointed out. Plus, that would give that heffa the upper hand in this situation, knowing that I lied to her and did not know about the purchase that my husband made, which would be humiliating. So, I decided to go straight to the source, our bank.

James and I had separate bank accounts, but I was listed as an authorized user on his account and vice versa. I had full access to his funds and bank statements. Still, I never paid much attention because I used his account mostly for pleasure spending and never bills. Well, it was high time I found out what was really going on with him and Keisha, and why didn't he tell me himself that he purchased the condo for her? I'm sure if he provided some logical explanation, then surely, I would be understanding, correct? Why all the secrecy?

As I walked through the bank doors, a sudden uneasiness set over me. I was afraid for the first time to find out how much I really didn't know about my husband. I sat in the lobby and waited to see our personal banker. Samantha, who was not our personal banker, greeted me with a smile. She was the assistant to the personal banker. She motioned for me to step into her office and asked how she could assist me. I began by asking how I could look for substantial purchases or down payments made on the account over the last 9 months. Samantha looked at me with cautionary eyes.

Samantha: Is there a specific reason that you have an interest in large purchases from this account, Mrs. Taylor?

Tabby: I think that's a funny question to ask me, but yes, to be honest, I do have a specific reason. I'm looking for the purchase of a condo recently and any other extravagant purchases that may seem unfamiliar to me.

Samantha: May I ask you to be more specific? For example, is there a question of fraud? Because I can assure you that all of Mr. Taylor's purchases are authorized by him personally. Does that clear up anything?

Tabby: To be honest, it does not. Now, as an authorized user on this account, I would like to see the statements and purchases on this account, as I have previously requested Samantha.

Samantha: My apologies Mrs. Taylor, I don't mean any disrespect, but although this account allows you full access, Mr. Taylor is a special client of ours. He has restricted your ability to view certain accounts.

Tabby: Is that a fact? And oh, and there are more than two accounts?

Samantha: Mrs. Taylor, you seemed surprised. Of course, there are.

Bingo! This was precisely what I had suspected! What in the hell was I dealing with? I really had no clue. This man had more than two accounts. Why didn't I know this tidbit of information? This was getting very interesting. I decided I was going to get those receipts, and little Miss Samantha was not going to stop me. This, however, was an upscale bank for the elite of the community. So, ranting and raving would more than likely get me put out first. I looked Samantha right in the eye, and remembered who I was; I was James Taylor's wife, and I belonged here. However, I was also the wife who obviously had more accounts here than she knew, but I didn't want to leave the bank with egg on my face, so I played it cool:

Tabby: Tell me something, Samantha. Do I have full access to all these accounts? If so, I demand to see the statements and go over in detail ALL the large purchases made in not only the last nine months but the previous year. And I REFUSE to take no for an answer. So, how can you help me?

Samantha: Mrs. Taylor, when I said I meant no disrespect, I sincerely meant that. And again, I apologize. You have access to 5 of the eight accounts, and I'd be more than happy to take the rest of this afternoon going over the large purchases.

Tabby: Wait a minute, 5 out of 8? What's on the other three that I can't see? What I'm looking for might be in one of those 3 accounts.

Samantha: Mrs. Taylor, that may be so, however, in the five accounts that you do have full access to, I am sure that what I'm about to show you will be more than enough that you will need to see.

Samantha winked at me and smiled with a knowing smile. It was a girlfriend moment between two Sistas at the bank. Oh, did you think Samantha was white? No, that's just her government name. Samantha Maria Evans was tall and slender and was mixed with African American and Latina. She had a natural wave to her hair that was straightened in a professional business style that extended beyond her back. True to her mix of Latina and black, she was very curvy in all the right places. Samantha had a small waist and her hips and booty, well let's just say that they were her stronger attributes. Samantha would be what you call thick in present times and had the kind of body that women would pay money to have. To me, Samantha looked more like a celebrity than an assistant at a bank.

Samantha was true to her word and spent the rest of the afternoon, giving me bombshell after bombshell. That sista even provided me with receipts; two copies. It turns out that Samantha had been James' assistant to this personal banker for the last three years. So, she recognized the patterns and irregularities in his spending. She also knew exactly which purchases went towards his baby mama, Keisha. And low and behold, he did more than purchase the condo. This motherfucker actually paid the airfare for her and Chris to come down here, and the hotel was purchased in advance, as well. That lying son of a bitch! This motherfucker acted like he was surprised that Keisha arrived in our city, and he had this planned the whole fucking time!

I looked at Samantha with tears in my eyes that were bursting to come out. She said she understood, but not with her words, but the knowing look in her eyes. We had another girlfriend at the bank moment, and she handed me a tissue. She told me to go see a girlfriend or go get a drink, but to think it through before I gave James the information that I got that day. I told her I would at least think about it, but I knew I was going straight home to start my own shit storm. I think she knew it too and gave me her business card. "It has my office and cell number on it. Call me if you need to talk," she said. I nodded and agreed. I thanked her one more time and walked out of the office with her business card in hand. And since that day, Sam and I had been second best-besties.

As I headed home, I thought about how furious I was. I couldn't believe James had lied to me all this time about how he had been taking care of Keisha. I sure would have wished I would have known that before we got married. That shit would have been a game-changer. How in the world was he going to explain this? The bad thing was, I was not able to confront him right away unless I went to the golf course if that's really where he really was. Everything I knew about James was beginning to be questioned. So, I had to think about my next steps.

When I got home, I decided to conduct business as usual. The kids had finished going through their things, and I had wrapped up as much sorting as I could muster up before the movers were scheduled to come and pack our things the following week. Here I was preparing to move into my dream home, with a man who I realized I had no clue who he was. He lied. He kept secrets, and he took no accountability for his actions thus far. Who was James, really? I thought about everything that I knew about him for a moment. He was polished, put together, and very well-spoken. He was also a man that, although he had his own set of issues, seemed to want to be in this marriage for the most part. But who is the man that I discovered today? That man was completely different. I would be in a beautiful home lying next to a stranger. Can a marriage survive something so deceptive? And if so, how was I going to move past this?

A few hours later, as expected, James arrived home in good spirits. Golfing always seemed to do that to him. I hated to be a bitch and bring his spirits down, but this could not wait. Before I opened my mouth to speak, James began to tell me how good of a day he had on the course, and how he and Pastor Doug talked about a possible business venture with some of the businessmen in the community that could be lucrative for him and the church. It would take a few years to fully develop, but he seemed very excited. That is until he saw my face.

James: Tabby, baby, what is it? You look like you've seen a ghost.

Tabby: Well, James, I got a disturbing phone call today…From Keisha.

James: Awe, man! Why am I not surprised? Here we go with this. When did she call you and WHY?

Tabby: She called to let me know that my position as "wifey" was not secure as she put it.

James: I knew that bitch was up to something. I gave her your number because she has been civil these past few months. I know you're not insecure about Keisha, are you?

Tabby: You gave her MY number?

James: Isn't that the number she called? And that's all you heard in the conversation? Why are you insecure about what that bitch has to say, we've been married over a year now?

Tabby: HELL NO, she didn't call my number! She called the home number, James.

James: Oh, ok. So, she called to ruffle your feathers a bit. Well, I will handle that.

James reached in for a hug. I took a step back.

Tabby: James, that's not all she mentioned. She also shared with me how you purchased her condo. That's a bit of information that you forgot to share with your wife. So, given that, how would I be secure in my status as "wifey"?

James: Are you gonna believe everything that comes out of that bitch's mouth? I thought you were smarter than that Tabby.

Tabby: Yea, James, you give me a lot of credit for being smarter than I believe I am. That's why I took a trip to the bank today. And I couldn't believe the shit I came across.

This time it was James who looked like he had seen a ghost. He looked at me in silence for what seemed to be about thirty seconds. I then saw a look of fear come over him immediately replaced with anger.

James: Excuse me, what do you mean you went to the bank today? You were supposed to be here packing.

Tabby: Well, James, after that conversation, I was smart enough to go down to the bank and find out some things for myself. You have 8 fucking accounts! When were you gonna reveal that information to me? Not only that, but you paid for Keisha and your son to come down here and relocate!

James: So, what! Yes, I paid for that, she's my kid's mother.

Tabby: But what I don't understand is why all the secrecy, James.

James: Because the accounts that I used that money from were MY personal accounts that I built before I met you. That is MY money, and if you have a problem with the way I spend MY money, then we're not gonna make it. I CAN'T BELIEVE YOU WENT BEHIND MY BACK AND GOT ACCESS TO MY ACCOUNTS! You have crossed the line, Tabby.

Tabby: Excuse me?

James: I can't even look at you right now.

James grabbed his keys and headed out the door. Fifteen minutes later, I received a text message saying he booked a room at Embassy Suites for the night. He had some late-night business he needed to wrap up and did not need any distractions. He also said that he expected to see me at church with the kids in the morning sitting in our usual spot. He said if I wanted to discuss things further, he would talk to me after church. And that's how the conversation went. I thought he would be sorry for his actions and beg for my forgiveness. However, he turned the whole situation around on me and made me the villain. What the fuck?

As I mulled over the conversation, I decided to get a second opinion via my girlfriend, Ebony. She confirmed that I had not lost my mind. As a matter of fact, she asked me what was wrong with him. I then got a third opinion by calling my new best-bestie. She first started by saying that I failed to do anything she advised and that if we knew each other better, she would call me a simple bitch for that. We both paused and laughed. She then asked what happened, and just like Ebony, she too thought James was a little touched. And not by an Angel.

After both conversations, I spent a sleepless night wondering what to do next. The only way to figure this out was to speak to James. But to do that I had to meet him at church the next day. Perhaps he just wanted to have a quick conference with Pastor Doug. Who knew with James? What if I decided to be rebellious and not go? That thought crossed my mind. I knew though, my lack of attendance at church would sound off some alarm not only to him but to Pastor Doug, as well.

Maybe we both needed to be in the house of God. Right now, I was feeling a lot of turmoil, and I couldn't push my way to happy, no matter how hard I tried. I knew I needed God or something, but right now, I just couldn't do it, especially not after today. I decided to search my heart. What would I be really accomplishing by staying at home? Although Pastor Doug still seemed a little off to me, some of his teachings had really helped. I decided to connect with God and be an obedient wife and meet him at church the next day. There is an old saying that hindsight is 20/20. And as I look back on that day, I wish that I had not stepped foot in those doors.

When the kids and I stepped into the church the next morning, James was already there. He was greeting some of the leaders with a hug, a "God is Good" and a "Praise the Lord." He greeted me with a kiss and took the children to kids' Jr. Church while I took our usual seats on the second row. As praise and worship began, James joined me with his hands lifted high. He seemed to be heavily into worship that morning, and I could see tears rolling down his eyes. I stood in awe and amazement. Perhaps, he was genuinely sorry, I thought. Perhaps God had spoken to him in his time alone, and maybe he needed solitude just like he said. A good feeling began to stir on the inside, and I began to lift my hands in praise also. Then, that's when the shenanigans began.

Pastor Doug came into the sanctuary down the middle aisle. He was dressed in a grey Giorgio Armani fitted mesh Suit with Ferrini Grey alligator shoes. He was draped in a purple mulberry silk robe that was surrounded in studded jewels. He also wore a gold studded crown with matching purple gems. I could tell that everything on that man's body was expensive. I must admit it was kind of a turn on. Pastor Doug had the type of swag that could make the weak-minded woman's panties melt. I saw firsthand how a lot of those women drooled over Pastor Doug and were secretly hoping his relationship with the first lady failed. But Pastor Doug had the "it" factor, the swag that appealed to the younger hip and wealthy up and comers. Some Pastors latched on to athletes and celebrities in this town, but Pastor Doug found his own niche. And believe me, it seemed to be working for him.

As he walked down the aisle of the sanctuary in a swag that could not be matched by any Pastor on the planet, he repeatedly chanted, "I am a king and a priest, and so are you, I am a king and a priest, and so are you." The congregation began to repeat after

Pastor Doug and started to get excited and shout. I looked over at some of the younger ladies in the church who were shouting real hard as Pastor Doug passed them by. One of the bustier women reached out and asked for a special blessing. Pastor Doug came close to the woman. He touched her head, then moved his hands from her head to her chest, then down her body. The lady "fell" in Pastor Doug's arms, and he whispered something in her ear, and his handlers laid her in an open seat in the pew. Pastor Doug continued to chant, and the rest of the congregation repeated.

I looked over at the first lady. The fact that she was a fair-skinned woman did not work to her advantage today as I saw her face turn a shade of red. First Lady quickly gained her composure, lifted her hands, and repeated the chants in solidarity with her husband, the pastor. As Pastor Doug came close to our seats in the aisle, he looked over and called us forward.

Pastor Doug: James and Tabby, I hear the Spirit of God for you. You're such a beautiful couple, amen? You are blessed and highly favored, and God has smiled upon you today. James, I hear the Spirit of the Lord saying that for all your hard work and all your good intentions that you will be rewarded and promoted. Everything you have done thus far has been for the good of your family. Tabitha, your man, is Abraham. Abraham wasn't a perfect man, but he sure loved God!

Upon the sound of that, the congregation began to roar, and James took off running around the church. He did 2 laps around the sanctuary and came back to his seat. James then proceeded to take his wallet from his pocket and dumped all his cash at the feet of Pastor Doug, who raised his hands and proclaimed "Hallelujah"!

Pastor Doug: Glory to the most-high God. I don't know about you guys, but He has favored me this morning! And as the Spiritual overseer of this house, I have a proclamation from the Lord! The windows of heaven are open this morning! If you have a need right now and you want a promotion right now, then sow children of God SOW!

. . .

Pastor Doug immediately laid his hands on James' forehead, which caused him to fall to the ground with the help of one of his handlers. I looked around in disbelief. The rest of the congregation erupted into shouts and proclamations and dug deep into their wallets in a hurried frenzy and ran to the alter to throw money at Pastor Doug's feet. There was so much combustion in the sanctuary that a long line had been formed in anticipation in laying money down for Pastor Doug.

I could overhear one young lady repeatedly saying in a drunken stupor, "If I could only just touch the hem of his garment. If I could only just touch the hem of his garment." Pastor Doug explained that she was talking about Jesus, and not him. But somehow, in the back of my mind, I couldn't help but wonder. As other congregants laid their money at his feet, they chanted things like "I'm a king and a priest," and "The windows of heaven are open for me" and the such like. His handlers immediately got the offering buckets out and began to collect to money laid at the altar.

Pastor Doug: Heaven's window is still open, but it's closing quickly, saints. Hurry children, sow while the window is still open. CHILDREN OF GOD BE OBEDIENT AND SOW WHILE YOU CAN!

I looked around the congregation to see a few straggling congregants gathering their money to take to the alter. There was an elderly woman who was struggling to get there. As she approached, Pastor Doug said, "The window is now closed daughter" in a somber voice, and she began to cry. He looked at her offering and pondered what he would say next. He laid his hands on her shoulder and began to speak in tongues.

Pastor Doug: ABA YATA…ABA YATA…come on saints of God! Let us intercede together on behalf of this woman…Lord PLEASE, PLEASE HEAR MY CRY!!!

The rest of the congregation began to lift their hands in prayer and intercession, along with Pastor Doug.

Pastor Doug: ABA YATA…"The window of heaven has a crack in it for God's beloved because he has heard her cry! Can someone match what the widow woman has offered? There will be a double blessing in it for you, the spirit of God says."

The woman's offering was $500. Immediately three congregants stepped forward to match the woman's offering. Pastor Doug then proclaimed a threefold blessing to not only her but the three congregants who matched her offering. The church erupted, and there was upbeat music, singing, dancing, and running in the church. James was still laid out on the floor during all this, so people just stepped over him. And to top things off, Pastor Doug's handlers then took the buckets of money and dumped them over his head as he said, "Let the rain from heaven rain down on us all"! If I didn't think things could reach any higher heights in one church service, I was obviously wrong.

What was I thinking at that moment? That this had become some sort of pageantry that I didn't want to be a part of. The only thing I could think was that this had become a three-ring circus, and I refused to participate in it. I watched the "spirit move" as a spectator for the rest of the service, praying that since it had a beginning that it also had to have an ending. It's only right, that's the law of balance.

As service ended, the congregants sang the "goodbye until we see you again song," and the church service was dismissed. James, still high in the spirit, asked me to hang tight while he greeted more leaders of the church. While I waited, many of the women came up to me to congratulate me on James' promotion in the spirit and how much of an honor it was for him to be referenced as Abraham, the father of many nations. "Perhaps he is called to be a Pastor like Doug! You would make an excellent first lady," some of the women said. I thought to myself, they didn't know James or me, so how could they assess our relationship based on what took place that day. And what was a "promotion in the spirit" anyway? James wrapped up his last few conversations and approached me in the sanctuary. James greeted me with a kiss. The kids asked if they could go home with my sister after church, and I agreed to give James and I some time to talk.

James and I sat in the sanctuary in silence for what seemed to be forever. He finally spoke.

James: Tabby, today was a good day, wouldn't you agree. The Spirit of God really moved today. I was not expecting the Lord to speak like he did. And to get confirmation that I am right where I should be Glory to God!

James looked up to heaven with a smile. He then looked at me, and his face turned dark. There was a chill in the air that I definitely felt. My spine tightened, and all my senses were on alert. It was like the whole atmosphere shifted from being warm to a distinct coolness that could be felt up and down my body, and I knew that this conversation would be different from the pageantry that I witnessed earlier.

James: Tabby, the way that God moved today was a sign; that you need to trust me, and I don't feel like you can do that right now. I feel like God is moving and speaking through me in this situation, Tabby. It's a lot to deal with, and I pray about it day and night. Can I ask you a question? How much time have you spent praying about this for me? Don't even answer because although you come to church, you don't pray like I do. I'm the spiritual head of our house, and you don't trust me. I am still so hurt and angry about the fact that you went behind my back and went into my personal accounts, how could you?

Tabby: James, wait...

James: No let me finish. That was uncalled for. Why didn't you wait and just ask me Tabby?

Tabby: James, wait for what? So, you could flat out LIE like you did?

James: The bottom line is this; you went behind my back,

which is a breach of my trust. It is also illegal because you technically did not have access to my statements, and you AND YOUR LITTLE FRIEND could face prosecution.

Tabby: My little friend?

James: Apparently, it seems you did a whole hell of a lot of talking to Ms. Burris at the bank yesterday who provided you with the details of the affairs of my accounts without my knowledge or consent. Therefore, Ms. Evans will no longer be employed with our bank effective immediately. It was either that or press charges. (James shrugs)

Tabby: You have got to be kidding me, James. This has nothing to do with Samantha.

James: Oh, so you're on a first-name basis now? This gets even better. Tabby, we are scheduled to move next week into our dream home, YOUR dream home. So, although we have this hiccup, we must move forward according to schedule. The movers will still move our things into the house and you and the kids will proceed. But right now, I can't be with you like this, it's too much. I have extended my stay at the hotel for another month.

Tabby: A MONTH! How the hell am I supposed to explain that James?

James: Just tell the kids that I am out of town on business. They will understand. I will work during the week and see the family on the weekends. My schedule has been hectic like that these days anyway. Perhaps we both need some alone time. Some God time. I just think this is best. Now, because the Lord has blessed me with the anointing of Abraham, I walk in authority to make these decisions. I prayed about it last night, Tabby, and I believe this is the will of God.

Tabby: You prayed about it, for how long? Long enough to get an innocent woman fired from her job? You really are a simple ass ni...

James: First and foremost, I need to remind you we are in God's house, and you will watch your tone with me. Secondly, I don't respond to the ghetto girl that you left behind in the hood. If you want to have a civil conversation, we can do that without all the extra stuff. Things in the house will be business as usual. I expect you to handle things at home, and I also expect you and the kids to be here at church every Sunday morning. We need to keep up appearances here. People need to see us worshipping together. How would that look if folks knew I was staying at a hotel? God is not a man that he should lie.

Tabby: James, I am trying hard to be a good wife to you. But you are trying my patience by putting all this situation on me? Yea, I went to the bank. But you concealed information and then lied about it.

James: I WOULD HAVE TOLD YOU EVENTUALLY!

Tabby: BUT YOU DIDN'T!

James: See, the fact that we are yelling in the sanctuary is a huge problem for me. That's why we need this time apart.

Tabby: James, I don't agree. I think we need to talk about this. Do you really think it's ok that you made all these decisions without consulting me first?

James: We are not here to talk about Keisha.

Tabby: What you don't understand is this conversation has NOTHING to do with Keisha. How could you decide to be away from your family for a month without even the possibility of discussion first?

James: Family? WOULD FAMILY DO WHAT YOU DID TO ME!!!!

Suddenly there was silence. I didn't understand a couple of things that were going on here.

1. Why was James so Angry?
2. If James and I were even having the same conversation.

The "would family do what you did to me" battle cry threw me off just a tad. Instantly in my mind, the psychologist in me tried to analyze some deep-seated issues that may be going on within James. Perhaps he wasn't loved enough as a child or bullied by his siblings. As I imagined him begging for the love of his father, suddenly, the wave of his hand in front of my face brought me back to reality.

Tabby: James, I'm confused

James: There is nothing to be confused about, Tabby. I have been pouring out my heart, and you haven't heard a thing I said. So, previously I laid out to you exactly how things will go for the next month. You need to give me this time with the Lord to work through this. Is that understood?

Tabby: First of all, James, I am not a child, and I would appreciate it if you didn't talk down to me like I was one. Second, it seems to me that you have already laid down the law as you put it in your newly found "Abraham Authority," why do you need my approval.

James: If you listened clearly, Tabby, you would know that I don't need your approval. But of course, you weren't listening. Oh, you heard what I said, but you never listen. I simply asked if you understood that these are the rules of engagement for the next month, no more, no less. All the extra added sarcasm makes you appear childish Tabby, grow up. So, if you feel like I talk to you like a child, then perhaps I feel like I must bring things to a childish level for you to understand.

This mother fucker was pushing my buttons in God's house. I wanted to beat his ass, and at that moment, I looked down the row. Besides a few free-standing Bibles, it was just James and I in the sanctuary. I thought to myself, "As angry as I am, I could probably beat his ass right now with one of those Bibles." I focused on the sharp edges of the hard-back bibles next to us. I imagined myself taking one of those free-standing bibles sitting in the row and beating him over the head over and over again until he bled out. I then would stand up and walk away and leave fate to decide what was next for him... Well, that was kind of sick, but you get the picture. I came back to my conversation and served James just enough childishness to drive his point home even further.

Tabby: Well, since we're still in God's house, then let me be the obedient wife. Why yes, James, I totally understand. These are the rules of engagement for our marriage over the next month. I will serve your house and God's house with my whole entire heart and soul. Is there anything else?

James: As a matter of fact, there is. I forgot to mention that I removed you from all my personal accounts. The only accounts you have access to now are YOUR checking account and OUR personal savings.

Tabby: So, the two accounts that I originally knew about in the first place and already had access to anyway?

James: And this Tabby is why we need a break. I'm done with this conversation.

James got up from the sanctuary pew and walked out of the doors. On his way out, I saw him greet two cute and obviously single sisters in the foyer area. I was a little flushed. But this time, I was gonna fight fire with fire. Somehow. I didn't know what I had planned, but I knew that we couldn't go on like this.

But my first piece of business was to check on Samantha. James was a low-down dirty bastard for getting her fired. I felt terrible because it was my actions that set her termination in motion. I pulled out her business card from my purse and gave her a call. The conversation with Samantha went very well. So well in fact that we decided to meet up for drinks. And that was the beginning of a beautiful friendship between Sam and I which got me through a lot of tough times over the course of my relationship with James.

Samantha was a fireball with a vibrant personality. When we met up for drinks, I imagined her heartbroken and crying. But no, she was bubbly and excited about what would be next. She felt like it was a sign. But what was interesting was that while we were drinking, she ran into a friend of a friend who was being promoted from her position as personal assistant to a local news celebrity here in town. She made a call to her boss, who had one conversation with Sam, and was offering her the job! "So, you see, your asshole of a husband did me a favor. What man means for evil, God means for good. How's THAT scripture for him."

We laughed and celebrated her new gig. There was something about Sam that made her easy to talk to. It was like we were already friends, and that was our official first meet up. Sure, we spoke last night, but that was a brief I told you so conversation. Today, we laughed and talked about our personal and professional lives and where they were headed. Samantha was more of a "fly by the wind" creative type who was into the same spiritual stuff Ebony recently got involved in. The congregation in my church says anything outside of the Bible is Satanic and goes against the word of God. But here I was, in an uncomfortable place in my life, and the two most genuine people I knew were non-traditional church folk. How was I gonna be able to balance my friendships, especially in light of my jacked-up relationship with James?

All I knew is that I needed another friend, a true girlfriend. In a few short hours, I had told Samantha things about my relationship with James that even Ebony didn't know. I don't know why I did. I just knew that I could trust her. Samantha and I wrapped up our conversation and parted ways, promising to keep in touch. We did just that over the years.

Over the next month, James did not waver and spent all his much-needed time at the Hilton Hotel. His conversations with me were limited to calling in the evening and having a goodnight conversation with the kids, as well as text messages with instructions on the move and the expectation as to where certain things went in the house. His demeanor was cold, and every night after speaking with the kids, he would talk to me about how hurt he was that I did this to him. Some nights he would cry, and others would get angry. But the conversation always ended the same; somehow, this was all my fault, and he had yet to hear me apologize or feel any remorse. And to be honest, I didn't. I wasn't the one in the wrong here. HE lied to me. What was there for me to apologize for?

What was also fascinating was seeing James turn into a different person on Sunday mornings for the spectators. He would pull out all the stops during service. He ran, he cried, and he threw money at the altar every Sunday. What I also found interesting was that every time he got in the spirit, there was a financial "move in the spirit." As soon as James got up and put money on the altar, the congregation followed. In the back of my mind, I started thinking there was a Ponzi scheme going on with James and Pastor Doug. "Nah, I'm just crazy," I thought. It did seem coincidental. That minute thought was overshadowed by the real issue at hand; my husband had hurt me and was living somewhere else.

Deep down, I really did love, James. And every week without him made me think more about him, his absence, and how much I was starting to miss him. What I couldn't understand was how he could be so cold to me during the week but pretend to be the doting husband here on Sundays. Every week he would greet me with a long kiss, and love on me in front of the rest of the church while ignoring me afterwards. He even pretended to be the "step-father of the year" by acting like he missed the kids. But maybe he did. I knew for sure that our lives could not go on like this; I did not sign up for this misery.

About five weeks later, we did our usual routine of meeting up in the sanctuary. This time I grabbed on to James' hand. He looked at me and his eyes begin to water, and I noticed his hand was shaking slightly. With tears in my eyes, I said, "Baby, please come home so we can work this out." He looked at me with a painful expression. "Let's talk about this later." I was crushed but hopeful. I waited for Pastor Doug to enter the sanctuary. Pastor Doug approached the platform and spoke into his hands-free microphone:

Pastor Doug: I have great news congregation! These past few weeks have encouraged me to start a Spiritual Father-Son mentoring group where I will be training up my leaders as spiritual sons that will help raise up our next leaders in the church. Glory to God! The father-son relationship is important in the Bible. And a good father has obedient sons; sons, who have proven they are trustworthy and can hear from God about their relationship with God, their finances, and their families. It's a wonderful day, saints!

The congregation erupted. Pastor Doug went into more detail about the program, its importance, and how he will use the offerings given to him over the last five services to invest in the mentoring program to make it a legitimate program to raise up everyone in the church to become leaders that desired to. I thought that was a pretty noble idea on his part. Kudos to Pastor Doug.

Pastor Doug: Now, to keep this program going, we may call on financial support from time to time. But the Spirit of God has already selected my first son in the gospel. Abraham…Well, you all know him as James…Please come forth.

The congregation cheered again. Wait, was James getting ANOTHER spiritual promotion? I couldn't believe this! To be honest, it had me second-guessing my sanity. Maybe I was the issue here. It seemed like things were going well for James, meanwhile I was miserable during our separation. I sighed at the thought of what was beginning to be my life; misery. I was unhappy and didn't know how to fix things. I wanted to run out of that church, sit in my car, and cry. But, at that moment, I couldn't do it. I had to keep up appearances for James, or things would get worse than what they were. So, I listened and smiled and congratulated James after service, as any good wife should.

He drew me in for a deep hug. He looked at me with sincere apologetic love and said, "I'm sorry. For my part in this argument that we've been having. I would like to come home and talk about things if that's ok." And just like that, my heart melted some more. I didn't fully understand this man, but I had married him and signed up for this madness. I thought about how this was just over year one, and how it takes most couples to hit the three-year mark before they got it right. "Maybe I haven't given myself enough time," I thought. And I decided to say yes to James and went home as a family and talked.

Our discussion that night was probably more about releasing sexual pinned-up frustration than solving the problem at hand. That afternoon and evening, we fucked and sucked the life out of each other, and I missed that. James was a little more aggressive than usual, however. His slaps on the ass were harder than I could previously recall. The slaps on the ass turned into pinching my nipples extremely hard and slapping me in the face a couple of times. I was into freaky shit, but GEESH that was ridiculous! I decided I was going to address that after we made love or whatever we were calling it.

After a brief conversation about the events of the past several weeks, James and I agreed to have a ceasefire. We decided to forgive each other and move on from this situation with a mutual understanding.

1. We agreed to keep all our accounts separate
2. For the moment, we would be in separate bedrooms
3. I would be responsible for all the financial obligations when it came to my children. James would pay all the bills, but my personal credit cards and any finances that pertained to the kids, including medical bills, were on me. I picked up my own medical policy at my job with my promotion upon his request.

His rules of engagement felt more like a roommate situation than a marriage, which brings me to part 1 of straw #2; the lack of sex. Over the course of the nine six years of our marriage, James spent time in and out of the second bedroom, his REAL bedroom. One can imagine that trying to be intimate with someone that lived in a totally separate bedroom would pose a challenge. Every time there was an argument or disagreement, he would reside there for weeks at a time. Once there, that beautiful external organ of his was on shut down, leaving me with many lonely and frustrating nights.

Our arguments were mostly about the same thing; his baby mama and her blatant disrespect, which led to straw #3. James never seemed to defend my honor when it came to her. When I tried to show him the error of his ways, it only made things worse. We would argue, and he would retreat. Once our arguments subsided, he would be solemn and remorseful and spring back to part 2 of straw #2, the Tiffany Boxes. I hope that you are following all of this. I had to mention these three together because they are intertwined in all my examples. Without the argument, he couldn't withhold sex. Without withholding sex, there could be no remorse. Without remorse, there could be no beautiful Tiffany boxes. All I know is that after repetitive years of this bullshit, I had gotten fed up.

Keisha had no respect for me or my marriage. Keisha would continue to call our home and James' cell phone at all hours of the night. If we were in bed together, he would get out of bed and go into his other bedroom. He seemed to demand complete secrecy with his conversations with her, and my gut always told me that James kept me on a "need to know" basis. Whatever Keisha had to say, it didn't matter to him because he gave her his immediate attention. But I thought he hated her?

Apparently not. I couldn't imagine myself leaving the room every time Travis called to talk about the kids. I wonder how James would feel if the role was reversed. Our arguments arose because I would ask about the secrecy. Why was she calling so late, and why did he have to leave the room? Well, this would enrage him about my lack of trust. He would then bring up all my sins of the past and ask me not to badger him. If he felt like I was, he would explode and sulk in his room for weeks at a time, only coming out to fuck me in cave-man style fashion to get his rocks off. This was frustrating for me because

1. We never resolved anything really
2. I wasn't getting fucked properly
3. I couldn't get out of that which I didn't really understand

James and Keisha had a love-hate relationship throughout the years. They would call and cuss each other out over little things, then stand together as "frenemies" when Chris started going down the wrong path. James would pretend to be her friend on the phone and talk to about her like a dog to me about her lack of parenting skills, how much of a bitch she was, and how she was misusing his child support money. Oh, during those times, our relationship had some resemblance of a marriage, although our finances were still separate. It was getting harder to keep my nest egg now that I was providing solely for myself and the kids. James had cut back on paying the utility bills, so they became my financial burden slowly over time as well. All the while, things seemed to be going well for James, or so I would overhear. James indicated he was making sound financial decisions that would have our family set for life. I felt secure in that information.

When things were bad with Keisha, however, they were bad with us on the homefront as well. James would be moody and withdrawn. When I reached out to offer my support as a wife, he would ask me to just pray for him and schedule additional counseling sessions with Pastor Doug. There were also times that I could verbally hear him yelling at Keisha in the other bedroom. When he spent time in our bedroom, this negro would get out of bed, put her on speakerphone, and take the call in the other room. Sometimes Keisha would flat out ask him if he was alone.

Well, one night, Keisha called at 2am as James and I were sleeping in bed together. We had just had one of our quickies, and I was lying in bed irritated, and sexually frustrated. The phone rang, and James jumped up in usual fashion and put the phone in speaker mode. Keisha was in hysterics about Chris, so James decided to take the call in front of me. It appeared that Chris had a warrant out for his arrest for not appearing in court for his recent drug charges. Wow, what a big surprise. The bail bondsman was at their door to collect $3000, or Chris was going to jail.

Keisha: Oh, baby, I don't know what to do! Do you have the money, James?

James: Keisha, give me five minutes, let me call you back.

James hung up the phone.

Tabby: Whoa hold up, did she just call you baby?

James: (yells) What in the hell has Chris got himself into now! Dammit, I paid the bail bondsman, I gave Keisha that money!

Tabby: James, Honey...Did that bitch just call you baby?

James: Not now, Tabby. She's trying to be ignorant, and you know that.

The phone rang, and it was Keisha again.

James: Keisha, what happened to the money I gave you to pay the bail bondsman?

Keisha: Babe, I made the down payment to the bondsman with the money you gave me, we needed the rest before his court date.

James: Keisha, stop calling me babe, baby, and anything else. Who the hell are you trying to fool Keisha? I paid the bond in FULL with the condition that he would appear in court.

Keisha: Do we really need to argue about this now, James? Our baby is being put in handcuffs, James, you must do something.

James: Keisha gimme a minute damn! Hold the bondsman off for a bit. I need to talk to my wife.

Keisha: Your WIFE! AWE HELL NO FUCK THAT!

James hung up the phone.

I looked at James in disbelief and shook my head. At least he corrected that heffa for once. But James already knew how I felt about this situation with Chris. I felt like these two were enabling Chris's bad behavior by always bailing him out. My kids didn't get that same luxury in our home over the years. They had to walk the line perfectly for the image of James' career, community presence, and his esteemed leadership position at the church. I found it funny that his own son always seemed to get a pass. In one of our counseling sessions, Pastor Doug told me that I was forbidden to even mention Keisha's name because it was a trigger for James and our relationship. I thought that was a bunch of bullshit. James looked at me with a pained expression on his face and raised his hands in surrender

James: Go ahead, Tabby, say what you need to. But you have to understand the predicament I'm in not only in the natural but the spiritual.

Tabby: You know what James, there's a lot I could say, but it's like beating a dead horse. So why bother? And now is not the time anyway. I know that you can't handle multiple fires under pressure. In business, yes. You're one of the most calculated people I know, but when it comes to matters of the heart; however, that's a different story. So, tell me, James, what is it in your heart to do really? Please be honest with me for once.

At that moment the phone rang. I knew it was Keisha. The phone rang three times while we looked at each other in silence. For once in our marriage, it was a good distraction for both of us. At that moment, I was asking James what was really deeper in his heart to do, and he knew that. James had to decide once and for all if he was going to set things straight in our marriage or allow me to begin to make some hard decisions for both of us. James and Keisha had played this cat and mouse game for years, and I was getting tired of it. James looked at me and then looked away and answered the phone.

James: Yes, Keisha.

Keisha: Are you taking this serious, James?

I sucked my teethed and mumbled under my breath.

James: Of course, I am Keisha, what's going on now?

Keisha: Well, they took him away, James. You took too long deciding, and they took him away in handcuffs!

James: Oh my God, are you serious?

Keisha: What's gonna happen to our baby James, I'm so afraid.

James: Calm down, Keisha, it will be ok.

Keisha: James, what if something happens to him? He could be getting jumped or gang-raped as we speak right now!

I chucked and said, "Is she so serious? They just took him away." James looked at me and put his finger to his mouth.

Keisha: Wait a minute. Is that Tabitha? Tell that bitch to shut the fuck up!

Tabby: Excuse me, bitch!

Keisha: Fuck you, project Hoe!

James: Keisha, calm down! I'm on my way!

James hung up the phone. He looked at me and said, "I'll deal with the issue when I see her," and he rushed out the door. Leaving me feeling utterly disrespected and disappointed in the situation. Did this heffa just call me out of my name, and my husband allowed shit to go down? Nah, somebody had to pinch me because I was surely dreaming. James returned a few hours later. He told me he was able to fully resolve the situation until Chis went to court in a few weeks. He also mentioned pulling a few strings with the judges to get the best possible outcome for Chris. But there was no mention of Keisha, her disrespect, and how and if he handled it. I decided to let it go because, at this point in our relationship, it was like beating a dead horse. The outcome would only be the same; I mention it, we argue, he shuts down, then there is an apologetic Tiffany box at the end to rectify the situation. It was a vicious cycle that I was tired of repeating.

After that evening, the disrespect continued. Keisha would call James at all hours of the night to discuss what was going on with Chris. Several times a week, there was a different sob story that had him running to their rescue. James was beginning to spend just as much time dealing with Keisha as he did with our family, sometimes more. Chris had gotten himself in a lot of trouble, and now apparently, he had a baby on the way. This new issue was apparently causing Keisha a bunch of stress. James said he had to be there to make sure she wouldn't lose her mind. It left me wondering what about me? What about the family we had created, did it mean anything to him?

Now that Chris had a baby on the way, it gave Keisha full reign to call whenever she pleased. The mother of the baby had nowhere to go, so Keisha took her in to live with her. She constantly complained about the added stress that having an extra person in her home added to her finances. So, James volunteered to go and have his child support increased. At the same time, my responsibilities around the house increased. James had transitioned all the bills to me except for half of the mortgage on the house. Things were getting a little tighter than I was used to. When I tried to talk to James about the extra strain being put on my finances, he would just shrug it off and suggest that I find ways to eliminate some of my debt. "Perhaps you should spend less shopping. Your monthly shoe subscription is something that can be sacrificed." He just didn't get it. But one thing was for certain. I was tired.

Keisha would call and consult James about all things concerning the baby. The two of them seemed to be getting along more, while it created distance between my husband and me. Our conversation now only consisted of what was going on in Keisha's house. In the years that had passed, and I couldn't remember the last time that James had taken me out and spent time with me. Hell, when was the last time he told me I was beautiful? I pondered that thought for a moment. I could count on one hand the number of times in eight to ten years that my husband had told me he loved me.

When I would ask James about quality time and compliments, his response was simply that because of all the chaos going on, it was hard for him to concentrate. James was not a multitasker. James told me he could not focus on us and our relationship as long as problems were occurring with his son. He expected me to hold down the fort until the rest of his life could get to a place of normalcy, happy. But where was my happiness? I felt like I had sacrificed so much already.

Intimacy with James became few and far between. When I tried to reach out and be intimate, he would explain how all the pressures of life were affecting his manhood. I had no idea this could occur, as I thought men thought about sex all the time. When we were intimate, they were a series of quickies on our scheduled days, with the sex session lasting about 8 minutes from foreplay to release. Hence, the introduction of Johnson. He was my constant lover these days. Johnson became to me everything that James was not. I spent more time with him intimately than I did with the man I took vows with. The bottom line, he still was not a real person with feelings and emotions. Johnson did the trick every time, but I have to admit that there were times I craved something more; someone more.

My ideas of infidelity, however, would only extend to my latex lover as I took my vows very seriously. I knew the only way for me to stay in this marriage was to continue to use Johnson and maybe add a little more to my arsenal. To be honest, I wanted more. It had been a while since I had my pussy licked, and James acted of late as if Boo Boo Kitty was a no-fly zone. It made me wonder what kinds of items were out there to fill that void. So, while James was helping Keisha set up the nursery for their grandbaby, I decided to take a trip to The Pleasure Palace. This local adult store had plenty of pleasantries.

Going to the Pleasure Palace was like an adventure. The Pleasure Palace was the most premium store in the city for adult entertainment. Their motto was, "If you wanna lay, come here first and play." I thought that was an odd slogan for a premium store. I guess it started out as a sleazy storefront, and that was their motto. As the pleasure palace grew, they kept their original motto, hence cheesy play and lay line. I also learned that the pleasure palace held most of the choice supplies there. From duck lips to dildos, the Pleasure Palace was the place for all your erotic needs.

As you walk through the doors of the building, you are greeted by an attendant. The décor in the store was set up like a bedroom with silk and satin sheets draped around several areas in the store. There was soft romantic music playing in the background, where each singer bellowed out melodic romantic melodies of pleasure and love. The pleasure palace was the ultimate place for lovers to not only set the tone for a night of pleasure but for lovers to pick up something extra to give that night an additional spark. They even had several risqué rooms in the back of the store where you can "watch movies" in the comfort of a bedroom. The whole atmosphere was a complete turn on.

As I headed to look for my arsenal of Johnson companions, I stopped at the costumes for role play. I came across a sexy cop outfit where the shirt sank to the navel, and the bottoms were nothing but tight short spandex material. I imagined myself in the cop outfit, and how sexy I would look. I took my finger and ran it up and down the top of the costume, imagining me beckoning my lover to come to take it off. At that moment, I felt an erotic whisper in my ear that made the hairs on my neck stand in pleasure.

It said, "I would let you arrest me, and do ANYTHING to me your pretty heart desires Mami." I turned around, and he smiled. It was probably one of the most handsome Puerto Rican men I had ever come across. He was tall, a shade of golden brown, slightly muscular with the prettiest set of teeth I had ever seen. He also had a beauty mark right above his lip that was a complete turn on. I couldn't help but admire this man from head to toe. Not only was he handsome, but as I scanned his attire from top to bottom, I couldn't help but notice what lay beneath the grey sweatpants he was wearing. I wanted to gasp. I blushed and tried to play it off. I told him, "Thanks for the offer, but I am a married woman." "All the more reason," he said. "But I already knew a classy woman like you would never make love to a stranger. In the end, all a man is left with is his desire. Take care, my love."

I opened my mouth to speak, and nothing came out. I thought about how sexy his accent was, along with everything else about him. Damn! He looked at me, smiled, grabbed my hand, and gently kissed it, released my hand, and passed me by. I felt an electrical charge when he kissed my hand that was dangerous. I was grateful that I was married because a part of me would have thrown caution to the wind and given in to my desire. But I also smiled on the inside, realizing that this girl still had it! I then proceeded to get Johnson a new friend, and perhaps a break from my pussy from time to time. By now, I'm sure he was exhausted.

The *Love Botz Robo Lick 5000 Oral Stimulator*. Now that was a mouthful, literally. The Robo Lick 5000 promised toe-curling clitoral stimulation with powerful g-spot vibration. Ooh, La La! The Robo Lick 5000 came with a rotating wheel of soft flickering silicone tongues and a super-flexible beaded probe that could be positioned to penetrate the vagina. I was sold already. In addition to that, The Robo Lick promised 6 patterns of rotation and 10 different speeds to choose from for the ultimate oral pleasure. SOLD! I grabbed that pink Robo Lick 5000, restocked on my massage oil, and headed home with a sense of urgency. But before I did, I had to make a pit stop. I pulled up in my old hood to see Ray-Ray. He was the local weed man.

Yes, this had become my life. With all the stress from work and my relationship, I had recently begun smoking weed again. I knew for a fact that some of my coworkers were doing more than that. Of course, I turned a blind eye to it because it was really none of my business. Cocaine, however, wasn't the drug of choice in my Sales and Service circle, but alcohol. Every meeting and event turned into an opportunity for us to have a drink. Half of the executive team at my job were functioning alcoholics. There were only a few that added coke to the mix, and the keyword for coke was "snow." Whenever I heard the terms "snow" and "ski" thrown around, I already knew what time it was. But again, it was none of my business.

Smoking weed was a secret that I kept from James, along with my fake man Johnson. Weed helped me unwind from the pressures of James, work, and so-called ministry. Did I feel guilty at church? Hell no, weed was from the earth. As my relationship with James became more strained, he became more visible in leadership at the church. The more visible he became, the easier it was for me to shrink in his shadow and do less and less there.

Did I feel guilty about keeping this from James? Absolutely. But, I felt that he had shut me out of so much of his life, and I didn't know what was real anymore. I also justified my behavior because he kept secrets from me. I knew he did, and I'm sure I could prove it. I just didn't care enough to try anymore. My phone vibrated, and a text message came through. It was James telling me he and Keisha still had a lot to do in the nursery. He agreed to stay on her couch for the night, and they would pick up in the morning. He was skipping church, and he had already touched base with Pastor Doug. How convenient. I decided at that moment that I would not let him ruin what I had planned. This worked out better for me. By this time, Victoria was the only damn near grown kid in the house, and she was staying at a friend's house that night. I decided to take myself to the ultimate pleasure zone with no interruptions. I had my weed, my toys, and my damn self! "Tabby take me to happy," I said.

I got home and set the atmosphere. I poured myself a glass of wine, turned on some soft music, and lit candles in the bedroom. I was ready for an enjoyable night by myself. Since I had all night, I took my time preparing; listening to soft music and imagining what sex would be like with the Puerto Rican man from the Pleasure Palace. I decided at that moment that he would have me tonight. I took my weed from my purse and rolled a fat blunt. I knew I wouldn't smoke it all in one sitting, but I would make sure I was nice and high. I took a hard toke in and held it. I breathed out and coughed a little bit, then a lot. "Damn, this is some good shit," I thought, and then took another hit.

After two glasses of wine and almost a whole blunt, I was feeling exactly how I wanted to, mellow and horny. I thought about the Puerto Rican, I imagined him approaching me again with his hot sensual breath on the back of my neck. My nipples got hard. I imagined him taking his tongue and kissing the back of my neck from the top of my hairline to damn near my spine. My nipples were standing at attention. I imagined how, if I was single, how my response would have been different to his question. How I would take him up on his challenge. As my juices began to flow, I undressed, took one last hit of the blunt, and got the Robo Lick 5000 ready to go.

I thought about my lover at the Pleasure Palace. I had to give him a name. I focused for a minute. Jorge? Oh, Jorge! No, that sounded awkward. Ok, let's see...I began to slowly massage myself and thought about my encounter with him. Damn, that man was fine. Who was he? I pictured him whispering in my ear again, inviting me to spend just one night with him, and this time I responded to his whisper in my ear:

Tabby: Don't you think that's a little forward? As a matter of fact, I am an officer of the law, and I am currently on duty (I picture myself showing him my badge as I move my hands down towards my vagina).

Esteban: An officer of the law, huh? Well, what is a fine officer such as yourself doing in a place like this on duty?

Tabby: I'm working undercover. I'm looking for perpetrators committing unlawful sexual acts in this place, we've gotten several reports. Could you be one of those perpetrators that I am looking to arrest?

Esteban: No disrespect, madam officer, but I only perform unlawful sexual acts on those who are willing.

Tabby: What is your name, sir?

Esteban: Madam officer, my name is Esteban.

Tabby: Well, Esteban, if you'll excuse me, I must get back to work.

Esteban: I totally understand. But perhaps I can be of some assistance to you? Rumor has it that the most lude sexual acts take place in the Risque rooms in the back. As a law-abiding citizen, I feel obligated to take you back there.

Tabby: Ok, Esteban, show me what you know about this place.

As I imagined Esteban grabbing me by the hand, I felt that same electrical charge I did in the store. Immediately, Boo Boo Kitty began to get wet. I started massaging her. I pictured Esteban and I entering one of the Risque rooms.

Risque room number 5 was dimly lit and contained a queen-sized bed, a flat-screen mounted on the wall, and a change in the bathroom attached to the room. I threw Esteban against the wall. I told him I needed to frisk him, to make sure he wasn't carrying any weapons. I made him stand against the wall with his legs spread apart. As I searched him from the back, and I couldn't help but admire how strong his physique was. I took my hands and patted him along the shoulders, and then took my hands and massaged his spine. My hands moved slowly down his backside and between his legs. I made sure to gently brush up against his manhood. I had to make sure he wasn't armed and dangerous.

I told him to turn around. I then took my hands and rubbed his chess and began to pat down his thighs. As I stroked his thighs, I lightly touched his Johnson which jumped in anticipation. I slowly stroked his manhood and asked, "are you carrying anything in here besides your internal organ? It seems to be a little larger than average." He moaned and said, I can strip and show you just to be sure." I told him no and kept gently stroking his cock as I looked into his eyes.

He reached up and touched my breast. He said, "It's only right that I do a search of my own. I usually don't tend to trust officers, and I don't want to be caught off guard." My nipples began to get erect. He circled them gently with his fingertips like he was admiring a fine piece of fabric. My juices began to flow, and I removed my blouse. Esteban said, "take it all off, I need to do a full body search." I objected, and my bra and panties remained intact in my fantasy. But I removed all my clothing, laid on the bed and turned on the Robolick 5000.

As I stood in the middle of the room, Esteban walked around me in a circle and stopped when he got behind me. He grabbed my shoulders and applied a soft massage that felt like heaven. I softly stroked Boo Boo Kitty as the Robolick massaged my pussy at speed 1. I then focused back on my lover, who took his hands and slowly moved them to my breasts while standing behind me. Esteban kissed soft kisses on my neck as he undid the back of my bra. I gasped at the touch of his hands on my erect nipples. He took them between his fingers. He circled them while playing with my neck with his tongue. My bra fell to the ground, and Esteban demanded that I put my hands against the wall, and I complied.

As I placed my hands on the wall, Esteban spread my legs apart, and I was at his mercy. As he licked me down the middle of my spine, he massaged my breasts and played with my nipples. I felt Boo Boo Kitty's tongue flicker. I thought to myself, "Not already. It had been so long." Boo Boo Kitty released a mini fountain and stood right back at attention, waiting for more. My body was on fire as the massager did its work. I increased the motion and speed and thought about Esteban. Esteban's hands moved from my breasts to my waist. He slowly took removed my panties and my body began to tremble. Esteban touched my sweetness, and my juices began to flow.

I massaged my Kitty and audibly began to call Esteban by name. "Oh, Esteban, damn baby, this feels so good." He whispered in my ear, and I felt his passion, his energy. He said to me, "We have all night, baby, let me take my time with you." I moved my lover in a circular motion, and I switched directions and changed speeds. The sensation in my body intensified, and I got back to my fantasy. Esteban took control and grabbed my hands behind my back, and escorted me to the bed. I stroked myself with Robolick as I anticipated what would happen next.

He threw me on the bed face down. He removed his tie and bound my hands behind my back. I began to resist until his hands began making their way from my calves, to my thigh to my love cave. As he stroked my button from behind, I couldn't help but to moan in pleasure to what he was doing to me. Esteban played with me for a while; he would lightly stroke Boo Boo Kitty until she reached the point of no return, and then he would take his fingers and place them in his mouth.

"This is some good pussy right here, I can tell Mami," he said, as he fingered my love box and flickered his tongue, he paused, and in one swoop flipped me over, so I was lying flat on my back in handcuffs. Esteban took my legs and hiked them in the air. He gently massaged my legs as he gave my thighs soft kisses. Esteban kissed my thighs slowly as he pushed my legs apart and positioned himself for a taste of the finest. Esteban edged up to Boo Boo Kitty who was flickering in anticipation. He took the first lick, and as I imagined this, I audibly gasped. It had been so long since a man had touched me in this way, I thought. I called out Esteban's name audibly again as he sopped up my juices with his mouth.

"You taste like pure chocolate, he said, as he took his time licking to the left and moving to the right. "And sweet, sweet cherries too," he said, as he moved his tongue in a circular motion around the edges of my vagina. "I love cherries, Mami, especially those that taste sweet like this pussy." He played with my Kitty, as he talked to me about how to please a woman, how to make love and care for her Kitty, and how he wanted to make me purr. I buried his face deep inside me. Esteban licked very lightly; just enough for me to feel my Baby Girl stand at attention. I begged and said to him, "please." He looked at me and stopped and moved his hands to Boo Boo Kitty's lips. His fingers flicked my center, and his tongue immediately followed. I changed vibrations.

As his tongue flickered in and out, up and down, and around, I could hear my juices scream in excitement. Esteban licked and sucked with masterful perfection, and I changed speeds. As I pictured him licking my body into a frenzy, I couldn't take it anymore, and the anticipation was building. I placed the Robolick 5000 directly on my center, and my orgasm began to build. Esteban, in my fantasy, licked and sucked and licked and sucked until I couldn't take it anymore. My legs began to tremble. Esteban grabbed hold of me with intensity. He dove in like it was a feast he hadn't had since the last holiday. As he licked and sucked me, I met the Robolick 5000 with every single stroke. I turned the dial to 8 and decided to take myself to happy.

As the Bot licked me from every direction, I moved my hips in a circular motion and pictured Esteban giving me everything he had. Our energies matched, and our bodies were in sync. I stroked Boo Boo Kitty until I simply couldn't take it anymore, and I yelled, "Oh Esteban! Fuck me, Daddy, Oh Baby, I'm coming! In that instant, my kitty gave her release, and a waterfall of goodness splashed out from inside me.

"What the fuck is going on here!" I looked up and saw an angry faced James standing in the doorway. He turned on the lights and looked at me in shock.

I was speechless. James was supposed to be sleeping on Keisha's couch that night. What was he doing home? Since I didn't know what to say, the only thing I thought to say was, "Care to join me, James?"

James: Hell, No! Is this what you do when I'm not around? And what is that smell?

James began to walk through the room, looking through all my belongings. I knew then that I was in trouble. As he rummaged through my things, he stumbled across my forbidden drawer, my secret drawer. James found the box, and my lovers were exposed. He opened the box to find Johnson and my stash of Mary Jane. He looked at me in disgust.

James: You whore!

James began to tear the room apart in an angered fury. He turned over drawers, flipped over the dresser, and began throwing my things across the room.

Tabby: James, calm down!

James approached me and pushed me. I stumbled and tried to run. He grabbed me again and threw me around the room like a ragdoll. I screamed for him to stop. James then threw me on the bed and tried to pin me down.

James: Is this what you want, huh!

James grabbed my naked breasts violently. I tried to swing, but he grabbed my hands.

James: Is this what you want! You want this dick, bitch? Answer me, whore!

James started applying sloppy kisses to my neck and face. I squealed, and we struggled. I screamed loudly, "Help, Get off of me." He yelled, "I thought this is what you wanted" James then got off of me, and I shrunk in the corner and began to sob. James stood over me, stooped down, and pointed his finger in my face.

James: Tabby, you listen to me. You hurt me, and I can't believe you did this to me! Here I am coming home to be with my wife, and this is what I see. You bring sex toys in our home! And drugs! And when I walked in, you were calling out somebody else's name! That's an act of adultery by itself. So, in my eyes, you are an adulterer and a whore!

I got angry as hell. This man had the audacity. James snatched me to my feet, and I jerked away from him violently.

Tabby: How dare you say that shit to me after all you've put me through. Then you have the audacity to try to rape me! Again! Who the fuck do you think I am.?

James: You are MY WIFE! I cannot rape you!

Tabby: What you just did was assault and rape.

James walked towards me, and I backed away.

Tabby: No, James, back off. I have a whole hell of a lot to say, but I will say this; Perhaps if you were handling your business as a man, then I wouldn't need accessories.

James: So, what are you trying to say?

Tabby: Does it really need to be said, James? Our sex life went from well to trash to non-existent.

James: That's not fair, you know all I've been dealing with.

Tabby: But for nine years, James? I have given you ample opportunities along with hints and direct talks to step your game up

James: So, you go out and have an affair?

Tabby: When did I have an affair, James?

James: YOU CALLED OUT SOMEONE ELSE'S NAME! Whether they are real or not, they are other than me, so you had an affair!

This nigga was insane, and I was convinced of it at that moment. He continued his rant.

James: And you bought drugs in our home! I didn't know you were smoking again. So now you're the one keeping all the secrets. What you did is unforgivable, and I don't know if I can deal with this.

James grabbed a bag and began to pack.

Tabby: James, where are you going?

James: Why the fuck do you care now? You weren't concerned when you were getting high and masturbating, which is also a sin. And for how long? I have no clue. So, your adulteress ways are telling me that I can go to hell. But for now, since it's so late and I can't get a hotel, I'm going back to sleep on Keisha's couch. While I was resisting the enemy, you were giving in.

I took that to mean he had an opportunity to sleep with Keisha that he turned down. However, he was on his way back there, and with a duffel bag full of items no less.

Tabby: So, you're gonna do what you always do, James, retreat? We need to talk about this because you're blowing this way out of proportion.

James: Right now, I'm so angry and hurt that I can't think about this. Don't make me stay and talk about this. You see what you already made me do.

Tabby: I made you..I'm not touching that James, take your ass on.

James finished packing and left the house. Here I sat, lonely, and no longer horny. I felt kind of dirty, actually. I thought about what James said about my toys and my weed. I then thought about how he almost raped me as a reaction to it. I looked at myself in the mirror and said, "I feel so dirty right now. YOU DIRTY WHORE," I yelled. Then, I laughed. I looked at myself in the mirror again, and I knew there was no truth to that statement. I laughed again, and this time at the insanity of the thought. I knew who I was. I was a woman who was in a marriage in which she was not happy. I also knew I had to do something to change this misery to bliss. But I didn't know how.

A few days later, I received a phone call from James. He said he was able to get into a hotel, and he had a talk with Pastor Doug. James also realized that our marriage was in trouble, and he really wanted to save it. He apologized for reacting the way that he did but wanted me to understand that he had never experienced what he did. He said that he was still hurt by what happened and didn't know how to deal with it. So he felt like our pastor would be the best spiritual mediator in the situation.

"Panty Drop Pastor Doug," I thought. Although James had the utmost respect for him, I had seen way too many times where he was way too friendly with the ladies of the church. I disagreed to no avail. James' suggestion was more like a command. I agreed to meet with them in a few days. In the meantime, James would stop by while I was out of town, to get some more of his things. He also scheduled our meeting where I'd have to fly right in and come straight to the church. I had an eerie feeling that this whole process would be painful.

When I touched down in the city, I headed straight to the

church. I noticed that the only car I had seen was James' BMW. That was odd because usually some of the staff were there. I tried the door, and it was open. As I walked back to Pastor Doug's office, I could hear voices, and again it appeared to be just James in the church. I thought perhaps they had a man to man before I arrived. That wasn't unreasonable. As I got closer to the door, I could distinctly hear the conversation happening. I wanted to ear hustle, but I wanted to also be respectful as I assumed my discussions with the first lady were confidential. I turned to walk away until I heard Pastor Doug say my name.

Pastor Doug: Tabitha will be here soon, so let's wrap this up a bit. (he breathed deeply). I heard all the things you have shared with me throughout the years, and I have prayed about this time after time, James. You have not totally walked upright before the Lord, and that is why this is happening. You see, you are Abraham in the spirit, the father of many nations. Has Tabitha or her children given you any seed?

James: No, but...

Pastor Doug: Now, let me finish. And then she goes off and keeps secrets that are filled with drugs and sex, which is soap opera drama that is not fit for this ministry. And you bring me the proof of her indiscretions, what is this? (I hear him pick something up) The *Love Botz Robo Lick 5000 Oral Stimulator*? What in the name of God!

I stood there for a moment in disbelief. This mother fucker went and stole my toys while I was out of town on business? Who does that? I wanted to storm right in there and cuss both of those assholes out, but my legs were frozen. I sat and listened intently.

James: I'm so ashamed, Pastor. What did I do wrong?

Pastor Doug: Last night, as I prepared for our meeting, I prayed to the heavens. I asked God to give me the word that he wanted for you in this situation, all of Him and none of me. I went to sleep, and I had a dream about guess who? Abraham! That was confirmation for me that God was speaking directly to me for you today.

Now brace yourself, my son, because what I must deliver to you is not tickling to the ear, but as the Prophet of God, I have to give you what thus saith the Lord!

I leaned in a little closer. Hell, Pastor Doug was so smooth that even I was intrigued about what he was about to say next.

Pastor Doug: In Genesis chapter 12:1, God told Abram to leave his house and his family, and he would make his name great. When he did that, he became Abraham. God promised Abraham that he would have a SON, a man of the promise. However, Abraham took matters in his own hands because he and his wife Sarah didn't believe…well, you know the story.

James: Yes, I know it well.

Pastor Doug: Well, I just have to come right and say it; you are not married to Sarah, you married Hagar. Tabitha is not the promise.

I wanted to yell, but I stopped myself by covering my mouth.

James: I'm confused, Pastor. Tabitha is my wife.

Pastor Doug: If you remember, Hagar was a slave girl, but having her child made her his wife. God showed grace in that situation. When Keisha touched down in this city, that was a sign God was working. Keisha has your biological child, and Tabitha hasn't given you any children, nor has she ever had any desire to. Tell me, have you ever been able to bond with her kids?

James: To be honest, not really.

Pastor Doug: Well, there you go. The master never forms a bond with the slave children. That was Abraham's problem. The slave woman became jealous of Sarah's child of promise. Tabitha had issues with you running to help your son. You see the similarities? If you finished reading the story, eventually, Abraham had to send the slave woman away. Who are you gonna send away James?

I had heard enough. At that moment, I walked right into the office. Pastor Doug greeted me with a fake "Praise the Lord, Sis" and asked me to sit down. I looked at the table and saw Johnson and Esteban looking up at me. And that was the straw that broke the camel's back.

Tabby: Pastor Doug, James, no need for me to have a seat. I have just gotten back into town, and I really need to get some rest. (I looked over at James). James, I'll make your decision really easy for you and end all this confusion and foolishness. Baby, (I smiled) I want a divorce.

I then looked down at the table again. I grabbed Esteban and Johnson and stuffed them in my purse. I looked at Pastor Doug, who was dripping in gold, which I hadn't noticed before, who had a look of both horror and disgust on his face simultaneously. I stormed out of his office and called Samantha, who suggested that I crash at her place until I figured out a game plan. I agreed and headed home to pack a few of my things. I asked Mrs. Landy if Vanessa could spend the rest of the week with her, and she agreed. Vanessa had no problem with this because her daughter Hayleigh was her best friend. I dropped off Vanessa and headed to see my second best-bestie.

Over the next few days, Samantha and I set the game planned for what was next for me. I went to the office and demanded a few days off and was scolded because the next two weeks would be filled with town hall presentation sessions that required my presence. They didn't know if I would have time to prepare if I took time off. I remember Marissa giving me the once over, then calling Becky and Amber into the office to strategize for a plan B. I was then released to take advantage of the PTO that I had worked hard for and deserved. That bitch acted like my personal life was an inconvenience for them.

I took my separation from James seriously. I was done. For those few days, he called and texted, cursed me out, told me how much he loved me, and he wanted to make things work. The whole experience was exhausting. Nonetheless, I put my big girl panties on and decided I loved me more than the James-Keisha element. I made serious moves to make this official, and Samantha was my saving grace. When I went to remove James from my personal checking, I found out I was blocked from our joint savings account. I was furious. Well, Samantha just so happened to still be friendly with her former boss, Chandler. Chandler was looking for some payback for getting Samantha fired, and this was just what he needed. Samantha always said it's not what you know but who you know. I swear that girl could negotiate world peace. He found a loophole that stated the account could not be frozen because it required both signatures. He lifted the freeze.

Of course, James was furious, and I got an earful. James knew I never touched that account but was using the freeze as a control measure. He was upset it didn't work, but he was also furious that he could not get Chandler fired because he was not the only elite client at the bank that Chandler handled. Plus, he legally did nothing wrong. But Chandler was not finished with James. My name "mysteriously" was left on account number eight that James had with no restrictions. He told me that James never went into that account, asked for statements or anything, and the money just continues to grow. Chandler then linked my debit card to account number eight. I logged in and checked my balance. TEN MILLION DOLLARS! Holy shit!

This negro had me struggling paycheck to paycheck to pay all the damn bills, and he had ten million dollars in this account alone! Where did all that money come from? James retired 18 months earlier. I know he had this food truck venture with Pastor Doug, and it was going well, but damn was this a food truck empire I didn't know about? I was furious, and it was time for a little payback of my own.

Samantha hooked me up with a realtor, and I looked at a beautiful condominium in the furthest development away from ours but in the same district. Perfect for now, I thought. I made an offer on the condo that was accepted within twenty-four hours. The buyer had relocated out of state and wanted to close quickly. We agreed to a closing date of ten days from then pending the home inspection. I called into work, left Marissa a voice message, and took the next week off. I knew they wouldn't be happy about it, but I didn't really care. The fact that Amber was present at all my meetings was starting to get me suspicious. But I thought if she wanted my job, she could do it over the next two weeks.

During my time off, I spent time at the house directing the movers while James was out of town on business. He took pride in mentioning they were expanding their business to yet another city. I rolled my eyes when he told me. Since he knew I was moving out, James made sure to have Pastor Doug present to supervise the occasion. James wanted to make sure I didn't take any belongings that could have been his before our marriage. He was one sick individual. Pastor Doug was there, but it was more his handlers that were keeping an eye on the movers and I. They were more like his bodyguards than armor-bearers. They went wherever he did, and it was often intimidating for those around him. Pastor Doug approached me to let me know that he was leaving.

Pastor Doug: Tabitha, I'm so sorry that it has come to this, I really am. You two were such an anointed couple.

Tabby: Is that a fact, Pastor Doug? If we were so anointed, then why did you tell him I was Hagar, and to put me away?

Pastor Doug opened his mouth in disbelief.

Pastor Doug: I know I heard from God for the two of you, I really did. But you see, man has free will. And the two of you are doing what you think the will of God is. Don't blame the demise of your marriage on me, Tabby. (Pastor Doug started to walk away and turned around) Oh, and Tabby, I think it's best if you took some time away from the ministry. This was James' home church first, and he needs time to emotionally heal from this terrible ordeal. (Pastor Doug shook his head and walked away).

After getting everything situated, I relaxed in the company of my second best-bestie. We talked and laughed mostly in between glasses of wine. We shared stories about our childhood and our parents. Her story didn't seem far off from mine. I was glad that I had Samantha to lean on then, and she was a great relief from what had been the last ten years of my life.

I thought about the last ten years. I got somber thinking about the drama, the fights with James, and the make-up Tiffany boxes. I immediately shut that thought process off and focused on what was next; happy. Or at least it was a start. I would take the next leg of this journey I called life and find my way back to happy. I had a lot to think about, though. It was just me now. Vanessa would be headed to college soon.

What did I want life to be like? Would I devote more time to my career? Hell, did I really want to? All I knew was I was going to have fun figuring it out. I would start by taking Pastor Doug up on his invitation to stay away from the church. That ministry was wacky anyway, so I was more than happy to oblige him. I thought about the fact that it was Sunday morning. I had to admit to myself that it felt good not putting on a show for once. I breathed deeply and smiled. And at that moment, Samantha burst through her spare bedroom with a bottle of wine.

Sam: You know I always say it's not what you know but who you know, right? Well, I know you don't go to that church anymore, Mami, but you need to tune in today!

Tabby: For what? And what is the wine about?

Sam: You might need it later, Mami. Pastor Doug is doing a special teaching. A girlfriend of a girlfriend goes to that church. They sent a text message blast on behalf of the ministry, encouraging people to tune in for his special message, "The Hagar Teaching."

Tabby: Are you for fucking real?

Sam: I knew it would get your attention Mami!

Samantha turned on the television. Pastor Doug had just asked the congregation to hold up their bibles and repeat after him. He then prayed that the spirit moved as "thou wilt" and asked the congregation to turn to the book of Genesis. True to the conversation that I overheard, Pastor Doug began to talk about Abraham and his two wives and their children. He encouraged the congregation to know the difference between the promise and the falsehood.

Midway during the service, Pastor Doug had a somber look in his eyes. He talked about the dangers of a woman like Hagar and encouraged the men of the church to beware.

He then asked Camera A to get a close-up on him. He looked at the camera and winked and said with a low, raspy voice that only a pastor could muster up:

Pastor Doug: We had a modern-day Hagar situation right here in this ministry!

The congregation gasped.

Pastor Doug: Oh, yes, saints. And the Hagar was nothing but a slut in sheep's clothing PRETENDING to be one of the flock…OH C'MON SOMEBODY

The congregation began to shout.

Pastor Doug: Oh, I feel the spirit moving saints! This Hagar teaching is spiritual, not natural, C'MON SOMEBODY! SHATA BO SHIYA!

Pastor Doug proceeded to air some of our dirty laundry without naming names. My name that is, as he painted James to be the picture of the wonder boy. I watched in disbelief as the man who was my overseer, the "shepherd of my soul," tore me down on national television. Pastor Doug then jerked his body.

Pastor Doug: Oh, I feel the spirit moving saints. I feel myself getting back to my roots…

The organ began to play

Pastor Doug: IIIIIIIIIIIIIIIIIIIIIII feel the spirit!

The congregation shouted as the Pastor hooped and hollered between the organ keys.

Pastor Doug: (began to hoop) I once was lost, ha, but now I'm found, ha, I got my feet, ha, on solid ground, ha. If she's the Hebrew slave, ha, then put her away, ha if you don't be obedient, ha, then Ya gotta pay, ha but saints I say, ha that ya gotta pray, ha but as long as I got KING JESUS ha, I'm A-OK! Ha! Oh, SHATA SHATA SHATA!

As the music cued down, Pastor Doug decided to bring the service to a close.

Pastor Doug: Oh, my beautiful saints, before I bring our time together and sing our song, I wanted you all to be aware of a disturbing situation in our congregation. My son in the gospel, James, is going through a tough time and needs your prayers saints.

I couldn't believe what I was hearing. Did this man just ask the saints nationwide to pray for my soon to be ex-husband? "AWE," I listened to the congregation say. Apparently, I had missed something as I let my mind wander, but the pastor continued:

Pastor Doug: Yes, yes saints, divorce is a terrible thing

He told the whole world that James and I were splitting up. I imagined some of the single ladies in the church, putting themselves next in line to be his wife. "Oh, Mr. Taylor, I'm so sorry for your loss," and "My God, man of God, you shouldn't be alone," came to mind. In anger, I tried to focus on the rest of what Pastor Doug was saying.

Pastor Doug: He is going to need all of our support and love right now. Let's stretch our hands forward. Immediately in unison, the congregation extended a prayer arm on behalf of James.

The camera zoomed in on him, and those that were close to him touched his shoulder. James broke down and cried, then fell to his knees. At that moment, I felt so bad for him, for us. The greeters came and covered him with a holy blanket, and James began to weep louder. Pastor Doug reached down and extended a hug to James and told him that he loved him. The whole thing was bittersweet. Until...

Pastor Doug: As we cover our brother in prayer, I have asked Sister Taylor to remove herself from our congregation, and she agreed. Mrs. Taylor is a woman of God, too, and she knows James needs this time of refreshing. Mrs. Taylor will no longer be welcome in this house while James is being restored. Her presence would only serve as a distraction for him.

"Hallelujah," one of the congregants shouted. I shook my head and poured the wine. Pastor Doug silenced the congregation and encouraged them to keep "Our" divorce lifted in prayer.

Pastor Doug: Now, this is no way about the teaching today. Ms. Taylor is still blessed and highly favored. This is just a big coincidence that God gave me this message on the same day I had to make this announcement. The camera panned the crowd. I could see quite a few people in the Super Dome laughing and whispering to each other. Pastor Doug did precisely what he set out to; try to humiliate me for calling him out on this silly bullshit in the first place. But what he didn't realize is that I no longer cared. He could take his Armani suits and gold crowns, his alligator shoes, and his Hagar teaching and shove it up his ass. I was done for a while, with James, with religion, with everything. I turned off the television, Samantha and I clinked glasses, and we toasted to my new life ahead.

LIVIN' IT UP IN L.A.

L.A., baby! HERE I COME! I smiled to myself as I touched down in one of America's most beautiful and busy cities. As I took in the view from my Uber on the way to my hotel, it was truly breathtaking! For the first thirty minutes of the ride, at least. Who knew that there were so many people and so much traffic in LA, Geesh! There were eight lanes of traffic, and they were all backed up. And to make matters worse, these drivers were bogarting their way through traffic like they owned the road. Welcome to LA, I thought. Despite the traffic, and thinking I needed to get to safety as quickly as possible, the scenery was still amazing.

LA is filled with many hilly roads lined with palm trees and sunny skies. As we took in the landscape, I admired the vast mountaintops that sat above the city but just below the clouds. The mountains were various colors of red and brown, and they seemed to just say "look at me" because of their stature alone. And I did just that and took in the beautiful mountaintops that seemed to transform into various figures with the movement of the clouds. I played a mental game with myself and analyzed what I saw. By doing this and focusing on the beauty of the landscape, I took my mind off of the apparent traffic that seemed typical for this time of day.

The heart of LA was filled with tall skyscrapers in which Manhattan came to mind. And just like Time's Square, the diverse population of wannabe's, superhero's, panhandlers, and the elite all blended together to make a wonderful melting pot. Further along, I saw the Hollywood sign in the distance; I couldn't help but get excited. LA was a place that people came to explore their inner greatness. Many have forsaken family and friends, careers, and everything they know just to take the chance at fulfilling a life-long dream. But it's also a place where fulfilling those dreams become a reality if you put in the work.

As I pulled up to my hotel, I couldn't believe my eyes. This was not the Hilton that I knew. It wasn't the Hilton at all, it was the Hollywood Hills Villa. At that moment, a text message came through. It was from Sam. She was welcoming me to the city in style to get the rest, relaxation, and fun that I deserved and needed courtesy of her boss, this A-List celebrity. But who was this person? And how did she pull this off without me finding out? I guess in the end, it didn't matter, and I decided to count my blessings and enjoy the upgrade.

I got out of the car, and the concierge took my bags. Before I stepped into the villa, I wanted to take in the view. The villa appeared to sit on the edge of the city, and as I looked around me, I took in the sight of the hills and trees that sat on top of the mountains. The villa itself was surrounded by exotic trees with multi-colored leaves and beautifully landscaped shrubbery. The birds were singing, and it was all very peaceful. I thought to myself, this was precisely what I needed.

As I stepped inside the villa, I was flabbergasted. The Hollywood Villa was a breathtaking 3,000 sq. ft. home with panoramic views, gorgeous wood-beamed ceilings, and spacious outdoor lounge areas. The villa overlooked all of LA, and there were various places to get a beautiful view. All three bedrooms had a view of the city and were surrounded by vast hills that seemed to go on for miles. The master bedroom had its own private bathroom with a custom tile centered jacuzzi. You could step right onto the balcony and right into the hills to get a dynamic view of the heart of the city.

I thought about this gorgeous place and the first thing that I wanted to do. I paused for a moment. I could shop, which always made me feel better. Or I could order a spa treatment. Now that I was in the city, I had no clue what I really wanted to do and who to do it with. Maybe Samantha had plans. Perhaps we could hook up later. I took a deep breath. I reminded myself that I came here to get away. All my trip itinerary didn't need to be decided in the first five minutes of my trip here. I told myself to relax, and I decided that I would take a nap, stay in, and tonight I would enjoy the city from up here in the beautiful villa mountains.

For the next few days, I got to know myself quite well. I had an in-home spa day, and treated myself to a full-body massage, a detoxifying body mud treatment, hair, nails, and make-up to boot. Hell, I figured since I was in LA I might as well get glammed out. My personal client ambassador took me on a personal shopping spree on Rodeo Drive, courtesy of James, and account number eight! I even signed up for a spiritual one-day seminar to get in tune with my inner self. I was looking good, eating good, and I also learned to relax a little. However, amid all this glitz and glam I still found myself a little bored. Although it was fun shopping, eating, and tuning in to my spiritual guide, I had not been with people. Not real people anyway. Everyone I was hanging out with were there because they were getting paid to be. What kind of loser was I? my only real friend in this town had flown out as I flew in, and I was beginning to think that this villa was more like a consolation prize.

Samantha was unavailable because her boss had a photoshoot in Italy that required her to travel. Who was this person? And why did she take my second best-bestie away? At least I knew it was a woman. Well, SHE had better give me some time with my friend or there was going to be hell to pay. Samantha assured me that she and I would hang out as soon as she returned. I was even her plus one to an exclusive celebrity party that was taking place in a couple of days. She told me to pick out something sexy, because this event would be like nothing I had ever seen before. The invitation details were on the way. "How mysterious," I thought. What was Samantha up to? I wondered what her new life was like in the thrust of the celebrity crowd. I had to admit, Samantha had the perks of the rich and famous and was living a fabulous life. Her philosophy of "not what you know but who you know" had helped her create the life she'd always dreamed of.

"Sex De Soleil: Edibles and Ecstasy" was the headline of the invitation that I received as the plus one for Samantha. Well, the invitation itself was more like a three-ring sex circus. And I mean that, literally. In addition to a beautifully crafted paper invitation came a personal greeting from a man dressed in a black leather ringmaster costume. "Hear Ye, Hear Ye, it's time for some PLEA-SURE." Then suddenly, the music cued, and sexy clowns popped out of the car, along with a bearded lady covered in nothing but tassels and a lettuce leaf over her lady part. There were naked acrobats with body art as their covering and I watched as they performed to the techno circus mix that played through the speakers. Once the music stopped, a royal horn blew, and the ringmaster begins to speak:

Ringmaster: All Hail Queen Lady G! Lady Gaga humbly requests YOUR presence for an exclusive night of entertainment. This year's theme: "Sex De Soleil." So, bring your sex and your Soleil and come, let's PARTAAY!

He paused and looked for me to respond. I was still in shock, though. Not from all the circus sexiness but that Lady Gaga was inviting me to her party! Samantha was Lady Gaga's assistant! It was Lady Gaga!

Ringmaster: Hello? Earth to star flake, come in….

Tabby: Oh, I'm so sorry! Of course, I accept! Who would turn down Lady Gaga? (I screamed) It's Lady Gaga!

Ringmaster: Wise choice my beauty, if one turns down Lady Gaga, one NEVER gets a second chance to make a first impression! Toodle-Loo!

And just like they appeared, the three-ring sex circus folded up their props, got back in their fancy clown car, and drove away.

Shortly thereafter, Samantha called, and she agreed to come to the villa for drinks. I really missed my girl. With all the stuff with James, she was right by my side. She helped me live and laugh a little when I was presented time after time with that Keisha bullshit. She was my ride or die, and James couldn't stand the fact that I had someone like that in my corner. Oh, he tolerated Ebony, because she stayed out of the way mostly. But Sam was never afraid to speak her mind and encouraged me to do the same. This sick dude even blamed her for the fact that I had started smoking again and had a "sex arsenal" as he put it. I guess it was easier to shift the blame than take responsibility. Samantha was tough though; his snide remarks and sarcasm went in one ear and out of the other.

When this opportunity opened for Sam, I knew it was big. She had to sign a non-disclosure agreement and everything to be hired. She then had to pack up and leave within 48 hours to begin her assignment. So, when she parted, we never really had a chance to get a proper goodbye. We had promised to keep in touch, but in the beginning her time was dominated by extensive travel and elaborate parties. So, it took several months for her to finally make an outreach. But since then, we promised to touch base at least once month, and stuck to that schedule.

Samantha Maria was still as beautiful as she was when I saw her last, even more. I was amazed by the glamazon the stared back at me in excitement. Everything on her shouted designer from the clothes on her back to the hair extensions and lashes that enhanced her already model style face. Sam looked like she went from a size eight to a four, but she really looked good. She explained that her position required her to be physically fit and certain sizes such as 2 and 4 were not only suggested, but strongly encouraged. When she explained what shows up on pictures and films and how the camera adds pounds, I totally understood.

We spent the next hour drinking wine and catching up on all the happenings in both of our lives and it was like we never missed a beat. Sam and I laughed, and shared war stories. Hers were a lot more exciting than mine, of course. But being with Sam gave me a feeling of elation. A sense of excitement about what lied ahead for my life. I was getting back to happy. At least I was gonna try. And I felt good just thinking about it. We shifted gears and I showed Sam this sleek little black dress that I had purchased for tonight.

"That black dress TAKES the SEX out of sexy," was her response to what I thought was an amazing purchase. "What do you mean, it's sheer lace," I said. She shook her head and said "it would never do," in her boujie LA voice. She then made a phone call, and within thirty minutes, we were having our own personal pleasure party. I watched in awe as the models appeared before us dressed in some of the hottest lingerie that LA had to offer. "So, no one is wearing real clothes?," I asked. Samantha laughed like I said something funny and began selecting a few pieces for me to try on. I must admit, I felt like a totally different person each time I put on something new. It felt good. To be completely honest it felt great.

I told myself tonight I was going to live a little. Hell, I was going to be in the presence of A-list celebrities. Maybe I would even give Johnson and Esteban a night off. Ever since I touched down in LA Boo Boo Kitty had been screaming at me, and all the meditation, self-discovery and shopping had not been able to quench that desire. She needed some penis, and tonight if she was lucky, her personal genie was gonna grant her request.

I tried on my last outfit. It looked damn good and I knew it was the one. It was a black and red baby doll camisole that crisscrossed in the front around the neck area. The v-shaped front was sheer black and red lace, and the back covered the derriere only. There was a simple X-shaped rhinestone stitched in the vagina area, and the outfit was completed with 2 black garters. When I approached Samantha she nodded in approval, and said, "Well, I believe somebody is getting fucked tonight. That's the spirit!." I agreed and we laughed, spending the rest of the evening sipping wine, and smoking Mary Jane until it was time to head out for the party.

We arrived at the party courtesy of our concierge. It just so happens, that the Sex De Soleil extraordinaire was occurring at one of the villas up the road. It was amazing to see this elaborate 15-bedroom villa transformed into a three-ring circus. I stepped out and took in all the sights from outside. The landscaping was still breathtaking; but as you looked to the villa you could see a full-blown festival in swing. I got a little nervous. I was going to be among celebrities for the first time ever. What would I say to someone who has everything? I just hoped that I didn't freeze up. I took a few deep breaths and looked at Samantha. She motioned for me. Well, it was now or never.

As we stepped into the villa, we were greeted by sexy women dressed in hot pink and black lace western style salon dresses that you see could through. The dress was accessorized with black fishnet stockings, hot pink stiletto pumps, a black lace choker and a rhinestone headband with a feather that made the whole thing go together. The western hotties walked around the party with trays of edibles for the guests to try at their leisure. It was actually quite a turn on seeing big busted ladies walking around the party handing out goodies while their "goodies" spilled out of their outfits.

The grand host had a one edible minimum requirement with a 6 edible max out. They had a neat system in place for checks and balances. Upon checking in we were given a card. The card served as a tracker for edible and ecstasy intake. Once you were served a treat you swiped the card, and the card tracked your usage. The host wanted to make sure there were no mishaps, we were there for fun and games and she wanted us to have a good time.

Where was she anyway? I thought it would be nice to get a chance to meet her. As I was deep in that thought I decided to take that opportunity to try my first edible. It wasn't too bad. I was waiting to see if these things lived up to their reputation. Samantha told me that these were a milder form of edible which would be equivalent to a joint. So, I got bold and took another one. Nothing, I thought. Sam and I decided to take in all the scenery and meet some fabulous people along the way.

As we walked through the party, I took in all there was to see. There were acrobats with fire rings and tightropes dressed in leather bottoms and body painted tops. They swung through the air in sensual and exotic stances that captured the attention of the guests. There were also several dancers and models dressed in animal print body suits that rode on live beasts in the yard of the villa. There were lions and tigers and elephants, oh my! They did juggling acts and acrobatic feats as they rode on the backs of the beasts. It was quite a sight to take in.

Inside, three of the lounging areas were transformed into dance floors with different music selections based on the preference of the guest. The techno room was filled with hype party goers dressed in neon lingerie with glow sticks waved to the electric sounds of the music. Another lounge area blared the top of the chart music and the celebrity A listers could be seen in VIP sections curled up doing unmentionable things. In the Urban lounge you could hear the latest hip hop and R&B music blasting from the room. Celebrity entertainers displayed their fame by hosting elaborate private lap dance parties in the VIP section of the lounge. Each room catered to the needs of the guests, and since the guest list was so diverse the celebrity host wanted to make sure everyone had a good time.

The Sex circus wouldn't be true to its name if there wasn't going to be any sex. What would be the purpose of having a Sex De

Soleil? The bedroom chambers were turned into private pleasure zones. Each room had a sex-centered theme and the rooms were dedicated to couple and threesome activities. The rooms were also set up peep-show style, where outsiders could peep through the see-through beaded curtains and the rules were very specific. If you enjoy what you see you are invited to come in, but strictly by invitation. I had never seen anything like this before.

There was also a taping of a porn session going on in a private room adjacent to the bedrooms. This special filming was by invitation only as well, and I watched famous celebrities enter that room with a special entrance ticket. Several well-known directors in the porn industry were also there and used it as a networking opportunity for their business. I thought the whole LA scene may be a bit much for me. Then when I came to the granddaddy of all the party extras, I knew it this life was much too fast.

The last sight to see in this beautiful villa was coined the Ecstasy Zone. This was a huge open space in the back of the villa. The floor was padded with plush faux red carpet, and there was an oversized sectional in the middle of the room where multiple guests made out. There were also decorated mini mattresses of multiple sizes neatly displayed around the room for those who were into watching and participating in in group sex. Couples were already marking their spots in the room, and you could see multiple people in various stages of sex. In addition, pornographic images that lit up the environment on oversized flat screen televisions bought the atmosphere of sex to life. There were also life-sized posters of hot sex symbols, and every song selection seemed to ooze lyrics of sex, drugs, and being free.

An oversized sign that hung down from the ceiling signaled the rules of engagement for the Ecstasy Zone; "Three AM is the bewitching hour: Where in lies EXTREME PLEASURE! Nothing is taboo. If you are not licking, fucking, or sucking you must exit! If you choose to stay, you must engage, NO EXCEPTIONS." I looked over at Sam. She gave me a knowing look and suggested we head back to the rest of the party. I agreed but swiped my card for a hit of ecstasy before we left. I mean we were in the Ecstasy Zone, right?

So far, I still wasn't feeling the effect of the edibles, and about 45 minutes had passed. Maybe my tolerance level was high due to my own personal weed usage. Whatever it was, it wasn't working. I decided to switch gears in my thoughts. I wanted to have some fun. I felt like I needed to hear some good music and dancing; be among my own people for a bit. So, Sam and I decided to venture into the Hip-Hop and R&B Room.

When we entered the room, they were in the middle of a live set with an up and coming band named Desire. The leading lady belted out neo-soul melodies that stuck to my spirit. I felt myself swaying back and forth to the music seductively as I felt every lyric in my soul. Wait a minute? Was it the music or the edibles? Did the ecstasy kick in that fast? Hell, I didn't know. While I was deep in thought trying to figure this out, I suddenly heard the most amazing guitar strings and I looked up. It was the FINEST young guitarist I had ever seen. He had to be about 30ish, was about 6 foot 2, brown-skinned, with a sexy frame and long dreadlocks that hung just below his shoulder. He seemed to be a simple kind of guy. He wore basic designer jeans and a cut off shirt, and his muscles and everything else was left to the imagination. He played that guitar with such intensity, that I felt my body pulsate with every single cord. I thought to myself, "this man is truly strumming my pain with his fingers," and I laughed out loud to myself, and then began to move seductively to the guitar strings. I pictured this man coming on to me, flirting with me, and making love to me. I swayed back and forth and started touching myself seductively as he continued to play my song.

Man, between the melody of the music and the rush of the ecstasy I felt good! I looked up and our eyes locked. At first, I was a little embarrassed, but I felt my inhibitions getting stronger, and my control less and less. I looked at him again, and he was still looking at me. I smiled. I touched myself again and subliminally beckoned him to come. Our eyes locked and it was intense. He understood my call without me saying a word.

When the set ended, I ventured over to the bar with Sam to have another drink. I also scoured the room to see if my secret fantasy was still around. He was across the room and I noticed him watching me. I tried to play it cool and whispered to my girl. Moments later he approached me and introduced himself. The handsome man that was strumming my pain was Samson and he was 38 years old. His voice was as smooth as butter, and every word that came out of his mouth sounded like pure pleasure. I was sprung already. This man could have my pussy, my money and my credit cards. Well, maybe not the money and cards, but the way I was feeling he definitely, well, let's see how the rest of the night goes. It turns out, he was originally from Detroit, and had been in LA for over 4 years. He enamored me with his tales of tragedy and survival in this dog-eat-dog city. He was homeless, with no hope and ready to end it all when his big break finally came. Since then he has not looked back. As Samson and I vibed to the thing he called his life, I noticed that Samantha had left the room and me alone with this handsome stranger. I didn't mind though, I was having such a good time.

Samson introduced me to the rest of the band, some close friends, and a few C list celebrities. I listened intently as they talked about life in LA and their struggles to their big break. What I noticed though was that through all their trials and challenges they were still there fighting for their dream. The whole scene was admirable. I took one more hit of ecstasy, downed a shot of tequila, and Samson and I headed to the dance floor.

As the popular lyrics of Gucci Mane, Travis Scott, and Jaquees hit the airwaves, I took that opportunity to show this young buck what I was working with. I grinded my hips against him to the rhythm of the music. He obliged and matched my energy. I dropped my body down low and touched him in places that made him wish I would touch him in others. As I rolled my body up slowly, I could clearly see what I could be potentially working with, and Boo boo Kitty began to awaken. He stuck to my body like glue and he touched parts of me on the dance floor that I was dying to show him privately.

I closed my eyes. I imagined being with this man as I danced seductively to the music. As our bodies swayed, I felt another partner coming, and I was sandwiched between the two. I opened my eyes to see a pretty red-headed woman grinding up on me as she touched my arms and back sensually from behind. Damn that felt good. Wait a minute this is a woman. But it still felt so good. I decided to let loose and go with it and enjoy the dance. It was only one dance, right?

The one dance turned into many, and I enjoyed the sensuality of both of my partners. Samson drew me in for a kiss. I felt an electrical charge go all through my body. As we kissed, we swayed to the music, and the pretty red head beauty stroked me from behind and kissed my neck, kissed my back. I wanted to stop her, but I wanted her to touch me at the same time, it was weird. I turned around and faced her. As the lyrics to "Little Freak" by Usher filled the airwaves, my defenses began to lower, and I put my arms around her and swayed to the music. She kissed me and I kissed her back. Samson played the back role and he touched all over my body while she kissed my face and massaged my breasts. "Be my little freak, be my little freak" was all I heard as I let the pretty red head's hands roam all over my body.

Samson kissed my neck, kissed my back, and took his hands from behind and stroked my pussy on the dance floor. This was getting intense. The whole thing had me so turned on that I let these two have their way with me on the dance floor. As Usher continued to remix we all danced and we kissed. Our bodies pulsated against one another to the music and all my defenses were down. I wanted them both and they wanted me. Once we all could not hold in our desire anymore, we all headed over to the Ecstasy Zone.

Samson, Pretty Red and I took a seat on the oversized sectional. We all took one last hit of Ecstasy and played and laughed until the effects of the drug started to kick in. The music in the Ecstasy Room had a playlist that oozed pleasure and sex. The classics like Prince's "Do Me Baby" filled the airwaves, but there were also songs of late, such as Tank's, "When We." The whole vibe in the room was sensual, and as we watched the other couples engage in foreplay and sex, not only did it get us aroused, but we took in their energy.

Samson sat in between us on the oversized sectional looking like an African King ready to be pleasured. He tilted my face to his and planted his hot passionate tongue down my throat. Every goose bump on my body began to stand to attention one by one. He then took his hands and began to stroke my body while still giving my mouth the oral pleasure it was seeking. Pretty Red took her hands and began to stroke Samson's body while kissing him on his neck and his ear simultaneously. Samson then turned to Pretty Red and kissed her seductively. His hands moved from my body and he lightly stroked Red's breasts while he made love to her mouth.

I switched gears. I kissed Samson's neck and ears, and my hands made way too his manhood. He gasped in between kisses, as I stroked his shaft up and down through his jeans. I fingered the zipper liner of the jeans as I ran my fingers up and down the print that had been formed which was continuing to grow through his clothing. I could fill his machine jump to attention. "Lady Marmalade" filled the airwaves. Pretty Red reached over and kissed me. It was a slow sensual kiss that got my juices flowing immediately. She then took her hands and massaged my breasts, as her tongue continued to do a slow sensual dance in my mouth. I moaned at her touch. As the singers belted in French, I said yes as

Pretty Red whispered in my ear. She nibbled on my ear and my body tingled again.

Samson allowed his hands to roam my thighs until they found their way to my sweet wetness. He stroked my wetness and placed his fingers in his mouth as he looked at me. He did it again, but this time Pretty Red took in his fingers in. She smiled and she kissed me again. I gasped at the intensity of the moment as Red masterfully kissed me and massaged my body while Samson took care of my love box. Pretty Red's mouth gave my nipples the attention they craved as Sampson stroked my Kitty feverishly. The whole scene was so intense.

Samson switched positions and got on his knees in front of the sectional. Samson hiked my legs up at the edge of the sectional and Pretty Red straddled me and massaged my nipples as she placed them in and out of her mouth. She took my large breast and drew it in for a kiss. She then kissed me and we both took my breast in our mouths at the same time. We played and sucked on my breasts until I was almost at the point of orgasm. The tempo of the music in the room picked up. The energy of our bodies matched the music. In the distance I could hear moans, as the seductress belted "I am getting so hot, I wanna take my clothes off." Meanwhile, Samson traced my Boo boo Kitty with his fingers causing my clitoris to jump in excitement. My juices started slowly flowing and I moved my hips back and forth as if to beg him for more. Samson did not disappoint as he spread my lips apart and began to lick my pretty kitty like it was a new lollipop. The effects of the ecstasy had me feeling every sensation, and my pleasure senses were on high.

Samson licked and sucked my little lady with tender loving care as Pretty Red kissed me and played with my nipples. Samson then took one hand and began to give Red's love box some attention by stroking and massaging her as he brushed lightly against my walls. She moaned intensely as his fingers stroked and massaged her. He stuck his fingers in her walls and swirled up and down, left and right as she bounced on fingers like they were the real thing. Samson released himself from Pretty Red and turned his focus on me. He spread my legs wide and looked at his prey. He looked up at me as if he was formulating a plan before he dived back into my cave. The flicker of his tongue on my center felt like pure ecstasy. As he flickered his tongue faster and faster my heart began to race. I felt my walls tighten and I let go in an instant shutter.

We switched positions again. "Motivation," by Kelly Rowland played in the background. Samson laid across the oversized sectional, and I positioned myself between his legs. Since he had been so good to us, I had to return the favor. I unbuckled Samson's pants, and he allowed me to strip him of his bottoms. I looked to see what I eventually would be working with, and Samson didn't disappoint. Samson's manhood was about ten inches in length and a nice wide, thick girth. His erection was thick and milk chocolate colored, one of the prettiest pieces of art I had ever seen. I stroked his manhood and had an intense desire put him in my mouth.

I smiled as I grabbed his shaft. I took my tongue and slowly licked his beautiful erection up and down and around. I pretended it was a microphone I wanted to sing in. I wanted to make love to him with my mouth. I teased his manhood with my tongue and his pre-celebration began to release. I put it in my mouth and tasted it. He moaned. I put the tip of his privacy back in my mouth and he gasped as he grew larger and expanded to his capacity. I slowly took him in inch by inch as I massaged him and went deeper and deeper down his wood as my mouth gave him oral pleasure.

As I continued to stroke Samson to the point of no return, Pretty Red placed her creamy wetness on top of Samson's face. Samson held Red by the bottom as he sucked her pleasure zone and took her kitty in and out of his mouth. She moaned moved her hips back and forth to his tongue, and Samson moaned as I continued to pleasure him with my mouth. I took him slowly and licked every single part of his erection. I stroked his manhood while my mouth licked his shaft up and down. I played with him. I sucked and stroked and released him from my mouth giving Samson a feeling of intense pleasure.

As Samson licked her goodness, Red's body began to tremble when he placed his tongue in and out of her walls and licked her clit with intense flickers up and down and back and forth. We all moaned simultaneously at the intensity in the moment of the thought of giving each other intense pleasure. As I stroked Samson he moaned. I moaned at his pleasure. As he licked Red she moaned. He moaned at her pleasure. Pretty Red let out an intense yelp and her love cave exploded. Red had her first release.

Pretty Red joined me in giving Samson pleasure. As I licked and sucked his shaft, Red began to massage and lick his family jewels. Red grabbed his manhood and began to stroke him slowly. As she stroked him up and down, I kept in tune with her rhythm as my mouth and my tongue matched her every beat. Samson moaned loudly and an audible "FUCK" could be heard. His breathing intensified as Red and I took turns licking and sucking and stroking and massaging until our lips made contact.

I kissed Pretty Red. And she kissed me back. Our tongues danced in a circular motion and my juices were stirring once again. Red and I began to touch each other in places that called out. She stroked my nipples and took them in her mouth, and I gasped. Samson took his hands and rubbed them down Pretty Red's back side, as she licked my nipples, and slowly made her way to my love box.

I inhaled deeply and let out an intensive moan. Red, had my lips in her hands. She massaged Boo Boo Kitty, as her tongue flickered her center zone intensely. Red's tongue was bull's eye focused as she sucked my button and licked my walls. I felt my body rock to the movement of Red's tongue, and it was like her oral pleasure was speaking a language of its own. Red ate my pussy so good, that I found myself moving in and out of her as she licked me into a frenzy. I wanted Red to please me. I was her little freak.

Samson entered Pretty Red from behind. She gasped and immediately begged for more. In that moment, I wanted him too, and I could feel his intensity through the focus she gave my kitty. Samson gently grabbed her by the hips and took her in and out slowly. She moaned. Red continued to lick me, and I could feel my juices build up. I closed my eyes. Her tongue flickered in and out of me faster and faster between her moans and I grinded into her and picked up the pace.

I looked at Samson. He picked up his stride also. As he moved in and out of Pretty Red, he looked at me passionately. I pictured him inside me, and our eyes stayed locked. Red spread my lips and exposed my center. She placed her mouth on my cherry and sucked until she gathered all my juices in her mouth. As she made love to my cave with her tongue, I looked at Samson. He pounded away faster and faster as Pretty Red licked me feverishly. I locked eyes with Samson as my legs began to shake and I had my release.

Samson laid flat on his back. I took my hands and slowly made my way on top of him. I took his manhood and gently rubbed it up against Boo Boo Kitty. Just the feel alone made me want to orgasm. I played with him and teased him for a little while. I stroked him while I sat on top of him and rubbed his shaft against my button. I would place just the tip of it in for a little bit, while stroking his manhood up and down. He looked at me with intensity as if to say, "please just fuck me, I can't take it anymore." I wouldn't give in though I wasn't ready for what he had to present.

Samson sat up. As I sat on top of him, he placed my twins in his mouth. As he sucked my girls, I stroked him and let his tip play with Ms. Kitty. I felt his pre-release, and I experienced some of my own. My love button began to flicker. I placed his shaft inside me and let out a moan of desire. This man felt so good inside me. Samson grabbed my hips and moved his in a circular motion. I matched his movement. He moaned and so did I. He moved back and forth and looked me in my eyes. Every thrust felt like pleasure and pain. As he shifted his body back and forth and all around, I met him with my movement. He grabbed my backside and pushed me deeper inside him. I moaned. Hell, I screamed this shit felt so good!

I looked at him. He started talking to me. He told me to give him that good pussy. I told him to take it, if he wanted it. I matched his deepness and increased the pace. He looked at me as if what I said was a challenge. He lifted my backside up and down on his manhood. I felt his deepness as I bounced on him and every stroke was intense pleasure. I found myself saying, "give it to me daddy" and he obliged.

We grinded deeper and deeper, faster and faster. Our bodies moved in cadence and our eyes locked. We moved harder, faster, and deeper, and as I rode that horse, I wanted all that he could give me. I said, "Fuck me Daddy" as my love box flicked with intensity and I felt his final thrust. Samson had finally given his release.

I laid in Samson's arms. Pretty Red joined me on the other side. We had one last intimate kiss, and we both gave Samson our love, as well. We all fell asleep in each other's arms, happy and satisfied. That was the conclusion of round one.

The following rounds were just as intense as the first one. Round two was Red and I by ourselves. We took our time exploring each other's every erogenous zone. That woman took me to depths of pleasure that I never knew were there. Until tonight I had never been with a woman, so I never knew what I was missing out on. A few hours later, I awakened to Samson, giving me oral pleasure. Round three was me and him. This man had moves I had never seen until tonight. This man sucked and licked me in places unimaginable. The ecstasy made some parts of my body a turn on that I would soberly think twice about. But I let this man have his way with me, hell you only live once.

The final round was one more three-some. We did add an inti-mate stranger, so I guess it was a foursome. We took one more shot of ecstasy and let the pleasure take over our inhibitions. Sex with four was much more amazing than three, and we took our time exploring one another until we had nothing left to give. That night, I felt like one of those women on the "Cinemax After Dark" movies that I would sneak and watch as a little girl. That night I imagined myself as Black Emmanuelle, a beautiful French sex Goddess. She was open and free with her body. For the rest of the night, I gave in to my every desire.

The next morning, I did the ride of shame back to my villa. I couldn't believe I had let myself get so free last night. I thought about the details of the night. Samson, Red, the stranger, the other stranger. I placed my hand on my head. I prayed on the inside that it didn't happen. Boo Boo Kitty began to throb. That simple bitch. I guess she wasn't gonna let me forget! I thought about last night again. I thought about how good I felt at that moment. How happy and free I was. Hell, I didn't care about what happened. As a matter of fact, everyone at that party was free, and no one judged the moment. I knew I couldn't take it back anyway. That experience was now a part of me.

When I stepped into the villa, Sam greeted me with her "hang-over special." We both sat in silence for the first five minutes. I asked her where she disappeared to. She told me that her boss had called her away for a business meeting during the party. She said it was a common thing. So at these parties, she had to keep her wits about her, unless she was told otherwise. There were a million people who would kill to have her job. I swear her life never stopped. We caught up on the events of the night, and she gave me a mental high five.

Sam: Sometimes, you need to unwind Mami. You have been way too tense lately. Last night was a way to release some of that frustration. Some people have a hobby, and others have sex. You used sex last night, it's all good!

Tabby: I don't think that's what happened. All I know is that I was waiting for the edibles to kick in, and the next thing I know, I had a big beautiful dick in my mouth.

Sam: Ok, we'll go with that. Tabby, it's ok. Don't judge what happened last night. This town is a little freer than others. That's what I like about it.

I thought about what Sam said, and decided that last night was no big deal. We moved on to better conversations, great food, and some shopping at LA's most elite spots. This was more like it, what I had come to do. I got to have some time quality time with my friend, which was long overdue. The last couple of days in LA were more of the same, and as my time was winding down, a sense of fear began to come over me. I couldn't understand why, but I was afraid of what was next. Although my time in LA was amazing, I knew I was going back home to so many unknowns. I took a few deep breaths. I told myself that I would be ok. I had a new life ahead of me, and it was up to me to paint the picture.

Sam and I said our goodbyes. I finished packing and headed to the airport to return to my life. I thought about what I would tackle first. I knew spending time with Ebony was a priority, but I also needed to find out how I would make a living, and what I wanted to do with myself. I was also preparing for Vincent to graduate. He was in his last semester of college, so there was a chance he would return home upon graduation. I tried to mentally prepare for that. As one was returning, the other was leaving. Vanessa's graduation was two months away, so I was making plans to send her off. I felt like although I was no longer going to be working that I still had so much that would keep me busy. I handed the attendant my ticket and took my seat in business class. I needed to quiet my mind a little. I put on my meditation music and drifted off to sleep as the plane took a flight home.

PART 1: THE DESTRUCTION

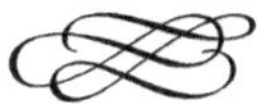

ow do you define destruction? Webster defines it as the action or process of causing so much damage to something that it no longer exists or cannot be repaired. Destruction can also be the process of killing or being killed. The third definition I have come across was being the cause of someone's ruin. In Greek mythology, the Trojan War was waged against the city of Troy by the Greeks after Paris of Troy took Helen from her husband Menelaus, king of Sparta. That one action set into motion a course of other actions that led to not only the ruin of marriage, and an affair, but also the destruction of a powerful city. Paris was willing to risk everything all in the name of love, but he didn't count the cost of his actions. Although this is a dramatic representation of the definition, I felt each one of these definitions based on what happened next in my life. I felt the weightiness of all that was occurring, and not only did I blame myself, but I was pissed at the world too. Well, you'll see what I'm talking about.

When I touched down in my city, I felt relaxed. I didn't know what my life would look like in the distant future, but I really didn't care. After spending a week in LA, I realized that sometimes you just must go with the flow of things, and I needed to try to do that more often. I had a million things on my to-do list, but I was going to try to tackle them one thing at a time. I felt like I came back with a new perspective on some things in life, so I felt like my mission was accomplished. Going to LA was just what I needed. Plus, I got to reconnect with my second-best bestie. I walked into my condo and was greeted by my housekeeper Maria, and a ton of unopened mail. Yes, Maria came with me in this separation. I guess she was tired of his shit too. Maria greeted me with a smile. She handed me a letter which she indicated required a signature upon delivery. It read,

"Jackson County Court of Common Pleas" Plaintiff James Taylor Vs. Defendant Tabitha Taylor in a petition for divorce. What the fuck? I looked at the date of the letter. It was dated the same day that I had taken my flight to LA. It was delivered three days later. The court date was set for two weeks from the date of the letter. With me being out of town for a week, this only gave me four days to find a lawyer and head to court to do battle with my soon to be ex-husband.

This was no strange coincidence. James had already filed for divorce before he invited me on this little Tiffany spree that he had planned. What kind of sick games was this man playing? As usual, this was part of his general off the wall antics, but this time he had gone too far. I decided to get on the phone and see how he would try to weasel his way out of this.

James: Good afternoon, Tabby, how are you?

Tabby: I'm good, James. I had an amazing time…Fuck the pleasantries, James. Imagine my surprise when I come back from my trip to find I have been served with divorce papers.

James: Tabby, what do you mean you're surprised? I told you I was going to file

Tabby: James, quit trying to mind fuck me, ok! We have never had a conversation about you filing for divorce. As a matter of fact, the little stunt you pulled before I went out of town is an indicator, we had no such conversation!

James: Calm down, Tabby. I'm sure we talked about this

Tabby: Are you really gonna make me do this, James? Ok, let's do it.

James: Do what, Tabby?

Tabby: Ok, here we go. First of all, you dragged me to Tiffany's, begging me to get back with you a week ago. The letter from the courts was dated the exact same day, which means you had this drawn up before we met up. Then, you have the audacity to have me served when I am not in town. Who does that? We have four days until we must see each other in court, James. How is that enough time to hammer out all our affairs?

James: Yes, ok, I admit I had this drawn up before we met. Pastor Doug said, to put the house on the market, I had to petition for a divorce.

Tabby: What the fuck does Pastor Doug have to do with all of this? And why would you be trying to put the house on the market? We have not had one conversation about how to move forward, and you went and filed for divorce.

James: Pastor Doug is my spiritual father, so you need to be very careful what you say about him. I know you don't like him, but there is no need to be disrespectful. The bottom line is you signed a prenuptial agreement in which Pastor Doug was witness to. The terms of the prenup are pretty clear since you didn't give me any children. I'm putting the house on the market to help you, Tabby. You'll need to liquidate if you want to maintain the lifestyle you currently have. I heard about your job elimination.

I laugh out loud. Of course, he would have heard about my job situation as well connected as he was in this city. But to bring this up right now while we were talking about the divorce was an all-time low for him.

Tabby: I don't give a fuck about what you heard! I don't even know why I thought it was worth my time having this conversation, James. I will see you in court.

James: You are so disrespectful these days. You are definitely not the woman I married. What happened to her?

Tabby: All the shit you put me through has made me the woman I am today, so congratulations!

James: The angry black woman is so unattractive, and you're way too pretty for that. Let me make this simple for you; since you cannot be civil, I am requesting that you cease all communication with me until the day of our court date. If you want to communicate about the terms of the agreement, please have your attorney contact mine. I have also emailed a copy of the prenup for your attorney to review. Now, is there anything else we need to review before we end this call?

I hung up the phone. I was pissed. I looked in the fridge for the bottle of wine but then thought this moment was way too intense for wine. I grabbed the bottle of 1800 and poured myself a shot. I downed it and thought about my conversation with James. He was smug as hell. He thinks he won this game, but he has another thing coming. I reached for my phone and called the girl who knows everyone. In a matter of a few minutes, Samantha hooked me up with one of the best attorneys in the city, courtesy of account #8.

Her name was Yvette Stevens, and divorce settlements were here specialty. She was so good that her success rate was likened to paternity tests; 99.9 percent! I forwarded Ms. Stevens my prenuptial agreement, and she agreed to get back with me within 24 hours with a game plan. I felt confident that Ms. Stevens would help me get what I rightfully deserved, whatever that was. I was personally willing to walk away and start completely over, that's how much I was over this marriage. James, however, had treated me like property the whole time we were married, and now was trying to make sure I had nothing. Something about that was just not fair. Don't get me wrong, I'm not trying to be greedy, I just want to live a good life. If James wasn't such a control freak, we could actually be civil. But Keisha was right, he is a man of extremes, the is no in-between with him.

As I was deep in my thoughts about the upcoming court date, a text came through my phone. It was from Ebony requesting that we meet her at her house today in two hours. I noticed it was a group text with me and her sister Katrina. I immediately became concerned. I knew on the inside that is was about her health, and I felt an uneasiness come over me. I felt sick suddenly and did not want to hear any more bad news today. I looked at the bottle of 1800 and contemplated taking another shot. I decided to wait to hear why Ebony was summoning me and Katrina. More like I didn't have a choice. I tried to occupy the next hour with duties such as unpacking and going through my mail. I then took a shower and headed for Ebony's house.

When I got to the house, I noticed that Katrina was already there, and a few other cars. Strange, I thought. As I got out of the car and headed inside, the uneasiness came back over me and hit me heavier. It made me wish I had taken that other shot. I rang the doorbell, and Katrina answered. We embraced each other for what had seemed like forever. As a matter of fact, it was considering it had been about fifteen years since I had seen her. We exchanged some small pleasantries and headed into the study, where Ebony was lying in her favorite lounge chair. I also noticed a couple of things:

1. We were not alone. There was what appeared to be a doctor and another healthcare professional in Ebony's study.
2. The feeling of peace that usually encompassed Ebony's home was noticeably missing today.

Ebony asked Katrina and I to join them in the study. Katrina and I took a seat.

Ebony: I called the both of you here today because you two are the closest people to me in life. I wanted you both to hear this information at the same time because y'all know I hate repeating myself. I also chose the two of you because both of you were the WORST thorn in my side growing up. You know how hard it was keeping the two of you out of trouble?

We both looked at her and laughed. I had to admit, she was right about that. I reflected on my former partner in crime, and how we always managed to get caught sneaking out to parties and trying to sneak boys in the house. Ebony even foiled our plans to have a party while her parents were away. We thought we had that one in the books, but somehow Ebony already knew what we were up to. She held that one over us for a while and made us her personal servants for 6 months! Although that was dirty, Ebony once again saved us from an ass-whoopin'. As I came back to myself, Ebony asked the doctor to explain to us what was going on with her.

Dr. Parker: When the cancer in the abdomen went into remission, there were small cancer cells that apparently attached themselves to the colon that were undetected. Throughout the years, those cells begin to grow and spread into other areas. Two weeks ago, Ebony came to the emergency room with bowel complaints. After further research and a colonoscopy, we detected the cancer cells.

Katrina: So, Dr., what is it that you are saying.

Tabby: Yes, Dr., we know that the cancer has come back, and Ebony has about six months with us. Are you here to discuss what she can and can't do over the next few months? Her bucket list is crazy, and I know she wants to get some last-minute travel in.

Dr. Parker: Unfortunately, I am not here to discuss travel. As I was stating prior, the cancer has spread to other areas of the body, which include the abdomen, stomach, and colon. The cancer cells in the colon are quite aggressive, and Ebony is in stage four of colon cancer.

Katrina: Stage four? What exactly does that mean anyway?

Tabby: Well, stage four is six months to like two years, right? I've been doing a little research since she told me a couple of weeks ago. But knowing Ebony, she's gonna be around for a while doc.

Dr. Parker: Typically, that is the case. However, because of the aggressiveness of the cancer cells, there's a blockage in the colon and a large mass. We tried everything to remove the mass, including surgery, both laparoscopic and invasive. But, due to its location, removing it would do more harm than good.

Tabby: Blockage? Mass? Dr. Parker, I'm a bit confused by all of this.

Dr. Parker: I completely understand how you feel. Let me see if I can clarify this for you. The blockage in the colon has hindered the digestive process. Ebony cannot take in any solid food at this point. Even the use of pureed foods will cause a buildup in the colon. She has been placed on a nutrition IV.

I looked over at Ebony. She had a solemn look on her face. This is the first time I had ever seen this expression from her, ever. I didn't know how to comfort her. My friend, my sister, was dying, and the realization was hitting me like a ton of bricks. I didn't want to hear anymore. Honestly, I wanted this all to be a bad dream that I woke up from on the plane ride home.

Dr. Parker: it is recommended that Ebony transition into hospice. With IV only nutrition, her life expectancy is about three weeks to thirty days maximum. Most patients don't survive beyond ten days.

The news dropped in the pit of my stomach like a gut punch. I sat there for a moment in silence. What do you say to something like that? I looked over at Katrina, who appeared to be physically sick. She ran out of the room sobbing and headed straight for the bathroom. Dr. Parker asked if I had any questions. I didn't know what to say. So, I said no. Dr. Parker left me his card and left me with Ebony and the nurse to make arrangements for the hospice services.

Ebony: Tabby, you are my very best friend. I need you to be strong for me in all this. A lot of people don't know, but when I put the post on social media to let them know what's going on with me, there will be a lot of people that rightfully will want to check on me. Let them within reason. I believe in giving folks their flowers while they're still living. Let them honor me. But I need you and Katrina to hold it together, ok?

I nodded. Katrina re-entered the room, and we sat with the nurse to make all the final preparations for Ebony's in-home care. Katrina and I took turns leaving the room and secretly sobbing about the news that we just got. We both wanted to put on a strong face for Ebony, but I know we were both quietly crumbling on the inside. I felt like someone had dropped a whole barrel of bricks on top of me, in which I could not unbury myself. I couldn't breathe. I felt heavy. I felt numb and sad at the same time. I felt helpless and confused, angry. I was forced to feel it all in a short period because I didn't know how much time I truly had left with my sister-friend. I needed to get away and process all of this, but I also needed to be with her too. I also needed to forget this was happening, and I needed to self-medicate. Thank God I still had my Mary Jane.

As we settled in for the evening at Ebony's, Katrina popped open a bottle of wine and poured three glasses.

Tabby: Is it ok for you to have wine Ebony?

Ebony: Baby girl, I'm dying. I can have whatever I damn well please. The wine will taste sweet going down, but it will just go straight through me (she chuckles). Tonight we're gonna have wine, smoke some weed, and be happy, ok!

Katrina: It's your world, Ebony, and we're gonna do whatever you like.

Ebony: Well, that's what I wanna do. I wanna listen to some music, smoke a little weed and get drunk tonight! All that's missing is a few good stories.

Tabby: Well, since you have nothing but time on your hands, and you're dying, as you mentioned...

Ebony: All facts (she giggles)

Tabby: Well, anywho! I got some juicy stuff to tell you. What do you want to hear about first, my upcoming divorce court date in a few days, or the fact that I had a threesome in LA?

They both went silent for a second. Then as Katrina had a look of shock on her face, Ebony burst out into laughter. They wanted me to provide all the details of what happened. I decided to tell them about James first. As we smoked, drank, and laughed, I got Katrina up to speed with my relationship with James and the never-ending baby mama drama, and the crazy relationship he had with Pastor Doug. I wanted to slowly build up to my trip to LA. We spent the rest of the night going over the juicy details of my escapades before we all dozed off in the study.

The following morning, the nurse came to check on Ebony. Katrina and I took that time to go over the details of Ebony's care. We both knew that the next few weeks would be delicate, so we both agreed to move in and split the day-to-day care along with the help of aides. We both wanted to spend as much time with Ebony as we could. I started to tear up, and so did Katrina. This was all happening so fast. Ebony was a strong woman who was a spiritual fighter also. She beat cancer before with prayer and meditation, I couldn't understand what was happening now. I wanted to collapse right there on the spot, but I had to be strong now. I felt like the weight of the world had just been placed on my shoulders ever so gently.

I thought about what was my new normal. I had gone from raising my own children to trying to have a brand new baby forced on me, and then the responsibility of taking care of a dying friend. I was terrified for a few reasons:

1. I had never had to take care of a dying relative or anyone close to me

2. I never really had to face a lot of death occurring around me up until this point in my life. I had lived in a bubble for the last 15 years.

3. I was scared as hell of losing my friend. I couldn't imagine life without her, she had always been there, and I did not want to watch her die before my eyes.

I took a few deep breaths in and out. I still felt the heaviness, and it wouldn't go away. Katrina and I continued to go over the finer details and reviewed Ebony's final wishes. As we talked and prepared, the reality of this whole situation began to sink in and out of my consciousness. I still didn't want to believe it, and I sure as hell wasn't ready to accept it, but here I was making plans for Ebony's transition into the next world. I thought about the fact that I would never see her again. Sure, they say we see each other again in the afterlife, but I needed her here with me now. Especially now. In my selfishness, I felt like God was being selfish and cruel for removing the one constant person in my life at a time when I felt the most turmoil.

I became a little angry, but I suppressed it because I knew that there was no time for that. I faked my way through the rest of the details that morning and then received a call from my attorney. Although I felt like the shit was getting ready to hit the fan with James, I felt like her phone call was a welcomed distraction from what was going on with Ebony. I excused myself from Katrina and went to take the call in what would be my bedroom for the next whenever.

Tabby: Thank you so much for getting back with me so quickly, Ms. Stevens.

Yvette: No worries, Ms. Taylor. This is what I do. How are you anyway? I can tell something is bothering you. Is it James?

Tabby: No, not at all. Not now, anyway. Full disclosure, to make a long story extremely short, my best friend is dying with a short amount of time to live.

Yvette: Oh no, Tabby. I'm so sorry to hear you are going through this. Is there anything I can do to make this easier for you?

Tabby: No, Ms. Stevens, it is what it is.

Yvette: Well, Tabby, my phone call isn't all pleasantries. I got back with you so quickly because time is of the essence. I looked over the details of the prenuptial agreement. I found a very significant loophole that would be beneficial to you, and I reached out to James' attorney. James hired Bradley Goldstein, who is one of the most prominent lawyers in this city.

Tabby: Well, I'm not surprised by that at all.

Yvette: Mr. Goldstein took that time to advise me that two days ago, a motion was filed and uncontested because you didn't have an attorney to have your court date moved to this morning.

Tabby: WHAT! That sneaky son of a bitch! I just talked to him yesterday, and he made no mention of this.

Yvette: Very sneaky, indeed. I filed an additional motion to have the court date moved back to the original date, which was denied. The judge did agree to move your time to early this afternoon. Can you meet me in the next hour? We need a game plan on how to move forward from here.

I agreed and ended the conversation. And just like that, the circus that had become my new normal was just beginning. Only this time, instead of ecstasy and edibles, I was left with death and divorce. I'd take the first two over the second any day of the week. I got myself dressed, met up with Yvette, and then we both headed to court together as a united front.

As we headed into the mediation room, there was an immediate coolness in the air. On the far end of the table sat James, his attorney, and none other than Keisha with their grandchild. Keisha was dressed in a Kate Spade black and white pinned striped jumpsuit and red bottom shoes. She was patting the baby's back as if she was burping him. I looked over at my attorney.

Tabby: Can I ask what Keisha is doing here?

Keisha: Are you so serious, Tabby? This is not the time for this.

I am here for moral support for James, and this is a public courtroom.

Yvette: Well, the mediation process is not. If you step out of this private mediation room, you will see the areas open to the public. This is not one of them. Please remove yourself from these proceedings as you have no relevance to this case.

Keisha looked at James in disbelief.

James: Uhm, I just got custody of my grandson, and I didn't have a sitter. Keisha is here as the grandmother and caregiver for my grandson.

Yvette: Fantastic! Now that we have all the introductions out of the way, the grandmother can kindly remover herself and the grandson from these proceedings. Please, and thank you.

Yvette smiled a wicked grin. I turned up a smile too and batted my eyes at Keisha. I had won finally. In a huff, Keisha began to grab the baby, and James assisted her with the stroller and the other things she needed to make her exit. I chuckled to myself. This was pure entertainment so far, and I needed a good laugh. Keisha had finally been put in her place, and I was there to witness it.

Our attorneys sat down with the judge-appointed mediator, and we all got to the business at hand. James demanded that we honor the terms of the prenup until he realized that I still had access to account number 8. He glared at me with an evil glare. At that moment, he knew that I had known for a while that I had access to this account he never checked. His face turned a shade of red, and he whispered in his attorney's ear. Mr. Goldstein responded.

Mr. Goldstein: My client has an issue with some of the details of the agreement. Account number 8 was created before his marriage to Ms. Taylor and should be treated as Mr. Taylor's assets prior to the marriage.

Yvette: I understand. However, during the marriage at some point, Ms. Taylor was added to account number 8, and the money that has been contributed to this account during their marriage should be treated as community property.

James: This is BULLSHIT!

Tabby: You know what is bullshit, James? How you orchestrated all of this.

Mediator: We need to stay focused on the terms of the agreement.

Yvette: It appears that this is not going to be resolved today.

Mr. Goldstein: I agree. My client and I are asking for a continuance on the grounds that assets in account number 8 were set up prior to the marriage. According to the agreement, since Mrs. Taylor did not bear Mr. Taylor any children, she forfeits all assets, and the home should be sold. The proceeds split 85/15 in favor of Mr. Taylor.

Yvette: That's fine, Mr. Goldstein. My client and I are filing a counter-motion to dismiss the prenuptial agreement altogether. The document was created and signed with the intent to deceive. The account in question number 8 has increased in value, not only since the marriage but also when he added Ms. Taylor to the account.

James: I didn't add her to that account

Yvette: This signature said you did.

James looked over at me, and I could see the rage in his eyes. He had been winning the battle, but I was setting up to win the war. And my girl Ms. Stevens came to play and to win. He handed the document to his attorney, who looked at him with questions in his eyes.

Mr. Goldstein: We will not be seeing the judge today. In light of this new information, my client and I are requesting a continuance of these proceedings. There needs to be a thorough investigation into account number 8.

Yvette: Agreed. Unlike you, Mr. Goldstein, I will not object to your motion. I believe you indicated the fact that I was not up to speed on the details of the case was no reason to push for another date correct? Well, here we are, and we are asking for some demands of our own. We are asking for all the finances to be reviewed and for Ms. Taylor to retain full possession of the house among some other assets we'd like to request. But we can hammer out the details of those things later.

Yvette winked at him. Mr. Goldstein knew he was in no position to dispute. The judge granted a continuance and scheduled it for 9 months from today's date. It was still not over, and I still, in some ways, felt like a prisoner. I so wanted this chapter of my life to be over, but it seemed to drag on just a little bit. The 9-month delay was typical in marriages where there were a significant amount of assets in question. My attorney advised me to brace myself, as these proceedings could take up to 18 months. I felt heavy again. I also felt nauseous, and after my conversation with my attorney, I headed into the bathroom to throw up, literally.

Upon my arrival into the bathroom, I ran right into my arch enemy, or so it felt for one last showdown. It was Keisha and her grandbaby. She looked at me and smiled as she rocked the boy back and forth, trying to calm him before putting him back in his stroller. As a courtesy, I asked her if she needed any help. She nodded her head no as if she was in complete control. Keisha laid the baby down and approached me.

Keisha: You know, it's such a shame that this couldn't be over today, I mean let's face it we both knew this marriage had an expiration date. I told James this long ago when he decided he wanted to marry you. You don't believe that anything happens in his life that I don't know about, do you?

In her last moments with me, this girl dropped another damn bombshell. This bitch never ceased to amaze me. She found every opportunity to throw shade at me she could, and the day of my divorce proceedings was no different. I looked at her and smiled.

Tabby: You know Keisha, I really don't want to do this with you today, especially in front of your grandchild.

Keisha: Since when have you really cared about my grandchild,

Tabby? Wasn't it you who walked away from James, and this situation? James is a good man. Yes, he has his flaws, but don't we all? You were not up to par to take the position of wife. So, say what you need to say, honey. Don't let that stop you because believe me, I won't be holding back.

Tabby: And just when I thought that because you had a baby in your arms that you had some type of mothering instinct like compassion. I should have known better than that.

Keisha: Let's not go there, you have no idea what I sacrificed as a parent.

Tabby: What? A lifestyle less lavish than you hoped for? Because that's what this is really about Keisha from the hood, let's keep it all the way real.

Keisha: OOOH... Now that's the bitch I've been waiting to talk to. Let's stop with the pleasantries, shall we? I told you from the beginning what it was with James and I, but you refused to listen. What would make you think that you could have what I built after less than a year of dating? Did you really think he was over me? That man talked to me and came to see me, spent time with me the whole time you were together. James had his own agenda, and I definitely had mine.

Tabby: Keisha, I really don't care about what you and James had going on before, during, and after. It is not my concern, I'm so over it.

Keisha: You think I really believe that? The fact that you didn't just walk away from everything tells me you're still in this Tabby. Now it must be dragged out another nine months or more. That's pretty selfish of you, Tabby. You need to leave James and our family alone.

Tabby: Bitch, please. What is selfish is for you to be...you know what, I'm outta here.

Keisha: How's your friend Ebony?

I stop dead in my tracks. How did this bitch know anything going on with MY best friend? I was fuming on the inside. What had he been telling this woman over the years? These two were having pillow talk, for real. I had to give it to her when it came to James, she must have kryptonite in her pussy. Or a voodoo doll. Either way, she had James under her spell.

Keisha: I know that she had recovered from her cancer, and now she is fighting again for her life. Wow, you must be going through a lot dealing with that, are you hanging in there?

Tabby: Bitch, you don't get to ask me ANYTHING about my best friend. Open your mouth and say her name ONE MORE TIME.

Keisha: I really didn't mean any disrespect Tabby. I just said that to prove a point. Everything that happens with you and James, I already knew about. James and I were friends first for a long time, even though we made the mistake of having Christopher and it was rocky, we always talked and remained friends.

Tabby: With friends like him, who needs enemies, Keisha. While he's talking to you about me, he's running your name in the ground as the money-hungry bitch who he pays all that damn child support to.

Keisha: And you really believed that about me?

I looked at her sideways.

Keisha: I'm sure you do like it matters. James and I have history, that's all. History you will never know anything about.

Tabby: And nor do I care to.

Keisha: You know, I think I kind of like this new Tabby. She's a bit feisty, stands up for herself, kind of cute. That tenacity will take you far, as you move into the next phase of your life as a single woman.

Tabby: I'm glad you like her because she has something else she needs to say to you, little bitch. You can have James.

Keisha: So Typical. I already had him and always have.

Tabby: So typical, but let me finish bitch. You can have James. When I'm done with him. You see, this conversation with you lets me know you think WAY too much of yourself. I'm not done with

James yet, hence the continuance in court. Now, as his wife of 15 years, I am getting what I'm entitled to, which is a whole hell of a lot more than what you have gotten over the years, and you've always had him right. So, take him, Keisha, when I'm done. You can have my sloppy seconds baby girl. When I'm done, you're gonna need a side hustle to keep your lifestyle going. You do remember what that is, don't you?

Keisha: Sweetie, I've never worked a day in my life, I didn't have to. So, this side hustle that you make mention of, perhaps…

Tabby: We're done here, bitch.

I grabbed my things and stormed out of the bathroom. I hurried to the elevators and pressed the arrow down. I could see Keisha walking up to James with red eyes. He touches her shoulder, and She looked up at me. The elevator dings, and the door opened. Three men in business suits exit, and before I entered, I looked at Keisha and James, lifted both hands up, and gave them both the middle finger. At the same time, I stuck my tongue out at them in a rock-star type fashion. They both looked at me in shock and surprise. Their attorney looked at me with horror and disgust. My attorney smiled, waved at me, and said, "I'll call you later." I stepped on the elevators and closed the door, and smiled.

I took a deep breath. I thought about what I had just done. I knew it was childish, but I felt good. That woman had played fucking games with me too many times throughout the years. But what was worse is that James allowed it. So, in my mind, they could both go fuck themselves. There, I said it. Even if only in my mind. How's that for a mind fuck! I laughed out loud. I made a joke I thought was funny. I laughed again, but this time at the realization that I was taking my power back from those two. I felt a sudden rush of adrenaline. My mind started racing, and I needed to get this energy off. Then I thought about the realization that I had to take care of Ebony. Immediately a heaviness crept in. I needed to release all that I was feeling, but I didn't know how. I decided not to think about it and called Katrina to check-in.

Katrina gave me an update on Ebony, who was currently entertaining some close family and other friends. I asked if she needed me today, and she said she had it handled. I told her about the events of the afternoon, and she encouraged me to take some time for myself. I agreed and headed for my condo. Since it was Friday, my first thought was to unwind by myself with a bottle of wine. I knew I didn't want to be alone, but I also wasn't feeling the club vibe either. My episode in LA was just enough to slow me down a bit. But only a little, I thought. I poured a glass of wine and listened to my messages.

Voicemail: Hey Tabby. It's me, Diana. I wanted to check on you since you left the company to see how things were going. I hadn't heard back from you and hope that everything is ok. I wanted to know if you got my message last week about my daughter's graduation party. She is finally done with college, and we're having some friends and family over tonight. You are more than welcome to come. Let me know, bye.

Diana was one of my only allies that I had in my department in this position. Probably because she was the only other African-American woman in our position in the same department. Diane tried to show me the tricks of the trade as best as she knew how. Any black person in corporate America knows that there is a unique protocol for the handling and care of white people. It's almost like caring for a gremlin; if you treat them really nice and play by their rules, then everything is fine. But the moment you deviate, then they can become your worst nightmare. I was almost certain that none of my Caucasian colleagues would attend this late-night bonfire. Not because Diana didn't like white people; she just didn't mix her professional life with her personal one.

I called Diana to see if it was still ok to come. With a resounding yes and a "Can you pick up a few items," I agreed to go to this bonfire and take my mind off present-day life. I picked out a cute little red polka dot sundress and headed to the party with my goodies in hand.

Diana's home was nothing short of amazing. Walking in the door of her home was a foyer entrance with twelve-foot ceilings. Her hardwood floors sparkled to perfection. Every item in her foyer seemed to go with the décor of the house. There was a poster-sized portrait of Diana and her family that hung in display, above the fireplace in the den area. Diana prided herself on being able to balance her career and her family life, and it showed.

I looked around her home and took in all the beauty room by room. As I made my way to the backyard, I noticed some familiar faces, but also some not so familiar ones. I noticed a few people from my old neighborhood that had done well, and I naturally directed my conversation there. While I was catching up with my old classmates, I noticed someone very handsome yet intriguing entered our space. Who was this handsome stranger? Immediately, I took a drink and became curious. I knew he had to be young, but just how young I didn't know.

I sipped my drink and watched this young man from across the room. I had a sneaky feeling I was about to get myself in trouble, and Boo Boo Kitty was cosigning. I wanted to yell down at her and tell her to calm down. But, how crazy would that look in the middle of this bonfire? Boo Kitty had been acting up these days, and she needed a reminder about self-control. I looked up and noticed Diana embracing this sexy young man.

Mario Hunter Jr. was 32 and a spitting image of his father, Mario Sr., Diana's husband. I felt the wind go out of my sails. For good reason, of course. Not only was this handsome stranger, my good colleague's son, but I was also technically old enough to be this man's auntie. For a moment, my hormones died down, which was a good thing. I decided to mingle and meet other guests that were around my age and engage in great conversation. I made my way through the home, assisting Diana when needed, and meeting new people. It was kind of fun, and I was certainly glad that I came.

Diana was an amazing host, and the food and drinks just kept coming. What I also noticed that kept coming was Mario Hunter Jr... As I moved from room to room, somehow, I noticed that this young man would make his way into my existence. Maybe I was paranoid, or perhaps a bit too confident? After all, this man was about 12 years my junior, so what would he want with me, especially with all these beautiful women his age running around the party? I watched him as he would engage in conversation with others from across the room. We never said a word to each other, but I felt his attraction to me, and I'm sure he felt mine. We played this little game until a few hours had passed.

Around midnight, Diana's brother decided it was a great idea for those remaining to take shots of crown apple. Of course, I was down, as I had my fill of alcohol all evening. Diana was not a drinker, so she excused herself into the kitchen to clean up since most of the guests had already left. The rest of us took several shots, and the playful banter turned into sexual flirting. As I began to feel the effects of the alcohol, I knew my defenses were down. I decided I needed to switch gears and went off to a private place outside to smoke a blunt.

On my way to finding happy, I ran smack into Mario Jr., who, in a lame attempt to get by me in a tight space, grabbed me by the waist and pulled me close to him. As he eased his body by mine, our bodies touched, and so did our energy. I let him pass me by, but as he did, I turned back and smiled. At that moment, Mario Jr. grabbed a bottle of tequila and headed in my direction.

Mario: While everyone was in there taking shots, I noticed that you didn't take one with me. We should take one together.

Tabby: I'm sorry, I see you have tequila. After taking a couple of shots of crown apple, I don't think it's safe to mix my liquor.

Mario: It all good, Ma. Just one shot of Cuervo won't hurt you.

Tabby: I don't really know you like that

Mario: I was headed out to smoke this weed anyway. You joining me?

Now how could I say no to that? Smoking with a mutual

acquaintance was harmless, right? Except that it was my former coworker's son. She wasn't just a coworker though, she not only mentored me in a sense, but she also had my back when all the crazy shit starts hitting the fan. I told myself it would be just a joint, and that was it.

As I headed to the deck, I noticed that Diane was watching us. I waved and smiled and waved my joint in the air. She nodded in understanding and looked at Mario with an inquisitive look. I smirked and headed to the deck. As we puffed and passed, I wondered what I was about to get myself into. I looked at his slender frame up and down. I have to admit, he was kind of yummy. And it was also very flattering that this hot young thing wanted to bed me. I smiled inside of the thought of a passionate tryst with him, but I was also conflicted because he was Diana's son. Who comes to their guest's home and fucks their son?

We took a couple of shots and got to know each other a little better. Mario basically was a nobody in his family; the oldest and the black sheep. All his siblings had gone on to greatness while he was still trying to find his way. He was a musician with the flighty belief that he shouldn't have to work at all to focus entirely on his gift. A grifter, I thought. I told him as little about myself as possible. Still, I don't think he was very interested as he became touchy-feely as I tried to engage in conversation.

I reminded him of who he was and where we were. He took that opportunity to let me know that he was a grown man, capable of making his own decisions, and he wanted me tonight. I thought briefly about the events of the day, and then of the week. I began to get tense and took another shot. I didn't want to think about or feel any of the events prior anymore. I looked at sexy milk chocolate. I noticed him eyeing me up and down, and I smiled. He drew me in for a kiss. Not bad, I thought for a man child. I wanted to kiss him longer, and he let me. I liked this already. He kissed me and fondled my body until his hands made way to my panties.

I grabbed his hands and pulled away. I let him know that this was not going to happen this way. He understood. Mario took my phone from me. He dialed his number and saved it to my phone. He said, "I'll be in town for a couple of more days. I would really like to see you." I said, "Maybe, we'll see." He grabbed me in for another kiss, and he headed back to the house.

After waiting several minutes, I headed into the house and decided it was time I said my goodbyes. I thanked Diana for having me, and I headed to my car. I smiled at the thought of sexy milk chocolate. I knew Johnson was gonna get it tonight when I got back to the condo. And sexy milk chocolate was gonna be the featured actor in tonight's performance. As I eagerly anticipated getting home to keep myself in the mood, I didn't notice that someone was standing on the passenger side of my car. I looked up. It was sexy milk chocolate. I unlocked the door and told him to get in. He hopped in the passenger seat, grabbed my face between both of his hands, and kissed me until I had to come up for air. I started the engine to the Mercedes, and she purred ever so sweet, just like my Boo Boo Kitty, that was revving her engine as well.

From the moment we hit the condo, it was on and popping. Mario could not keep his hands off me, and I got excited by his every single touch. Mario had a tall, slender frame that was screamed of instant sex. When he removed his shirt, I noticed his chest and arms were covered in tattoos. I took my hands and rubbed his arms and chest slowly, as I touched and admired every piece of artwork on his body. Mario responded by removing my dress and taking his tongue and kissing and licking in correspondence to my sensual touches. As his body was close to mine, I noticed his scent. His cologne was wild and exotic, and the smell had me hypnotized as he continued to shower my body with kisses. Mario lifted me in the air, and I wrapped my legs around his body. We kissed like that for a second, and then he walked me into the bedroom.

As he laid me on the bed, he positioned himself between my knees. Mario rubbed my stomach, my thighs, and the inner workings of my panties. I begged him to take them off. He refused. Mario, begin to place soft strokes on Boo Boo Kitty, and my panties began to get moist. I begged him again, and he refused. Mario pulled my panties to the side. He opened up my Kitty's lips and went right for her center.

Splash! After a series of flickers, Mario sopped up my juices like he was the biscuit, and She was the gravy. Mario kept sucking as she stood to attention again. He took his tongue from her center to her lips and flickered in a circular motion. I moved my hips to match him. Mario came up for air only long enough to tell me how good my pussy tasted.

There it was again, cherries and milk chocolate. Ok, so I must let you in on a little secret. My lady part has a special potion that has been passed down in our family for many generations. This potion has been proven to bring any man to his knees. Or so we believe anyway. It obviously was working because that cherry-chocolate swirl had Mario down there forever. Plus, I just had some good pussy too. What can I say? Mario took his time sucking and pleasing until Kitty gave her release a few more times, and I felt it was only right to return the favor.

As he laid on his back, I was astonished at the piece of equipment that was staring before me. Mario's frame may have been slender, but his manhood was thick, long, and beautiful. I have to admit, I was a little intimidated by what I had come across. At that moment, I knew I was going to have fun, but two decisions were made at that moment:

1. I was not riding that horse. I valued my insides and wanted to keep them.

2. I was already committed to pleasing him orally, hence him laying flat on his back. I decided that I would use all the tools in my arsenal to make this one of the best experiences he ever had; if I was able to take all that in.

I focused on that beautiful piece of equipment in front of me. I stared at it. I decided that I would not suck his dick tonight. I would make love to it. I looked at that milk chocolate piece of steel. I took it in both hands. I massaged it and stroked it. I looked at it like it was the love of my life before I took it in my mouth. I took my tongue and licked his shaft from the tip all the way down to his anal cavity. He moaned in pleasure.

I looked at his manhood again and took him in my mouth. I added additional juices, and he went crazy. I sucked and slurped and stoked on his Johnson. As I tickled his tip with my tongue, my hands massaged his twins as my finger circled his anal outing. His dick throbbed in excitement, and his toes began to curl.

My Kitty got wet instantly. As I stroked him, licked, and played with his balls, Mario went insane. He kept uttering words like, "damn, Oh shit, and Fuck." I didn't think I was doing so bad considering the enormous package in which this chocolate was wrapped. As I sucked and licked him, I gave the illusion of taking him all in. I made sure all his manhood was satisfied, and he held my hair back as I pleased him. He was such a fucking gentleman.

"I want to feel you inside me," he said. He lifted me up and drew me in for a kiss. He moved his tongue from my mouth to my neck, and then to my breasts. His mouth felt like ecstasy. My girls stood erect, and Mario feasted on them like they were the last supper. As he sucked on my ladies, I took his shaft and rubbed it up against my cave. As I rubbed him back and forth, we could hear the creaminess of what was becoming my explosion. Boo Boo Kitty flickered and was ready to welcome her guest.

I laid on my side, and Mario entered me from behind. He moved in and out slowly and I felt every stroke. I moaned in pleasure as my hips moved in cadence to his movement. He said, "damn baby, your pussy feels so good." I said, "ooh baby, yes," and he moved a little faster.

Mario grabbed my hips and dug deeper into my walls. I yelled, "damn baby this feels so good. Don't stop, baby PLEASE don't stop." He grabbed my breasts from behind. He massaged my nipples as he stroked in and out and around and around. I matched his movement with my hips. I backed my ass up into his and he slapped it. I said, "Ooh, fuck me, Daddy." The thrusts felt so good inside me that I didn't want him to stop. Mario grabbed me by my hips. He began to pound hard and fast. The tip of his manhood hit Kitty in her spot, and she began to scream. I felt him pulsate, and he gave his release. Mario and I laid in each other's arms like we had been lovers forever for the rest of the night. He gave me a beloved forehead kiss, and I fell asleep in his arms.

The next morning, I had to get back to reality. Although our encounter was brief and magnificent, I knew I had to take this man's child back to his momma's house. I dropped him off a few streets over, and we promised to keep in touch. We both knew that wasn't happening, and I wished that man child well. I thought about the events of the day before and got a little sick to my stomach. How did I let myself sleep with Diana's son?

Everything in my life was dragging me to an all-time low, and I didn't know how to stop myself from spiraling. I was barely surviving, pretending to be happy. Sure, I had small bursts here and there since James and I separated. But I still was not happy. "What was it gonna take"? I thought to myself. That was a question in which I didn't have an answer. I just knew too much was happening way too fast. The only way I knew how to cope right now was to just exist.

I headed straight to Ebony's house. Katrina was already up in the study. "How is she this morning?' I asked. "The same as last night," she said, and we went over Ebony's plans for the day. Since I took the night off, Katrina agreed to spend the day with her family. It was my job today to make sure that Ebony took her medication, and to empty her colostomy bag when the time was right. I thought about what our friendship had come to and became very sad. I didn't know if I was built for this; watching my best friend cease to exist. I wanted to run, but I couldn't. I felt like a helpless child trapped in a nightmare in which I couldn't wake up from. I was asked to be strong, and I didn't really know how. In the meantime, I would pretend and hope I got it right.

Throughout the days, there were plenty of visitors to keep Ebony occupied. She had made such an impact not only in her family but in her community as well. Although Ebony was not affiliated with any religion, she had strong personal ties to a lot of churches. She also, at one time, sat on the board of directors for one of the largest nonprofit organizations for domestic violence. Ebony lived a full life. If I had accomplished half of what Ebony did, I would look back on my life and be proud. As I watched her entertain her guests in good spirits, I was amazed at her strength. I watched her comfort and console during her own trial. That was just like Ebony. Even in her death, she was always concerned about your life.

As the last guests made their way to the door, I took in a deep breath. I finally would get some alone time with Ebony. She was still in good spirits, but I could tell she was tired.

Ebony: I love the fact that all these people want to show me love, but it is truly exhausting.

Tabby: I know Sis. I can see it all over you. How about we take a break tomorrow? Would you like that?

Ebony: Yes, I would. I love em, but they're getting on my nerves. Tell Aunt Maple the next time she comes to leave them badass grandkids at home. They ripped and ran the whole time and gave me a headache!

Tabby: I'm sorry, Ebony, I will make sure that's taken care of for you.

Ebony: If you don't quit treating me like a patient! What happened at court yesterday?

Tabby: Since you're already sitting down…

I began to give Ebony the details of my court date, and what happened afterward. She looked at me and closed her eyes. I could tell she was a bit taken back; by everything. She said, "Don't let what is happening to you get the best of you. You will come out on top, I promise." Then she closed her eyes again. I asked her if she was tired. "A little. To be honest, I feel like there is nothing else to do here, and my body knows that.

Earlier that day, the nurse had notified me that Ebony was no longer digesting the liquids that were going through her body. Cancer had created a block in her abdomen and colon. It would now be only a matter of days. We would begin to see a rapid change in Ebony, in the ways of her behavior, personality, and level of care needed. She told me to prepare myself for what may lie ahead. Considering I had no experience caring for a loved one in this manner, the only thing I could do was listen carefully to the nurse on what to expect and then try to act accordingly. I could also drink every now and then to cope with all this. But I thought that I owed my friend better than that, much better.

I looked over at Ebony. She looked at me and smiled. I knew that I wouldn't be able to have many more meaningful conversations with her alone, so I thought about asking her something that I could take with me when she left.

Tabby: As you look over your life Ebony, is there anything you would have done differently?

Ebony: To be honest, no. As I look over my life, I realize I came to do and be exactly who I am. There is nothing that I would or could do differently.

Tabby: That's fair. Well, is there anything that you regret about this life?

Ebony: Regrets? Ah, yes, regrets. I have spent a lot of time over the last few weeks thinking about regrets. Sure, I could focus on the material things, or the people, but those are not the things that I regret. What I regret most is time wasted. I spent too much time focusing on others in some capacity. I worried about them, mothered them, and made them an intricate part of my life. Not just close family and friends, but EVERYBODY. In the end, it took a toll on me mentally and physically. So, life is what it is, my dear.

Worrying only takes away from your life, so try to avoid it if you can.

Tabby: Ebony, I'm so sorry for making you worry about me.

Ebony: Stop it! You are my BEST friend. I was gonna worry about you whether you knew it or not. There is nothing you could do about that.

Tabby: I know, but I worry about you too. Its human nature.

Ebony: Well, breathe, dammit!

We both laughed. I knew what she was saying to be the truth. I needed to breathe more. When she had her first bout with cancer, I saw Ebony's whole perspective on life change. She did less and was happier, while the rest of the world still moved at an accelerated pace. My entire relationship with James kept moving while she adjusted in the fight for her life. She was telling me to slow down, and I needed to heed her message.

Ebony: If there is any advice I can pass on to you, you might ask?

Tabby: Uhm, I didn't ask, but I am so sure you were gonna give your two cents anyway.

Ebony: Glad you know! (She winks) My best advice for you is to love yourself and do your life's work. Find out who you are and what you want to be and be that. On your life's journey, you're gonna have naysayers, and you're gonna bump your head hard along the way. But it's ok, pick yourself back up, and laugh at yourself along the way. Often. Don't spend too much time worrying about what you didn't get done but celebrate the things you did accomplish. We spend way too much time creating the life we want, and not enough time enjoying the life we are creating. Stop and smell the roses, my dear.

I looked at Ebony. She smiled at me again and winked. I took a deep breath in and out and took in what she had said. I smiled back at her. At that moment, I had peace, and I knew my life would be ok. She knew it too. We sat in silence for a minute, and then I got up and removed the blankets from the den closet.

I got into bed with my best friend and said, "Oh no, my dear, you're not off the hook that easy. I am about to tell you all my deepest darkest secrets, the ones you don't already know about, AND you might hear the juicy details of the other stuff too! Prop yourself up darling!" for the rest of the night, I entertained her with the good, bad, and ugly of what had become my life, and we laughed until we both fell asleep holding hands. That was the last intimate moment I had with Ebony.

Over the next few days, Ebony's strength began to weaken a bit. Katrina and I went from alternating days of care to both being there full time. Ebony went from being able to bathe herself, to needing assistance. She was also not able to walk on her own, and she was beginning to lose weight at a rapid pace. Ebony had lost thirty pounds in the last few days. Everything she took in her body was going straight to her colostomy bag. She was still Ebony, though, and wanted to partake of her vodka and smoke her medicinal herbs. The doctor advised against the weed, but since Ebony insisted, who was I to argue?

On day four, Ebony began talking to herself. She mentioned her high school love who had passed and how she saw him. Then she asked me if her Aunt Daisy was in the room because she heard her. When I said no, she told me she was starting to get delusional. By this time, Katrina and I decided to limit the visits to very close family and a few friends. Although Ebony was a fighter, I knew she didn't want to be seen like this. Plus, all the visits were really putting a strain on her. Although she appreciated the love, I knew that it was taking away her energy.

One day five Ebony surprised us all. She yelled from the study for Katrina, and I. Ebony had a grand idea of having a party. She wanted all her closest girlfriends there, and she wanted to listen to music and reminisce. Katrina and I didn't know what the evening would be like but thought why not. We called five of her closest girlfriends and invited them over for food, love, and celebration. They were more than happy to oblige. Once all the ladies arrived, we all rallied around Ebony and let her know how much she was truly loved, and then the celebration began.

We turned on Pandora to one of the old school stations. As the melodies played throughout the sound system, we all talked about every song and what memories they held for us. Some of them were intertwined, while others held a special place with just Ebony and one of the ladies. We drank and talked about life and loves we lost along the way. As romantic songs bellowed, we even got up and danced to the music. Ebony waved her hands in the air and belted the lyrics to her favorite tunes. We all laughed and cried.

Then, in an instant, when "Adore" by Prince hit the airwaves, Ebony jumped out of her bed and let her body sway from side to side as Prince sang the melodies. We were all in shock. With caution, we all watched Ebony make sure she wouldn't fall. She took two steps forward. Then three to the side. She swayed from side to side as she sang " I'll give you my heart, I'll give you my mind; I'll give you my body, I'll give you my time." We knew she was with us and somewhere else at the same time. We all could feel it.

And just like the song, Ebony's energy also had an ending. Ebony got weak and collapsed, but we were right there to catch her. She said, "Where's Eric? Where did he go, we were dancing"? Eric was her high school boyfriend, who had passed away when we were teenagers.

Eric was shot in a fight that went left. He was Ebony's first love, and she saw herself being with him forever. She was able to keep one piece of him. Shortly after she passed, Ebony found out she was pregnant. Although she was devastated, Ebony gave birth to a handsome baby boy, little Eric and she decided in her heart that no one could truly take that man's place. So, she lived the rest of her life as a single woman.

"Eric, come back," she said. She yelled his name again. "Don't worry, I'll be with you soon." Ebony looked up at us and smiled. "I love you girls, all of you are so sweet. Now somebody take me to the bathroom I have to pee." Two of the ladies helped Ebony in the bathroom, and we all had a good laugh. We spent the rest of the night listening to music and holding on to the hope of having our beloved friend with us for just a little while longer.

The very next day, her condition began to deteriorate. When I approached Ebony, I could barely understand her. I became concerned, so I called the nurse. I explained how yesterday she was coherent and now appeared to be in a and out of consciousness. The nurse said that Ebony was in her final stages on this earth. Most patients in hospice have a burst of energy, followed by an accelerated deterioration of life. It can be confusing to the care-givers, but she shared with Katrina and I what to expect next. We both prepared ourselves with the somber reality that Ebony only had days to live. It felt like a ton of bricks had hit me in the chest, and I found it extremely hard to breathe.

I wanted to die with her, especially with all that I had going on. But what would that prove? I thought about my last conversation with Ebony. Life happens to us all. Well, apparently, death does too. I thought about Katrina for a moment. Not only was she losing a best friend, but also a sister. I got up and hugged her tightly. I decided that not only did I need to be there for myself, but Katrina needed me too.

The next couple of days were light, yet emotionally brutal. I went in to give Ebony her bath, and she didn't want to get out of the bed. I sponge bathed her and gave her an intimate massage with lotion. I noticed she smiled at times and winced at others. Her skin was colder and appeared to be rough to the touch. Certain spots that I touched, I could tell she was in pain. She opened her mouth, but no words would come out. I talked to her and tried to be as gentle as possible. Once I finished her massage, I covered her body and got her comfortable. She looked at me and smiled, closed her eyes, and went to sleep. For the rest of the day, Ebony was only awakened to administer her pain medication. The nurse explained that we needed to be precise about her medication and that she needed to take her medication on time from here on out. Her body would experience pain, and the medication would make her comfortable.

At this point, all visitors had ceased. It was Katrina, and I on watch waiting for the end. The feeling was uneasy, and I was reminded at that moment what Pastor Doug always said about death and life; they both held the same power, and for both, no man truly knew the day or the hour. I hated Pastor Doug, but he wasn't wrong in that statement. I thought about the waiting part. At this point, we were just making her comfortable. I wanted Ebony with me, but I also didn't want her here like this. I got mad suddenly. I thought about the unfairness of the situation.

Ebony was one of the best people I knew. Why did her life have to end so abruptly? It seemed like it was always the good ones that were taken away so early. Then I thought about what her life had become. There was still our love and prayers, but no quality of life. Ebony would not want to go on like this much longer I knew it. As I was engrossed in my thoughts, I looked up to see a teary-eyed Katrina. She said, "Call the doctor, Tabby. Ebony is not breathing."

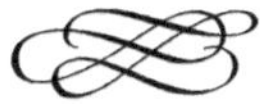

The aftermath is defined as something of consequence or the after-effects that follow an event, especially one of significant, unpleasant nature. For example, the aftermath of what occurred on September 11, 2001, will forever be etched in your memory if you're an American. In the wake of the September 11 attacks, the aftermath of that event caused other events to be set in motion. The initial response was of shock, sadness, and horror. Then people rallied together to become a community. First responders and ordinary citizens alike all band together to create beauty in that chaotic event. What also happened after that was the war on terrorism. Whether you agree or disagree with the outcomes, the aftermath of an event is designed to bring awareness and action. My aftermath of the unfortunate events of my life also created the same kind of reactions.

By the day of Ebony's homegoing, I had reached my wit's end. Ebony had passed almost a week ago, and I had to play nice, and be strong for not only Katrina and her son Eric, but for the rest of the host of family and friends. All the arrangements were already in order before Ebony passed per her request. She had asked me as her best friend to say a few words on her behalf, and I knew in my numbness I had to yet be strong again. I was tired of pretending. A part of me wished I had a motorcycle that I could hop on and ride off into eternity. Well, first I'd have to learn to ride a bike. At this point, I'd settle for the back of the motorcycle with a hot guy attached to it. Anything to take away this pain I was feeling. Ok, Tabby, focus on the task at hand, I said, and thought about what I would say to encourage the people. I thought about it and cried. Who was going to support me on this leg of my journey? I didn't know, but I know I missed Ebony already.

Live, laugh, and love were the words of comfort that I spoke to Ebony's host of family and friends. I thought about our relationship, and also our last conversation. Above all else, Ebony truly wanted me to live and be happy. I thought to myself, even if I don't currently share the same sentiment, I wanted the people to be encouraged. For a minute, I thought this must be what Pastor Doug and other pastors had to go through in their own personal trials. I felt a little sorry for Pastor Doug and men like him. They seemed to always have to put on a brave face when they could be dying on the inside. Well, not me. Not anymore, I thought. I would get through the speech, and then I would live life unapologetic whatever that meant. I took a deep breath, got dressed, and prepared to say goodbye to Ebony one last time.

During my message, there was not a dry eye in the place. I could see the congregants engrossed in my stories of our childhood and friendship, and how they tied into the message of Live, Laugh, and Love. I also challenged each of them to embrace their own memories of Ebony. In those, they can find life, laughter, and love. It was all very moving. So much so, that as I exited the podium, I noticed that James was standing there waiting for me crying. I thought to myself, "what in the hell," but I wanted to assume positive intent, as she was my best friend for many years, and he knew that.

James: (Crying) Oh Tabby, I'm so sorry for your loss (he hugs me)

Tabby: It's ok James, it will be ok

James: Ebony was always good to me. I remember when I was going through my own personal stuff after you left me, she was right there.

Tabby: I know James. She will be missed

James: Oh, Tabby (begins to sob). If you need me, I'm here ok

Tabby: Ok James

James: I mean it Tabby, I'm here for you. Tabby, I know you're going through a lot. Maybe you should just stay with me after the homegoing, get your mind off things.

Was this negro serious? So, I was supposed to forget that we were in the midst of a heated divorce? He's got to be joking. I was still trying to assume positive, so I would let this negro down gently.

Tabby: I appreciate the offer James, but maybe I just need some time to myself

James: You sure? I can have Rosanna whip up something real nice...

Tabby: I'm positive, I just need time alone

James: Well, we still are husband and wife, Tabby. I am here if you need me.

And just like that, the conversation ended. By this time, my emotions were on overload, and I just wanted to get out of here. I was tired of fucking pretending, and I didn't want to do it anymore. My face began to get flushed, and I couldn't breathe. I felt trapped suddenly, and I kindly excused myself from the rest of the family. I stepped outside and felt instant relief. The atmosphere in the homegoing was just too much for me to take in. I needed an outlet, and I didn't care what happened next. I texted Katrina and told her, "I have to leave, I can't do this anymore, sorry." I ordered and UBER and headed to the nearest bar.

When I got to the bar, I looked around. There sound of Trap

Music was playing on the jukebox, and there were only a couple of customers present. I sat at the bar and instantly smelled the down-home cooking coming from the kitchen, and I knew that this would be my home for the rest of the day. "A double shot of Cuervo, please." The bartender obliged. I tilted my head back and took in the tequila. It went down smooth and refreshing considering it had been a few weeks since I had a drink.

I asked for another double, took it back, and then ordered some food. "It's gonna be a long day mam, I might as well introduce myself now. I'm Tabby, and I just buried my best friend." "Well, I'm Tara, and I make the best drinks around here girl. I'm so sorry for your loss. The first round was on me. Now, if you don't mind, I'm gonna keep my eye on you. Pain is a hell of a drug. You don't wanna add fuel to that fire. I stared at her for a second. I said, "Ok Tara, keep an eye on me. As a matter of fact, make me something good."

Tara: Oh, I can definitely do that. Since you're in the spirit of Tequila, let me make you one of my signature drinks. You seem like you could use an uplift, boost your spirits per se. I call this drink, "getting back to happy." Its tequila, lime juice, and pineapple juice. Goes down real smooth, but has a powerful punch, be careful.

Tabby: Sounds right up my alley. (I got teary-eyed). More than anything else, I wanna be happy. Tara, make me one of those and keep em coming.

Tara: Coming right up.

The next morning, I woke up with the biggest hangover. I sat up in bed with my head spinning. I looked over and saw a big light-skinned awkward shaped lump lying next to me. What in the hell have I done? Wait a minute, is that Fred from high school? Freaky Fred? No! Say it isn't so. I looked over slowly at the mysterious man lying in my bed next to me. Yep, it was him, Fred Forrester aka Freaky Fred from high school.

But how the hell did he end up in my bed? Ugh! I knew how,

but I couldn't remember the details of the night before. "Think Tabby. I went to the funeral, then to the bar, had a happy drink, then..." the rest of the night became a blur, even down to the details of waking up with a high school chum. "Tabby, ya gotta do better than this," I thought.

I eased out of bed and tiptoed to the bathroom. I grabbed my phone to get some clues from the night before. I looked to see 10 missed calls and 20 text messages. The ten missed calls and the first seventeen text messages were from James. First, indicating he still didn't think I should be alone. Next, he professed his undying love saying life was too short, and Ebony's passing was a reminder of that. He asked me again to get back with him via text. I responded with laugh emojis. He then switched gears calling me a dirty whore who wouldn't get anything in the divorce settlement. Then the last text message was an apology for his behavior.

Typical James. The last three texts were from Tara at the bar. She was making sure I got home safely as the man I was talking to swore we were high school sweethearts. She asked me to check in when I got home, and apparently, I did just that. I responded to her text with one of my own: I MADE IT HOME, AND NOW FREAKY FRED IS GONNA SUCK THE SOUL OUT OF MY VAGINA. I was so embarrassed. I decided that I couldn't let this happen again. It was not one of my finest moments. I looked down at my phone, and I peeked out of the bathroom. Fred was lying in my bed with his head propped up on his arm and smiling. Fred had pop-bottle glasses, and he was still as nerdy as ever since high school.

Fred: I can't believe I got with the prettiest girl in high school

Tabby: Fred, you're way too obsessed, stop it.

Fred: Obsessed, I am. I had an amazing time last night. I can't believe I came home with you, you acted like I wasn't even alive in high school. Did you know we had Spanish together?

Tabby: Fred, that was many years ago, so no.

Fred: I remember everything about you. I was in love with you, still am.

Tabby: Ok this is a bit odd

Fred: (laughs) Don't worry! I love you like a high school crush. Since I'm married now, I know we can never be

Tabby: Married? So, shouldn't you be getting home

Fred: My wife knows I stayed too long with the boys, she's ok. But I'm ready for round 2.

Fred kisses me, and I feel a slight electrical charge. As he kisses my body, I noticed that Boo Boo Kitty was springing into action already. This nasty bitch will take any dick that's thrown at her. Since he was touching me so well, I decided to let Kitty do the talking. I wanted to feel this man suck my soul out of my vagina like my text last night mentioned. So, in all fairness, I decided to give freaky Fred another shot. I reached for his manhood. I stroked him sensually but noticed nothing was happening. I touched him again. Still nothing. I didn't want to put in the extra work, but it appeared for the first time I would have to. I was not used to men not getting aroused at my touch, and it felt awkward and frustrating. Fred grabbed my hand to stop me.

Fred: Tabby, it's not you. I promise I am so turned on. But I don't think you remember me telling you last night that I have diabetes. Diabetes affects my erection, and I must give myself a shot. So, if you'll excuse me, I'll be right back to finish what I started.

Wait a minute. Did this man just tell me he has a wind-up penis? There is no way I can be with a man that I can't get hard, that's way too creepy. I decided that after today I would not see Fred again. I wanted a penis I could make love to and control, and his was not it. This man had to wind it up to get it started. Too much work for me, especially since he was not my investment but his wife's. I headed to the kitchen and hurried and took 3 shots of tequila. I had to erase from my psyche that this man had to have penile assistance. I imagined him winding his dick like Jack-in-the-box, and I chuckled to myself.

As Fred emerged from the bathroom, I took that moment to take in his frame. He was funny built with a big stomach, and skin hanging in the arm and thigh areas of his body. It looked like he had gained in some areas and lost in others. Age was not very kind to him. I looked down at his Johnson. Fully erect, it seemed to be about 4 inches. I was very disappointed and knew after today, I would have to ghost this fool.

Our lovemaking was confirmation he had to go. Don't get me wrong, when it came to eating pussy, he truly snatched my soul. But there was not enough penis to sustain what Boo Boo Kitty needed. And to make matters worse, Freaky Fred had an awkward conversation during sex. I can deal with the usual "you have good as pussy, fuck me harder, and come all over this dick," those were given. But Fred had a way of wanting to pretend we were in high school all over again. he was saying things like, "if you met me in gym class, would I get your number," and "If we had a chance to work on our big Spanish class project together, would you have been my girl?." That was incredibly creepy, but I played along to get the act over with.

When we were done, he kissed me, told me he loved me and asked me to dinner. I told him I would think about it and call him later. That later never happened as I deleted Freaky Fred's number from my phone. That was a nightmare that I didn't want to relive again. I promised myself that I would do better over the next few months not only to make Ebony proud but for my own sanity.

Over the next 6 months, however, I found myself not doing better, but heading down a path of self-destruction instead. The memories of Ebony were constantly flooding my head, and I felt out of control. I began screening my calls, also thanks to James. Since the funeral, he took every opportunity to text and leave messages about what a horrible person I had become. He knew this because he had me followed. He also threatened to use whatever he knew in court against me and was pressuring me to take the terms of the prenup.

After talking to my attorney, Ms. Stevens assured me that we had a solid case and that James' contact could be considered harassment. She sent a letter to his attorney advising James to cease all activity. It didn't help, however, and James called me at least three times a day. I would let him go through his love-hate cycle, but the pressure from his harassment sure didn't make things any better during this time.

I was also able to pick up two new friends; Tara, the bartender, and the drink, "Getting back to happy." I found myself in the bar almost night and day trying to mask the pain of what had become my life or lack thereof. I felt like I had no friends anymore outside of the bartender and the drink. Sure, Sam and the kids had been calling me over the last few months, but I didn't want to talk to anybody. I was angry, hurt, and had emotionally checked out.

The only constants in my life right now were the happy drinks and the men that I fucked along the way. I kind of called them my casualties of war. Whatever it was, this six month period had been way too much for one woman to take in. As I sat and thought about the course of my destruction, I got a little sick on the inside. I wanted to get off this path but felt like I couldn't. I reflected on the men I entertained recently; I got even sicker. It was reflecting on these encounters, though that helped me see things from a new perspective.

Freaky Fred was the first man I hooked up with. Although he had a wind-up penis, my promise to cut him off went on deaf ears for a while. The bottom line was that Fred didn't have much to work with. But, he sure knew how to feast on my Kitty. I kept him around for a while for that, until the sex kept getting creepier. Not only was Fred fixated on our high school years, but he always wanted to act out a scene from "Grease 2" or "High School Musical," pretending that he and I were in the leading roles. And to top things off, Fred always wanted to find a way for me to put items in his butt. Fingers, remotes, fruit, it didn't matter. It got to be a little too much for me. Fred really crossed the line; however, when he kept saying he loved me and wanted to leave his wife. That had made me uncomfortable, and I ended up blocking his number for good.

The next notch on my pussy scale came from a man that I coin the young anaconda from the country, or Southern Hospitality, I like to affectionately call him. Corvin was the 26-year-old dick that I met on social media and flew into my home town all the way from Biloxi, Mississippi. Kinky, I know, but I spent most of my time drunk. I met Corvin in an adult chat group on a social site. It was one of those places where they request pictures of you in all kinds of forms. Since Tuesday was "Titty Tuesday" I decided to show the men and women in the group what I was working with through my lace push up bra. Corvin liked my post and immediately hit my inbox.

We talked lightly back and forth for a while, and then our sexuality went into full peak. It started with me sending a boob pic which I had never done before. Then he sent a penis pic. Next thing I knew as the days went by, we were having video sex. Johnson and Esteban would put on a show for Corvin, who then showed me what his man could do. We both were skilled at pleasing ourselves, and it was so exciting seeing him get aroused at watching me giving myself delight. When I turned on my video, it was lights, camera, action! I swear I could have been a video vixen in another life.

We both had decided that we wanted to take things to the next level. Corvin got a one-way ticket from Biloxi to my city. We both agreed to leave that would be best just in case things didn't go as we planned. When he touched down, I met him at the airport, and we stopped for something really quick to eat. After that, we skipped the pleasantries and went right into action. Corvin was everything I imagined a 26-year-old to be, young, gifted, and full of energy. I swear it was like fucking the energizer bunny! Everything Corvin did was a little more aggressive and slightly immature.

For example, when he touched my body, he was a little rougher than I was used to. He also wanted every stroke inside me to be a real pounding. No matter how much I said slow down, Corvin had one pace; jackrabbit speed. Our first night together, he had so much energy that after two straight hours of getting pounded in the doggy style position, I looked back at him and begged him to hurry up and cum. That was ridiculous.

Before and after that encounter, I had spoken with my new girlfriend, Tara, who cautioned me against bringing in young meat for entertainment. "Be careful with that, mama! You never know what you're gonna get." After I slept with Corvin the first time, her words came back to haunt me immediately. I have to admit, I was flattered by the attention that he was giving me. He was yet another hot young man turned on by me, and it was over-whelming in a good way.

I felt attractive and sexy, something I had long stopped feeling when I was with James. That attention meant nothing, however when I felt the constant pounding of his rod. Corey seemed to go on for what I considered forever, and it was way too much for me to handle. Of course, I got the "I told you so" from Tara, and I hate to say it, but she was right. There were red flags that this wasn't a good idea from the beginning.

The first dick pic that he sent me where his penis was the same length as an aerosol can should have been an indicator that I was in for a ride, literally. I learned the hard way (no pun intended) that every anaconda is still a snake, and if that snake is way too big to fit in your mouth and your vagina, you may want to rethink dancing with the snake. I spent precisely five days with this young-ster, which was way more than enough time to get felt up, slob-bered on, and pounded. By his last night in town, I put on my Moo Moo dress as an outward sign that his penis was no longer allowed to enter my vaginal walls. He saw the dress and understood.

Although the young anaconda was not my finest moment, there were also some other near misses that left me just as shameful. There were the fuck boys who slept with me once or twice and never called again and blocked me on social media. The fuckboys were equal opportunity dogs, and they didn't give a fuck who they hurt in the process, hence the term fuck boys. Fuck boys came in all age ranges, and I couldn't distinguish what was worst, getting dumped by a young or old fuck boy. I determined it to be far worse dealing with an old school player.

At least with a youngin, you could chalk his behavior up to silly immaturity. But with an old school player, one is left feeling like a fool and angry. I so hated them both young and old, and it seemed to be a whole lot of them out there. On the other end of the sex spectrum, there were the stage 3 clingers who fell in love at first sight and taste of this sweet kitty juice. That was not good for my image, either. These men were stalkers, followers, texters, and followed your social media-heavy. I already had my ex harassing me, the last thing I needed was another string of lovers to be stalking me as well. I was looking for something in between and could never have a happy medium.

One of the most undesirable moments in my drunken stupor, I called the Ebony and Ivory doubleheader. Yes, we women have names that we coin for memorable sexual encounters. At least I do anyway. What is the Ebony and Ivory Doubleheader, you may ask? Well, I made the mistake of sleeping with two men at two different times in the same night, one white and the other black. Hence, the term doubleheader. Two penises, two heads. Although it was not one of my finest moments during the aftermath, it was sure a wakeup call.

That night in the bar, I was feeling terrific. I had already eaten some good food from the kitchen, and I had three happy drinks already. As I was on my way to the fourth, the cutest little white man approached and asked if he could buy me a drink. I had seen him in the bar a few times as a regular, so I obliged. His name was

Pepe, and he and I were around the same age. We got to know each other better at the bar that night, and we decided to keep in touch. We drank, exchanged numbers, and went along our merry way. I stayed in touch with Pepe and was proud of myself for not handing over the family jewels the first night we were together. I was trying to do things differently, so I wanted to make him wait some.

After a few weeks, I agreed to meet Pepe at the bar again for drinks. While waiting for him, I was being entertained by a hot 27-year-old fuck boy who was upfront and honest about his intention to "fuck me." I could respect that, as there is nothing more frustrating than someone pretending to be interested. I took Peanut's number intending to call him sometime soon. He bought me a couple of drinks and continued celebrating with his best friend, who was celebrating his birthday. I sat and waited for Pepe to arrive.

Pepe entered the bar with a pair of jeans, a leather jacket, and a fitted cap. Typical wanna be white boy, I thought to myself. I also thought that at forty-eight, he was too fucking old to be dressing like that. But who was I to judge? Pepe's Story was interesting. He was a small business owner who grew up in the hood. He always hung with black people, so his attraction has always been to black women. He also mentioned that he was waiting on a massive settlement of over a million dollars from some previous accident. In my opinion, I think he was just using that line to get some pussy. He must have taken me for one of those hood rat chicks.

What he didn't and would never know is that I had my own money and did well for my damn self. Especially since I still had access to account number 8. At least for now. So, what Pepe didn't know was that, in essence, I was out of his fucking league. If I decided to fuck him, it would be on my terms, and more than likely a sympathy fuck. To be honest, I just wanted to add a white man to my arsenal. I had heard raving reviews about their head game, and I wanted to see what his mouth did.

I finished my drink, "Getting back to happy." I then downed the shot that peanut purchased for me. I looked over at Tara, who gave me an evil smirk. Pepe excused himself to the bathroom. Tara looked at me and said, "Now, this should be interesting." I smiled and said, "Girl trust me. If I take this one home, it will be a one-time-only deal." She said, "Trust me, from what I've heard, I'm sure you're right. You know these stools do all the talking. But that's all I'm gonna say about it. Enjoy, my love." We both had a good laugh and moved on to other business at hand, such as my upcoming court date, and if I had thought about another outlet as opposed to sex.

Tabby: So, have you become my therapist now?

Tara: No, but I have become your friend. All the drinking you've been doing lately is really self-destructive. I know you're going through a lot, but you gotta find another way to deal with it. The alcohol leads to one-night stands, and then how do you feel afterward?

Tabby: Can we not get into this tonight? Look, I PROMISE to do better, ok? But tonight is not that night.

Tara raised her hands in surrender. I looked at her in a loving tone and told her I really appreciated her advice, although I was not heeding it tonight. Pepe approached me from behind and whispered in my ear. He asked if I was ready to go, and I nodded. I said goodbye to Tara, and she smiled and waved in response.

Pepe's head game was AMAZING! It was everything I had imagined and more. I had cum five-time from Pepe's love and affection that he showed my kitty. He stroked her and touched her and sucked and licked. It was like he knew every spot to touch, and Boo Boo was getting her fill tonight. Pepe had me so worked up that I wanted him to give it to me raw in that moment, fuck the consequence. So, I said, "c'mon baby, show me what you're working with." He said, "You want some of this big cock?." I said, "Yes, baby yes"! Pepe undid his pants, and they fell to the floor. "Tighty-whiteys," I thought. Kind of interesting. I laid on the bed with my legs spread in anticipation of my lover's manhood as he dropped in undies.

Wait. "What is that?' I thought. I looked at Pepe and at his little friend. And I mean little. Like Stewie from family guy little. I thought about Tara for a split second, and I tried my best not to burst out laughing. Pepe approached me, and I had to figure out what my next move was going to be. It was too late to say no thanks, sir, as I just begged for the dick seconds before. I decided to let this thing happen and pretend to enjoy every minute of it. How could a man with head game like that have such a small and very disappointing penis? I left Pepe's place feeling disgusted and sexually frustrated at the same time. So, what did I do? I gave peanut the fuckboy a call. Hell, there is nothing like a fuckboy to finish a job that a so-called grown-ass man couldn't accomplish.

And just like I had anticipated, Peanut did not disappoint. Although young and a little inexperienced, Peanut had dick for days. There was not a lot of foreplay, as I answered the door naked after I hopped out of the shower. This man was immediately aroused and began playing with my lower lady. Ms. Kitty got wet instantly. As he played with her, I stroked him through his grey sweatpants. We kissed and made out and ended up on my couch, where I rode this young buck until the sun came up. We ordered breakfast, ate, and said our goodbyes. I thanked him for an amazing night, and neither of us made any promises.

Once Peanut left, I sat and thought about my transgressions from the night before. I had fucked two men in one night. What had gotten into me? Sure, I had always enjoyed a good dick, but I had never been "that girl." I started thinking about my conversation with Tara. The weightiness of the truth of her words began to sting me in the back of my throat. I had to find another way to cope. I realized in that moment that I had not been sober since the passing of Ebony. I had been drinking every single day. The pain of losing her was too much to bear alone.

And then there was James who had been calling and harassing

me about settling out of court. He had threatened me once, and even had that tired ass bitch Keisha call me to give me advice "one woman to another." On top of that, I hadn't looked for a job at all, and I had no clue what I wanted to do with my life, no direction or purpose. How was I happy? I wasn't miserable, but I sure wasn't happy either, except when I was drinking. But the drinking masked all the other shit that I didn't want to deal with.

All I knew is that I was at a crossroads. I could no longer go on the way that I was. I wanted to do better, and I wanted more. I wanted to be happy. I thought to myself about what it was I truly loved to do, and my mind came up blank. "Great! I have absolutely no purpose in life," I thought. Surely there was something I could do. In the meantime, I decided that I needed to get back into my best shape. I didn't want to hit the gym though, there were too many hard bodies. Sure, I could hire a trainer, but I also didn't want someone I really didn't know to be in my personal space right now.

I thought back to high school when I was on the cross-country team. That was one of the best and worst times of my life. My family being poor, I had to grow up starving, having no electricity half the time, and having to fight off older cousins and uncles to keep my sexuality. Long-distance running was a way back then that I learned to cope with all the harshness in life that the hood had to offer. I figured if it worked back then, perhaps it was worth giving a shot now. It had been so long, though, that I knew I would die. I figured I had to start somewhere, so I dusted off my running shoes and headed out for the first time in a long time on the journey to find happy.

That first run was a beast, but the runs after that became easier and easier. It had been a little over a month, and I had become comfortable in my new routine of things. It didn't take me long to get back in a groove so much so that I found myself running on most days, and I was surprised at how good I felt. I would turn on my positive affirmations, and the rest was history.

When I first started out, I would walk for 28 minutes and run for two. Now I was running 30 solid minutes every morning without blinking an eye. Getting in a five-mile run in the morning was starting to be the best way for me to start my morning, outside of meditation, that is. Yes, I had started meditating. I figured if I wanted to stop drinking and being reckless sexually, I had to fill that void with other things. For the most part, it seemed to be working, although every now and then, I still felt the urge to merge.

With the release of more positive endorphins, there was also some insight into the direction I wanted to take my life in at least the immediate present. I decided that I wanted to run a marathon. Sure, I had been running for only a month, but I felt if I had a goal to concentrate on, that would give my life some sort of purpose. At least until I figured out the rest. Just the thought itself gave me a good feeling, and I decided to explore my options. As I looked up information on marathons, I had to decide how soon I wanted to embark on this endeavor. It just so happened that there was a marathon occurring in the next 5 months. Perfect. That would give me plenty of time to train for the event, and it would also serve to celebrate my freedom from James. My own personal divorce party.

I got on my shoes for my morning run. I pictured myself running this marathon. I visualized myself crossing the finished line and felt the sense of accomplishment that came with it. Then I envisioned again me crossing the finished line, but there was no one there for me. I looked around as all the other runners had their support system come for them. I thought to myself, "Who would be there for me"? Both of my kids were off to college, and my very best friend was gone. My second best-bestie had a glamorous life in LA, so who was left for me? No man, no kids, and no friends. What had my life become?

After my run, I decided to switch gears and head for the bar. Yes, I still went to the bar, but not to get plastered. Tara and I had developed a weird friendship, and I came in for non-alcoholic drinks most of the time and to bounce my ideas off her. Tara had been the one to suggest something constructive, and when I hinted about the marathon, she thought it was an amazing idea, and encouraged me to sign up. I was coming in for my weekly checkup visit and to let her know that I had stopped being a scaredy-cat and decided to take her advice.

"Well done," she said. She even agreed to be there when I hit the finished line. I smiled. Just hours before I was having a pity party about having no one and here the universe was showing me that I really had people in my corner. I smiled and said, give me a double of my recent usual. "Isn't it a little early for a shot Ms. Taylor, especially a double, my goodness."

I recognized the voice a little and turned around. The face was very familiar. It was the face of a blast from the serious past, and I couldn't help but laugh. Rico Green was the face of one of the boys in my old neighborhood. Rico lived a few streets over, and he hung with the Anderson boys, two of the cutest guys on the planet. Or so we thought back in the fifth grade. Manny and Tim Anderson were that deal to every girl in the neighborhood. I can remember the countless amount of marriage and baby games that we girls played where Mammy and Tim were at the top of the list for potential husbands and baby daddies. I had a crush on Manny, and we even "went together" for a few months, which took my popularity up a notch. Ah, those were good times.

Rico, however, was not much to look at back then. As a matter of fact, he was more like a sidekick to the 2 cute superheroes he called friends. He was kind of annoying, and I remember him taking every opportunity to pick at me or make my life miserable. But here he was in the flesh and in my face after thirty-plus years. I laughed at him in recognition, but I also looked him up and down and admired how good time had been to him.

Rico: Are you gonna answer my question, woman?

Tabby: Excuse me? Just because I know you don't mean I have to give you an answer, the last time I checked, I was grown.

Rico: Still feisty, I see. You lookin' good woman, what have you been up to?

Tabby: You want the long version or the short?

Rico: I would say the long version, but you are ordering drinks already. It ain't even noon woman

Tabby: If you don't stop calling me that

Rico: You know I'm messing with you

Tabby: Something you obviously haven't forgotten how to do

Rico: Damn, who hurt you?

We both looked at each other and laughed. When my drink came, Rico realized it was a double sho; of a special energy smoothie that Tara had begun whipping up for me since I had started running. I drank my smoothie, and Rico and I got reacquainted. Rico had never been married, had a quiver full of children, and lived most of his adult life as a player. He was a massage therapist and a jack of all trades handyman who bragged about the ability to fix anything. According to him, he had done a lot of damage in the streets and, as of recently, made the decision to slow his life down some. He had admitted to spending a little time in jail. He was looking to rebuild his life, which was becoming quite difficult because of his arrest record.

I felt a little pity for him. I got Rico up to speed on what had become my life and the direction I was headed, which outside of the marathon, I really didn't have a clue.

Rico: You know we used to go together, right?

Tabby: What?

Rico: Yea, we went together in middle school, you don't remember?

Tabby: I sure don't remember that

Rico: Tabby, we did things to each other back then that little kids shouldn't speak of

Tabby: What the fuck are you talking about?

Rico: I can't believe you don't remember us going together.

I thought to myself, not another Freaky Fred. I was gonna cut this off before it even got started. At least that was my thought process, but the more Rico kept talking, the more I was intrigued to know more about his life.

We sat in the bar and talked for over two hours about our lives, where we were headed, and what we wanted in this next phase. It was kind of refreshing having a mature, intelligent conversation with a man outside of sex. Rico was clear that he was looking for a wife. I was honest with him and let him know I was still married. He told me he appreciated my honesty, and we both exchanged numbers. We decided that we were in a unique place in our lives, and we could both use a friend. I took his number, and Rico and I began to chat every evening about the old neighborhood, our family dynamics, and what tomorrow looked like. Rico had 12 children, all of whom were grown except for two. I often wondered how a man like him was able to financially take care of all those children. In the end, though, it was none of my business.

After a few weeks of talking on the phone, I finally felt comfortable enough to invite Rico over for lunch. I had just taken a ten-mile run in preparation for the marathon, and I was starving. My body was starting to take a shape that I was proud of, and the running had been paying off. I admired myself quickly in the mirror. The belly was coming down, and my legs had definition. I smiled back at what I saw. My body temperature began to rise a bit, and I already knew what time it was. It had been two months, and my kitty had been really good at restraining herself. But I had a sneaky feeling that today she may not be on her best behavior.

It was ok, though. I really liked Rico. He was familiar, an old friend from way back, and we really had a lot in common. He was safe, and I knew that if I was going to put myself out there sexually again, it was best to do it with someone safe. Rico also made me laugh. I don't know if it was the happy endorphins from exercising, but being with him added something positive to my life. I wasn't drinking nearly as much, and I was happy for once. Rico and I also knew each since we were kids, how much safer can you get?

I prepared spaghetti and a small salad. I also had a bottle of wine chilled in the fridge. I had on something cute, but casual, and my nails and feet were done as I had just left the spa earlier that week. The door rang, and I checked the mirror one more time. I looked at myself for approval and answered the door. Rico had a big smile on his face, and we laughed and gave each other a big long boisterous hug. Rico was a bigger guy than he was in middle school. Back then, he was a puny chocolate boy with oversized teeth. But this man had grown and matured into his complexion, his teeth, and his frame.

Rico was about 6'0 with smooth dark chocolate skin, a salt and pepper goatee neatly trimmed around his sensual lips, and a semi muscular frame that screamed he could get it if he really wanted it. Rico's goatee salt and pepper was sprinkled just enough to know that a woman was dealing with a grown man. I looked at him in admiration. He looked at me, and he smiled. I could tell he liked what he saw. We sat down, I poured the wine, and he rolled the weed. Our lunch date was sweeter than sweet.

Rico talked mostly about what his life was like after he left our neighborhood. He moved from the southside to the north, so he created new allegiances. Rico was affiliated with some of the biggest dope dealers on the north side of the city. Rico wasn't a drug dealer himself but made a lucrative living for a while as a transporter. He talked about the fast lifestyle, the quick money, and the string of women he had along the way, hence the twelve children. For some reason, the fact that he had so many kids didn't bother me. I figured since they were grown, he didn't have many financial concerns with them. Plus, I thought it was perfect because my kids were grown, and I was not trying to start over; with anyone. I listened and smiled as he shared the good, bad, and ugly of his life with me. After being enamored about his many tales of life after he moved out of our neighborhood, we decided to switch gears. Rico went to his car and returned with a massage chair.

Rico: I want to thank you for lunch, Tabby. And to show my gratitude, I'd like to offer my services and give you a massage.

Tabby: A massage sounds nice, and I have been negligent in that area.

Rico: I could tell by your body language that you had a lot going on. Then when you talked about Ebony and your husband, I could tell you were tense. Let me do this for you as a gift.

Tabby: Rico, that's a nice gesture and I accept. However, I ain't sittin' on no stiff ass table.

Rico: Oh, so you wanna do this, right? Well, let me put the table away. You get fully naked and meet me in the bedroom.

We stared at each other for a second. He said, "My massage can go one of two ways; Either you will be my client, or we will cross over into something else. I will let you decide that." I said, "Take the board to the car and come back, and we'll let fate decide." He smiled and took his time putting the board away. This man was slow and intentional, I could tell. I felt a little excited, and so did kitty. I wanted this man, and today he would have me.

I laid on the bed, totally exposed on my stomach. I watched as Rico mixed exotic oils together. He asked me about my music selection, and I told him to surprise me. When I heard the sexy melodies of Jodeci, I knew this man wouldn't disappoint. As "Cone and Talk to Me" filled my airwaves, Rico slowly massaged my feet and my legs. I melted at his touch. By the time he reached my shoulders, I was in heaven. Rico put love in every single touch to my body, and I thought about all my life's pressures. Slowly one by one, I could see them fading in the distance, and it felt like healing was taking place. I sunk into his touch and allowed myself to be free. Rico was very professional, and I could tell he took his craft very seriously. He talked to me about my stress points as he masterfully kneaded and massaged those parts into submission. I laid there grateful and happy. I smiled and moaned to show my appreciation.

It was time for me to turn over on my back, and I looked Rico in his eyes as his body towered over mine. His eyes were piercing, and I felt like he was trying to look directly into my soul. He stood between my legs and spread them apart. He grabbed the oil and applied the oil to one of my legs, and began to massage. I closed my eyes and let out a deep sigh as his fingers brushed the crevice between my thigh and my labia. Rico applied pressure as he massaged my inner thigh, and I could imagine his lips on my secret place. Rico repeated the motion with the other leg, and the feeling I experienced became more intense.

As "Sex Me" hit the airwaves, I felt Rico spread my legs further apart. In one sudden motion, his tongue swarmed down on Boo Boo Kitty like an eagle diving for his prey. Just the flicker of his tongue made my body shiver. Rico stroked my center with masterful perfection, and my juices flowed from Kitty like a volcano. Rico slurped up my juices as "Moments in Love" played from his playlist. He flickered his tongue in a back and forth motion, then moved from side to side, and finished in a circle. My little hottie throbbed in anticipation of the pleasure this man was giving me. Finally, I couldn't take it anymore, and I moaned in pleasure as his tongue stroked me until I came to a climax.

Rico released his pants from his waist. I'll have to admit I was not impressed. On a scale of 1 to ten - I give him a 5 for size, a 7 for width, and a 6 for overall appearance. Let's pause here for a second. Statistics show that either men have an amazing head game or amazing dick, and the two rarely meet. Sometimes you run across a bigfoot or a unicorn, and the stars align where you're fortunate to have both. But most women know they concede one for the other. At least until you're lucky enough to find teachable one. Unpause.

Rico looked at me again with that same intensity, and my body began to heat up. He entered me with intense, powerful strokes that felt, well better than ok. Was the earth shattering? No. But he was the little engine that could. Rico got up, and we switched positions. I found myself on my knees with my back arched, and Rico sat right on top of my back. Rico massaged my back and my shoulders as he showered my neck with kisses.

Immediately I felt drunk again by the magic of his hands. As he massaged and kissed, Rico entered me from behind. I thought my body was going to go into a seizure from the pleasure of it all. Rico continued to massage my shoulders. His manhood stroked me from deep, and I felt pure pleasure at his penetration. He was the engine that could indeed. His package may not have been in a huge box, but that gift he was giving me had my body shivering in ecstasy. I found myself saying," oh Baby, as the female artist bellow, "Baby, baby baby baby baby." He whispered in my ear, "Damn baby, tell me that it's good to you." I said, "oh yes, baby," as our bodies moved in rhythm with the music.

Rico grabbed me by my hips as he dug deeper in me. He pushed deeper and faster and deeper and faster until my body couldn't take it any longer. My love cave exploded, and so did he quickly thereafter. We laid in each other's arms for a few hours after and talked, laughed, and played.

For the next several days, it was more of the same. Rico and I would spend hours on the phone, he'd come over for a meal, and we'd fuck like crazy. That man had his way with me in all parts of my condo. He ate my pussy on the island, bent me over the dryer, had his way with me on top of my office desk. I was so into this man, and I even entertained the possibility of us taking our relationship to the next level once I freed myself from James. The court date was coming up by the way, and I had forgotten to return Yvette's calls over the last few days. I also had neglected my running schedule, which also wasn't good. Although I was in bliss with Rico, I couldn't help but notice that he had become a distraction from not only the bad things happening but also the good that I needed to focus on. My spidey senses went off a bit, and I decided to call one of my girlfriends to get a second opinion. Just as I was about to dial, Rico dialed in.

Rico came to me excited about a new investment he had made. He was recently approved by the bank for a loan on a space he had been eyeing for his massage business. I was excited for him as well. "I have the money for the building, and I have most of the equipment, but I just need the place decorated, you know a woman's touch. Would you mind helping me out with that"? And how could I say no? of course I would help decorate. I even spent about $2500 of my own money on his renovations. Rico and I were headed in a good direction, and we had this unspoken agreement that once I was divorced, we had planned to move forward with our relationship. Was I ready? I had no clue. But I was going to trust the universe to allow things to fall into place or not.

I decided since I had finished the decorating that I would surprise Rico with a pop-up picnic lunch. He mentioned that he didn't have any clients for a few hours, so why not. When I walked through the doors of the shop, I was surprised to see Rico in the arms of another woman, a little woman. I looked at him puzzled, and he looked surprised to see me. I said, "So, who is this little cutie, your granddaughter?'. He looked at me and said, "No, Tabby. She's my daughter." I stood there in shock for a minute. I mean, I knew he had 12 children, but he told me they were all grown.

Rico: I know what you're thinking Tabby

Tabby: What am I thinking, Rico? Could it be "Why did you lie to me"?

Rico: I didn't lie Tabby I do only have 12 children. I just didn't tell you how old she was because I didn't know where the relationship was going.

Tabby: Is that a fact.

Rico: I know I'm wrong, but I was going to tell you.

Tabby: Rico, we've been dealing with each other for almost 2 months now, don't you think you had ample time?

I looked at his daughter. She was looking back and forth at me and him. I decided that I didn't want to discuss this in front of her, as I didn't want to be inappropriate or disrespectful. I grabbed my picnic basket and told him I would call him later. When I had no clue, but I really needed to process all of this.

As soon as I left the shop, I gave my girl Sam a call. I gave her the details of my relationship with Rico and what I had just discovered. Sam confirmed how I felt about the situation; if he withheld the fact that his daughter was a small child, what else was he lying about? For all, I know he could still be in a relationship with the baby mama. I needed answers, but I didn't really want to address this with Rico at this time.

Thank god I had Sam in my arsenal. She has always said it's not what you know, but who you know. Sam suggested that I allowed her to use her resources to do some digging into Rico's background. I thought that it wouldn't hurt to find out who I was truly dealing with. I gave her all the information I knew about Rico, and Samantha assured me that I would have the answers I needed about Rico within 24-48 hours. In the meantime, I thought it would be best if I avoided him altogether.

The more I tried to avoid Rico over the next 24 hours, the more he called me. Finally, he demanded to see me by just appearing at my doorstep.

Tabby: Is there something I can help you with, Rico? The last I recalled, I didn't invite you here. Don't you have a small child to take care of? Where is she anyway?

Rico: That small child has a name. Her name is Mariah, and she is two years old. You're so disrespectful right now.

Tabby: Disrespectful? Ok. So, respect would have been telling me you had a child under 10. Given the amount of time we've been dating, don't you think you could have found some time to mention that to me?

Rico: Tabby, yes, we have been kind of seeing each other. We have been getting to know each other again, and I really enjoy your company. But the way you are acting about the fact that I have a baby girl makes me question the true nature of our friendship.

Did this mother fucker say friendship? He has been bringing his tired ass to my house almost every day for food and this good pussy for the last seven weeks. And, he is questioning the nature of our friendship? Get the fuck out of here.

Rico: Tabby, did you hear what I said?

Tabby: No, my friend, to be honest. I tuned you the fuck out. How about this; take your newly friend-zoned ass out of my home and away from my presence. Unlike you, I don't sleep with my friends, it just confuses things. So, if that is where we stand, just know that as a friend, we will NEVER sleep together again. Thank you, and good night.

Rico stared at me. I looked back at him with a stare that dared him to open his mouth to challenge what I was saying. I was done with him, and I meant it. I opened the door, motioned for him to leave, and he walked out the door. And just like I closed the door on his tired ass, so did I to that weak ass relationship. I took a deep breath in and out. I looked back on the time that I wasted entertaining yet another man from my past and vowed at that moment to never look back. What was done was done, and I couldn't take it back. I got myself ready for bed and thought about the information that Sam's contacts would uncover about Rico. At this point, did I really want to know? Did I care?

The next morning, I woke up feeling refreshed. I meditated for twenty minutes and put on some music to get me in a good mood. I looked at myself in the mirror and smiled. I felt like a weight had been lifted off me. Making the decision to let go of Rico was somehow refreshing. When I thought about it, I knew we were in two different places in life. He had a small child to raise, and I was just finding out who I was outside of being a wife and mother, the roles I had taken on for over two decades. Plus, I just thought his character was sketchy. Anyone who can conceal information about a child they gave birth to was a real piece of crap in my book. That was something I couldn't get over, and it was definitely a deal-breaker. My thoughts were interrupted by the ring of my cell-phone. It was Sam. Immediately my stomach got queasy on the inside of the nervousness from what I would find out. Perhaps it would be nothing, and this man was squeaky clean. Either way, I was prepared for whatever when I answered the phone.

Tabby: Hey, Foxy!

Samantha: Hey, Sexy, Mami! Have I got some info for you!

Tabby: Well, spill the tea Foxy!

Samantha: So..it turns out that not only does this man have a two-year-old, but he also has a set of twins that are teenagers.

Tabby: What! Oh, hell, no!

Samantha: Yeah, girl! I have pics of him from the baby mama's social media page and everything. They look kind of cozy if you ask me. But that's not the big thing I found out, are you ready.

Tabby: Well, what the hell can be worse than that?

Samantha: I know you know Rico spent some time in jail for child support, right? Well, that's not the only thing. He went to prison for fraud a few years back. Two women claim that he scammed them out of thousands of dollars. As a matter of fact, he has a pending case right now where another woman claims he scammed her out of five thousand dollars.

I was speechless. That smooth-talking mother fucker was a con artist. He had got me to furnish his spa that son of a bitch! I thanked Samantha for the information and tried to figure out what to do next. I called Rico, and it went straight to voicemail. That fucking bastard. I wanted to confront him with everything I knew. Then I thought about it. What good what it do? I was done with him anyway, and he probably had already moved on to his next victim. I decided that the best way to get revenge would be to let karma take care of him. That bitch always does.

I put on my workout gear and tied my running shoes. I had no time to slow down now. I had a marathon to run in a few in a couple of months, and my court date was creeping up the next week. This had been a long nine months, and a long time coming. As I got into my run and hit my stride, I thought about what lied ahead and took it all in stride. I sensed that although I hit a few bumps along the way that good things were on the horizon. I was full steam ahead with a new focus on happy, and I was for damn sure nothing was going to stand in my way.

To be happy means to show feelings of pleasure and enjoyment of your current situation. It also means having confidence or satisfaction with someone, something, or an amazing outcome. Also, happiness can be defined as a state of well-being or contentment, usually implying a state of pleasure or pleasurable satisfaction. Happy is a state of mind, and it's up to us to figure out how to navigate our way to it. But once you're there, life seems to take hold of you, and for the first time, you experience sugary bliss. At least that's what I imagined it feeling like. All I knew is I was tired of struggling to find myself and what happy was, and I decided to release myself to the universe. I wanted life to take hold of me for once.

Over the next week, I was laser-focused on two things; my upcoming court date and the marathon in the very near future. I spent much time in meditation and prayer and made sure I stayed on my running schedule. Too much had happened over the last nine months, and for once, I decided to focus on myself. To be honest, it felt good. I was alone most of the time, which kind of took some getting used to. Still, over the last week, as I ran in preparation for the marathon, I had really gotten to know the person I had been running from, myself.

I had eliminated the alcohol completely, and I had seen a significant increase in my run speed. I was impressed. I was able to run a full marathon of 26 miles in roughly over 2 ½ hours. Not bad for a beginning runner, I thought. I decided my life needed to shift gears from alcohol and sex, and I would be the only one to change it. I put on my affirmations and tuned in to my running path, and nothing else seemed to go on in the world.

When I'm running, I am in control. I control my breathing, my pace, and how long I plan to run. On my runs, I'm alone with my thoughts. I can take in the scenery and quiet my mind. On my runs, all I have is me, and I like it. My thoughts are not clouded by the opinions of others. Running is my own safe place to be.

The rest of my life situations, on the other hand, are not so easily controlled. My marriage deteriorated because it takes two to make a thing go right. I was not in control. My position was taken from me because I had no control over how I was perceived at the job. I wasn't in control. My best friend died because she is her own person, and I couldn't control when it was her time to go. Damn, that's the only other thing I wish I could have controlled. Running had become my great escape from all the things I couldn't control, and in the end, it always made me happy.

As I took off my running gear and to head for the shower, I looked at myself in the mirror and smiled. I was pleased with what I saw. The running was paying off to a nice slender body that I hadn't seen in quite a few years. Almost since I had the kids. Sex appeal oozed out of me as a sense of satisfaction crept over my aura. I was happy for the first time in a long time. Yea, me, I was happy!

Then I remembered today, and I put on my game face. It was D-day. The big divorce. Today I would find out if I was pinned to the terms of the prenuptial agreement, or if the judge would extend some sort of grace to me and give me over and above.

Alimony, the house, anything would be nice considering the hell I had been through with James and Keisha.

James found out that I had been using money from account #8. He was furious. He demanded as part of the divorce settlement that any award proceeds would be used to pay back the funds that I had withdrawn from that account. He had also tried to put a block from me using money from that account, but it was a little too late. Keisha's ass even called trying to "check me" on the situation as if this was any of that bitch's business. The whole thing was a mess, and I was ready to close this chapter of my life completely.

I stepped off the elevator at the courthouse dressed to the nines. I was wearing a black and grey Gucci pin-striped timeless suit with a one-button blazer. I had on a pair of black Christian Louboutin's with the Prive patent red soles, and a matching bag. All this was courtesy of account #8. Hell, I figured, if I had a chance of losing access to that account or must pay it back, I was going to go out with a bang. But the one-two punch of my outfit was the $200,000 bracelet that James had expressed to my home. James was probably going to shit himself when he saw it, but I didn't care. I thought to myself that I may need to sell it later to live off, but for now, it served as my good luck charm.

Yvette Stevens greeted me at the elevator. She escorted me into the courtroom where James, his attorney Mr. Goldstein, and Keisha were already sitting at the table across from us. Why the hell was she here anyway? She wasn't part of these proceedings, so the least she could do was take a seat in the general area. But no, that would be too much like respect. She looked at me and smiled, then took James' hand for support.

He looked at her with endearment and took a deep breath. The whole thing was sickening. "Oh, just get a room why don't ya," I yelled across the room. Both attorneys looked at me as if to say, "Leave it alone." I whispered to Yvette that I needed to go to the bathroom, and I excused myself. Keisha got up from the table and followed behind me until we both found ourselves looking head-on at each other as I stopped dead in my tracks and turned around.

Tabby: Is there something I can help you with?

Keisha: Tabby, always the sore loser, and always making it about you. No dear, there is nothing you can help me with, you have already done that.

Tabby: Look, if this is about that tired ass negro in there, I'm here to end this. Bitch, you can have him because clearly, you have been

Keisha: Excuse me? Tabby, I am a lad…

Tabby: Stop with the games.

Keisha: Tabby, I told you a long time ago to play and know your position. James is out of your league. He's a man of wealth and means, and he needs a woman that is going to compliment that. You weren't it for him, I'm sorry

Tabby: Girl bye

Keisha: See, that's what I mean. You had too much hood in you, Tabby. Just because you came from there doesn't mean you had to stay there.

Tabby: What are we even talking about? You wanted him, you won! Congratulations! You can have him, Sis.

Keisha: I was never worried about you, Tabby. Just know when we walk away today, no matter what we win.

Tabby: Well, good for you.

Keisha: You look nice by the way, I see you're tailor-made today. How much was that Gucci suit, about six grand? Oh, and the shoes? I know those set you back some. Well, probably not since you've been dipping into the account, you weaseled your way on to. Oh, I have friends at the bank too, honey.

Tabby: And your point would be?

Keisha: I could go tell James, and it would be over for you.

Tabby: Bitch, run, and tell, I don't care. The only person James has power over is you, my dear.

Keisha: No, you're mistaken, I hold all the power. That's a nice bracelet, by the way. Tiffany's? I can spot a gem from a mile away. It's from the Blue Collection, right? It's beautiful, where'd you get it? Oh, don't tell me, the same account? You may want to hold on to that after the proceedings. You may have to cash it in to live the lavish lifestyle you've become accustomed to. That should hold you over for about a year.

Tabby: Thanks for admiring this piece. Yes, it is a beauty. Costs about $250,000. So you're right, it would take care of my needs for just a little while. Oh yea, I got this courtesy of James a couple of weeks before the divorce proceedings. He shut down Tiffany's and offered me anything I wanted in the store to get back together. I declined. He was nice enough to have this delivered by arm guard that same night as a gesture of his love for me. You know James, he can be sweet like that.

I winked at her, and her face turned a shade of red. She looked me up and down one more time and strutted out of the bathroom. I laughed and looked at the bracelet again. That bitch felt like a fool. She had no clue that James had asked me back, or that he had dropped $250,000 on me himself. I know she was pissed. I guess this was my good luck charm, after all.

I stepped back into the courtroom and sat next to my attorney just in time for the judge's arrival. I looked over at Keisha, who was still heated, as indicated by her resting bitch face. I smiled and winked as the judge reviewed all the details of our case. I tried to over exude confidence, but I was nervous as hell.

While the judge reviewed the documents, it was so quiet you could hear a pin drop. Yvette, my attorney, was pretty confident we didn't have to honor the terms of the prenup. Still, the judge, we had, prided himself in being fair, by the book, and doing the right thing. Yvette cautioned me that because there was an agreement in place, any request in addition to the prenup could be null and void. My arms begin to perspire as the judge asked both of us and our attorneys to stand.

Judge: In the matter of Taylor vs. Taylor, I have issued the following ruling; The prenuptial agreement is considered void due to the lack of willful consent. This document was signed without Ms. Taylor's knowledge and therefore is invalid. Mr. Taylor, you and your spiritual advisor that prepared this document should be ashamed of yourself, so I am ruling and ordering the following:

Ms. Taylor will maintain full and complete possession of the property in Clareville Estates. Mr. Taylor will be responsible for maintaining the mortgage in that home, along with $30,000 a month in alimony for the next 18 months or until Ms. Taylor remarries, whichever is sooner.

I am also awarding Ms. Taylor, the beach house in Atlanta, and twenty-five percent of Mr. Taylor's retirement. Mr. Taylor, I understand your hardship of raising a grandchild. That is why Ms. Taylor is only getting 25% of the retirement. But understand this; that is your grandchild and not your child. You are making a choice to allow the parents to not be responsible for their own actions, and that has nothing to do with these proceedings today.

Now concerning account number 8. I am awarding Ms. Taylor 50% of all the funds deposited into this account from the first date of the court proceedings. I was able to take an in-depth look at the account, and I saw that money was being transferred out in significantly large chunks, Mr. Taylor, and that is not acceptable. I instruct you to transfer the three million dollars that you moved into your personal account back into this one. You have 30 days to make the complete wire transfer of Ms. Taylors' portion of the funds to her bank account. Failure to do so will leave you in contempt of court. This judgment is final.

I had won! I really won. Like I had won so big, I wanted to do the happy dance, but I kept my composure for the judge. I looked over at James, who looked defeated. Keisha looked at me with disgust on her face. For an instance, I felt sorry for James. Until he signed the papers and threw them up in the air before they could be handed to my attorney. Talk about a sore loser.

He then jumped out of his seat and stormed out of the courtroom. Keisha chased behind him. After our attorneys gathered the papers, I signed them and thanked Yvette. I looked over at the elevator to see Keisha and James arguing with each other. The elevator doors opened, and I watched them get in, hoping that was the last time that I would ever have to see those two again. I know we lived in the same city, but a girl could dream, couldn't she?

Over the next couple of weeks, I rode the cloud of happy. James didn't waste time turning over the deed to the beach house, and I was making plans to visit after the marathon. I decided that the best way to celebrate my bucket list accomplishment would be to take a drive to Atlanta with minimal bags packed and enjoying the open air along the way. I was a cute, single, and newly wealthy. For once, the sky was the limit for me right now, and it felt amazing.

Going to the beach house in Atlanta sounded nice, gave me a good vibration. Since I had been running and meditating, I had learned to just go with the things that felt good. Taking a much-needed breather after running a marathon would be just what I needed. And why not take some time at the beach house, it was mine now.

I imagined myself running on the sand. I pictured the resistance of the sand on my legs, but I also imagined the wind hitting my face from the seawater. I felt an immediate calm come over me. I could take the time at the beach house to figure out my life's journey beyond the marathon. So much had happened, I had not taken any time to breathe and figure it out.

Between the death of Ebony, the divorce, and the string of unhealthy relationships, I had formed as a result of the alcohol abuse. It had taken its toll on my emotions. And in the midst of that, I had to put on the brave face of graduating one kid from college and sending another off to school. Vincent had graduated with honors and had relocated to Arizona with an amazing career opportunity based on his internship. It just so happened that Vanessa had transitioned to a college in Arizona, so her brother would be there and promised to look after her. They were both so concerned about me after Ebony died, but I pretended that I was fine. I didn't want them to know how much I was suffering, and I didn't need them seeing me self-destruct. As I focused on the destruction that had become my normal during that time, I became extremely grateful for what I had bought myself through.

Later that night, however, I felt like my accomplishments were going right out the window as my body started to develop "the itch." The last man I had been with was Rico, and Boo Boo Kitty was feeling the urge to merge. Nothing I did seemed to make a difference, and at 3am taking a drive or putting in a 10-mile run didn't seem feasible. I tried to calm myself by having a glass of wine and turning on a movie. The movie was blah, so I decided to scroll through social media to take my mind off things.

I came across a post from one of my guy friends who talked about 3am being the hour of the freak zone. I looked at the post for a moment and went to his profile. He was a handsome guy. Since I didn't know him personally, I went to his personal information, and a light bulb went off. I had seen this guy's profile before, and I thought he was hot. I lusted after him as a matter of fact until I realized how old he was. The man was only thirty, and I knew with me being 45, this would be nothing but trouble.

I looked at his post again. I looked at his picture. He was so freaking sexy! Something in me told me to respond to his post, and since the feeling felt good, I hit the comments. "Well, everyone isn't freaky at this time. Some of us are being constructive. I am preparing for a marathon, no freak in that." I hit send. A few seconds later, he responded. He asked me what made me run a marathon, and he seemed very interested. We had small talk back and forth on his page, and then he said, "While some of us like to run, others like me like to ride." Wait a minute? Was my Boo Boo Kitty's antennae going up? Was this man flirting with me? I responded and put a feeler out there. He responded back, and he flirted back. At this point, I was intrigued, and the flirtatious banter went on for several minutes. I could tell he was feeling me, at least I thought he was.

The whole time we conversed, I also had a conversation with myself. I kept telling myself how crazy this was, that I didn't really know this guy, I also was trying to talk myself out of this because he was only 30. It was a struggle. I imagined the good and bad version of Tabby weighing out all my options as I continued to flirt, and the bad Tabby was outweighing the good. I wanted to have fun, it had been so long. The good Tabby had served her purpose, keeping me on the straight and narrow, but sometimes I had to unleash the bad girl. As I was mulling over all this in my mind, my young hottie thanked me for a great conversation on his page and said to have a good night. Just like that, it was over. Damn, I didn't want it to end, though.

I went back to his page again and looked at all his pictures. He was so damn fine. I thought about our conversation and how I felt his energy. He wanted me, I could tell. Then I thought about the age difference again. He was 15 years younger than me. Perhaps he was flirting just to be nice, to stroke my ego. That was always a possibility. He probably felt sorry for an old ass woman who was throwing herself at his fine young ass. I looked at him again and felt his energy. I wanted to see if my intuition was on point, and there was only one way to find out.

I wanted to have a conversation with him, but I didn't want to be the one to reach out. So how was I going to make that happen? I clicked on his messenger and looked at it. I willed him to reach out to me, but of course, he did not. I had to find out, though, as curiosity got the best of me. What would I say? I had no idea. So, I said nothing. Instead, I sent a wave to him in the messenger as if to say, "Hi."

My young hottie waved right back and engaged in conversation. Wow, he made it easy for me. He introduced himself, and I did as well. I also took that time to address the age difference between us, to make sure there wouldn't be any elephants in the room. It turns out that he was inter older women. He said he was at an age where he wanted to be more settled, and the women his age were into playing games. He also mentioned that he thought older women were more confident, sexy, and knew what they wanted.

I thought about my life for a minute. I had no clue where it was headed outside of the upcoming marathon. This young man probably had it wrong, if he was basing what he wanted off my life, I thought. I decided though to just go with it, as the reality of things were that he was only 30, and I was 45. The two of us could have a little fun, but beyond that, I couldn't see magic.

He gave me his cell phone number, and we decided to take the conversation offline. It started out as a "get to know you" session that turned into something just a tad bit steamier. My young hottie had a name; Jaquan. He had literally turned 30 several days before and was living with his older brother. He didn't live too far from my condo, and I thought that was convenient. He also smoked weed, and I knew then that we would hit it right off. We got comfortable with each other very fast, and our conversation quickly turned to what things were a turn on.

I pictured myself smoking with him, then I looked at his pictures again as we texted back and forth. I was smoking, and so was he. I pictured what it would be like to have this man inside me. My body tingled. The more he talked about taking his sweet time with my body, the more I got aroused. Here it was after 3am, and I was really feeling this guy. So much so, if he would have asked me to come to him that night, he would have been in trouble. Hell, if he wanted to come to me, I would have more than obliged. We talked for several minutes more, and then he asked to see me the next day. I agreed, he told me goodnight, and I slept well looking forward to this hot young man that would occupy some of my time.

The following evening, we agreed to meet up. Although it was later than I had anticipated, we still agreed to take some time to get to know each other; at around midnight. I agreed for the first meet up to go to his place. He had a roommate, so although it was late, his spot could be considered neutral. At least that's what I tried to tell myself. But if you don't know by now, Boo Boo Kitty always has plans of her own.

He texted me directions to his house, and I showed up without any mishaps. Jaquan was even better looking in person. He was about 6'1 dark-skinned with the most intense eyes. He had a beard that was neatly trimmed, and he smelled fucking fantastic. His frame was smaller than I would have imagined, but I could tell that he was physically fit. He looked at me and smiled. He drew me in for a hug, and his touch was very tender. I think I liked him already.

Jaquan lived in a townhouse with his roommate. When I stepped in his place, the décor seemed basic, like a simple bachelor pad. It was nothing impressive, and I had to remember that everyone had not been exposed to or accustomed to the life I had created for myself. The living room had standard living room furniture designed by someone unknown, and the place seemed tidy enough for two men occupying the space.

We headed straight for his bedroom, and I was even more unimpressed. Jaquan's bedroom consisted of a full-sized bed, a television, a game console, and clothes spread throughout in tubs with lids. Typical young boy habitation, I thought. I looked around and told myself not to judge, but a part of me wanted to run the hell out of there. This was not the kind of man I was accustomed to.

He asked me to sit on the bed, and he lit a few candles. My mind slowed down a bit, and I thought he couldn't be half bad. He sat next to me, and we had a small conversation while he rolled a blunt and lit it. Jaquan was living here as a temporary situation. He had just purchased his first property, and he was in the middle of a renovation. I asked him what kind of job he had to acquire such an accomplishment at 30. He said, "He has never had to work for anyone, and he has always had to make his own way." I left that conversation alone and didn't want to imply what I thought I knew. This went on for about thirty minutes, and I was really feeling the conversation with this young man. Or maybe it was the weed.

Jaquan leaned in to kiss me, and I didn't stop him. I felt an electrical charge go over my body like I had never felt before. I was surprised and yet impressed at the same time. Jaquan's kiss was slow and methodical. He took his time exploring my mouth, and the rest of my body got aroused at just the affection from the kiss. Jaquan touched my face gently. He kissed me like we were lifelong lovers, not like strangers having a one-night stand. I kissed him back with the same intensity. I let his hands roam from my face to my neck, to my back and my chest.

His touch was amazing, and my body tingled every time he reached for me. We kissed for what seemed like hours, as we let our hands explore parts of each other's bodies that only lovers should touch. He touched my wetness, and I melted. I opened my legs to receive all of him, and he took his time playing and exploring my love cave. I wanted to get freaky, but I didn't want him to think I was a hoe either. I stroked his shaft while he played intensely with my garden. He looked me in my eyes.

He kissed me again, and I melted. His mouth felt like ecstasy, and he made love to me like I was his. Jaquan entered me in missionary. He looked me in my eyes. With each stroke, he kissed my mouth and gave me intensity until I couldn't take it anymore. Jaquan stroked me slow. He looked at me, and I looked back at him. Every thrust gave me electric energy, and I felt we were connected, not just in our bodies, but on a celestial level. I couldn't explain what was happening at that moment, but I could tell by the look in his eyes that we were both feeling it. As our bodies continued to move in sync, Jaquan looked me in the eyes and showered kisses all over me. Then suddenly, he jumped up and gave release.

Our conversation afterward was sweet. He told me that he wasn't seeing anyone and that although he was only 30, he wasn't into games. I took what he said with a grain of salt, as I knew to be that young, I felt he really hadn't had a chance to live. So, I just went with the conversation. He asked me out for lunch the same day, and I was surprised. I was expecting this to be a one-night stand; however, romantic it had turned out. I agreed to lunch, which he also paid for, and we said our goodbyes and agreed to see each other later that night.

The following night it was more of the same. We met up late for a smoke session at his place, and he had candles lit and great conversation. I felt I could get used to this. He spent most of his day occupied, so whatever I had planned wasn't interrupted by constant communication, etc., like I had experienced with Rico. I was able to get my run in and do other things without feeling the pressure of having to be in constant communication with someone. So far, this thing I was doing felt good. Although it was only 2 days in, it felt better than anything I had done previously, so I decided to go with how I felt.

We got to know each other some more that night. This time we talked about our families and the things that shaped who we are today. Jaquan's conversation was so refreshing that I forgot that I was engaging with someone 15 years my junior. He made me feel so at ease with him, so it was no surprise when he got me naked again for the second night in a row.

This night was a little more intense. Jaquan and I were still feeling each other out, so although he had me under his spell with every touch, I still tried to proceed with caution. He started again with the kisses that made my body melt. I have always appreciated a good kisser. Jaquan had beautiful full lips that were amazing. And his kiss was just the right speed for our intimacy. His hands roamed my body. But not in an immature fashion, but like a man who knew how to touch a woman. Jaquan took his time, and I matched him by getting to know his body as well. Our hands roamed each other's bodies, and we both moaned in sync, in pleasure. Every touch sent surges through my body.

I touched his manhood. It was fully erect. He moaned in my ear," damn," as I stroked him up and down. He let his fingers trace my nipples. My wetness started to build up as his kisses filled my mouth. He moved to my love box. He fondled my kitty intensely as I continued to stroke him up and down. We looked at each other in the eyes. We both moaned. I closed my eyes and experienced the intense pleasure of all that was happening. I wanted Jaquan and was ready and open to receiving his amazing package. Jaquan laid on his back, and I looked over him. Tonight, I was the lion, and he was the gazelle. I wanted to devour him, all of him. He pulled me close to him, and I prepared to enjoy the ride.

I looked down at him as I eased onto his shaft. I took my time and moved slowly as I leaned in for a kiss. His penis felt like pure magic, a perfect fit. As we kissed each other, our bodies moved in sync as his manhood filled up all of me. He moved his mouth from my lips to my chest. He took my breast in one by one and devoured them as our bodies moved in cadence. I moaned out loud, and we talked shit to each other:

Tabby: Damn baby, your dick is amazing

Jaquan: Nah baby, it's your pussy

Tabby: Ooh baby, don't stop this feels so good

Jaquan: I won't, baby. I don't wanna stop

Our bodies continued to move together in pure ecstasy. I moved my hips slowly in a circular motion, then increased the tempo. Jaquan moved with me. He grabbed my breasts and played with them. "I love these big as titties," he said. I moaned. He said, "Give me that pussy," and I obliged. Our bodies thrust in and out of each other, and my explosion began to build. I increased the tempo yet again, and we both went insane.

The bed moved intensely to the cadence of our lovemaking. And I leaned in for another kiss. Jaquan lifted my hips, held me in place, and stroked me from the bottom. He moved in and out faster and faster. I moaned as his manhood filled up all of me. I yelled, "Oh, Fuck me, Daddy," and he did just that. He stroked and stroked until Boo Boo Kitty couldn't take it anymore. Now it was his turn. I said, "Come for me, Daddy." I bounced up and down and in and out. I moved my hips in rabbit speed. Jaquan began to moan intensely and yelled, "damn baby. Damn"! Jaquan gave his release, and I collapsed on his chest.

As we laid there together in silence, I played with the hairs on his chest. I looked up at him, and he kissed my forehead. It was erotic yet loving. I felt like at that moment, I was at home in his arms. He said to me, "I want you to know that I am not out here as a typical 30-year-old, I have had my fun in my twenties. I'm not seeing anyone, and I'm not out here playing games. If I'm into you, it's just that."

I think I knew what he was trying to say. He was into me, and he wasn't seeing anyone. I took that time to let him know I hadn't seen anyone in a few months as well. He asked if we could do something later and I said yes. As I thought about what this was, we were doing, I smiled. It wasn't defined, but it was good, I knew it. I could feel it.

Over the next ten days, I moved along in pure bliss. I got up every morning and did my meditations a pre-marathon run. I was making great strides, and even I surprised myself with my timing. I was focused, and I knew that I would feel such a sense of accomplishment once I completed the race. I didn't care if I placed or if I came in last, as long as I did what I set out to do. I also saw Jaquan a lot, and things were going well.

Our relationship was perfect, so it seemed. He spent most of the day at his property renovating, which left my day free to do anything and everything I wanted. We came together at night to smoke, chill, and get to know each other. He also added the right amount of steamy to each of our nights as well. I was worried if I could match his energy because of the age gap. But so far, I think he was trying to keep up with me.

I felt comfortable with Jaquan and opened up immediately about my life, my pain, and the love that had come and gone. I also shared with him my passion, the one constant over this last year; my running. Jaquan seemed genuinely interested in what I was doing and even agreed to be there when I crossed the finish line. That meant so much to me to hear. For the first time in a long time, I felt like I had support, someone who was in this for me this time. I had never experienced that before. He also opened up about his own personal struggles. He went into detail as to why he was put out on his own at age 17.

It was Thanksgiving afternoon, and he was watching television with his older sister and her boyfriend. In usual fashion, his mother and stepfather were arguing. He heard his mother say she was trapped in the room, and his stepfather refused to let her out. He also heard banging, and he heard her scream for help. To be more detailed, she specifically called to him for help. Jaquan indicated that he kicked the door down.

After a long struggle with his 300-pound stepfather, he prevailed. What was his reward? Being kicked out of the home. Jaquan opened his heart about sleeping in his car in front of his home. And, when his mother went off to work, she didn't even acknowledge his presence. It was all very sad. I felt like there were pieces in me that Jaquan was looking for that he missed from his mother. Maybe that explained his attraction to me. After all, I was old enough to be his mother. A small part of me begin to wonder, was there a motive with this man too? After all, in the past, I really knew how to pick em. But, I also thought about the way I felt with him. I decided, for once, to just go with that.

Being with Jaquan made me feel young, attractive, and alive. Whenever we were together, he made me feel like I was the sexiest woman in the room. He constantly told me how beautiful I was, and he showed me by spending every available time he had outside of his renovation with me. He was also mindful of the things I had to do and made plans around my schedule.

Around day seven, he began spending the night with me. As I watched him sleep peacefully, I thought about the happiness that this man made me feel. It was something about his presence that made me feel safe and secure when he was there. he had a commanding aura about him that was not only authoritative but sexy as well. Jaquan was the type of person who was so handsome. His presence demanded your attention. And that alone made him powerful.

Over the past 10 years, I had been introduced to the life of the wealthy and cultured. Being with James meant I was connected. This man appeared to be a nobody with no connections. To the rest of the world, it would look like I was taking a step backward. But to me, this all felt amazing.

I decided it was time to share my happiness with my girl-friends. So, the next morning I Facetime'd Samantha. She immediately knew that something was different and asked if I was getting it on the regular. I smiled, and she said, "Oh, I can tell Mami! Who's laying that Mandingo"! I told her about Jaquan. I laid everything I knew about him and how I felt when I was with him. Her response was elation and that she sensed good vibes. I told her I felt it too, but I still needed some assurance, as I hadn't made the best choices lately.

She asked me if I knew if he had a criminal record or not. I told her I didn't but based on his background, I could imagine there was something there. I wanted to see how bad it was to make sure it wouldn't be a deal-breaker for me. Jaquan and I had never discussed his background; therefore, he had not been allowed to be dishonest. I just wanted some peace of mind because I really liked him and thought that maybe this could possibly go somewhere. Sam agreed to run the background, and I headed to the bar to see Tara.

Tara was in full swing serving drinks to the lunch crowd when I arrived. I decided to patron the place and ordered lunch, and ate at the bar. When Tara had a break, she joined me in the stall next to me. She asked me what had been going on, as she had not seen me in the last couple of weeks. I reminded her about the marathon coming up, and then I told her that I had met someone. As I was basking in the glow of my conversation with Sam, I thought that the same energy would spill over into this one. I was not so fortunate.

Tara: So..You met a man on social media, and you slept with him the next day? Now the two of you damn near living together?

Tabby: Must you be so dramatic Tara, he just spent the night for the first time a couple of days ago.

Tara: And you think that's good?

Tabby: Well, yea, considering that we have been together ever since we met. It's not like all we do is have sex, Tara.

Tara: And how old did you say he was again?

Tabby: I don't believe I mentioned it to you yet, and I wonder why.

Tara: Oh lord! He must be a youngin. You ain't learned your lesson, girl.

Tabby: Can I ask why you're being so negative?

Tara: As your friend, do you want me to be honest? Of course, you do, so I'm going to give it to you raw. I have watched you come in here and be a hot ass mess for almost a year. And don't get me started on the number of men I have watched you take in and out of here. Do you honestly think that a man is what you need right now? You need to be by yourself. Sit down somewhere and heal.

Tabby: While I appreciate your raw honesty, don't ever insinuate that I'm a hoe. And furthermore, if you feel that way, I don't care. Bitch, I wouldn't care if you watched me fuck 69 men over the last year you have no right to judge me or think you know what's best. Just like you gave it to me raw, I'm telling you don't judge this situation until you really know.

Tara: Listen, you're my girl, and that's why I'm saying this. You need to slow down

Tabby: I have, but you hadn't noticed. Since I seem to have a parade of dicks in me, tell me this; how many men were there between Rico and this guy? None. That was about two months of me, my running, and sometimes my vibrator. So, I think I spent plenty of time getting to know me, Sis.

Tara: Well, I said what I said, but we will agree to disagree. Girl, you can't keep a man these days anyway. Two months from now, either he will be gone, or you'll get tired of them. Come talk to me after the two of you have been together for six months or more.

I then changed the subject, because she started bringing up all the guys I had slept with. Who did this bitch think she was? For some reason, I felt attacked by her, and I couldn't understand it. I moved on to a more pleasant topic; the marathon. I confirmed with her the date, and then she told me there was a big chance she would not make it to support me that day. What was really going on? She mentioned that the owner would be out of town that week. It was her responsibility as a manager to pick up the slack.

I understood, but inside I felt just a little slighted. The only person I could rely on for support for my bucket list was a new friend. Everyone else was leading their lives. I felt the pang of hurt as I thought about Tara. I then started thinking about what was really left here for me in this city. And before I knew it, I wanted to burst into tears. I excused myself from the bar and headed back home.

I processed both conversations that I had with my girlfriends over the next 24 hours. I knew both cared for me, but both of their reactions were so different. I thought about Tara's response the most. Her attitude appeared to come out of nowhere. I tried to understand it all. Perhaps since Tara has never seen me outside of being drunk and reckless, that she has no other guide to go by. Whatever her reason, it still pricked my consciousness like a needle. My phone buzzed, and I looked down. It was an email notification from Samantha that read CONFIDENTIAL. I clicked on the email and prayed for the best.

Domestic violence, and possession of a controlled substance. This was my Prince Charming. As I looked over Jaquan's record, the same reoccurring theme kept appearing in his record outside of a few traffic violations. I put my hands on my head, asking myself how I could be so stupid. Hadn't I learned anything from the Rico situation? The drug possession didn't surprise me because of his background, but domestic violence? And according to the record, the man had a history. This was definitely a deal-breaker. I thought about my lover for a minute. My heart instantly panged. I really liked him and was rooting for him. Now I had to eat crow with my friends, especially Tara. That bitch would take pure satisfaction in being right.

Later that evening, I met up with Jaquan. We had an amazing time at a Japanese steakhouse, and then we returned to my condo for drinks. As much as I was enjoying the evening, I still could not let it end without addressing MY elephant in the room. I opened the tequila and took a shot. I had an eerie feeling that it would not end well. Would he attack me violently? Who knows what someone with a record like that would do? I looked over at Jaquan, who had a puzzled look on his face.

Jaquan: What's wrong, baby?

Tabby: Oh, nothing's wrong

Jaquan: So, you gonna lie to me? I can tell your energy is off, so what is it just say it.

Tabby: Why didn't you tell me you had a record?

Jaquan: We never got around to discussing it

Tabby: Well, don't you think that was important enough to talk about?

Jaquan: We're talking about it now, right? What is it that you want to know?

Tabby: Ok, I'm just gonna be honest, you have a lengthy domestic violence record that I am not comfortable with.

Jaquan: What the fuck are you talking about? I have one domestic violence charge that goes back 10 years ago.

I pull out his rap sheet and throw it at him. He looks it over and looks at me and shakes his head. He immediately got angry. And that was what I was afraid of.

Jaquan: Where did you get this?

Tabby: Don't worry about all that, just know I know EVERY-THING I need to

Jaquan: Actually, you don't know shit

Tabby: Such a disrespectful mouth you have. I know your momma raised you better than that.

Jaquan: Oh, you haven't seen disrespectful. And you should know, considering you and my momma could be sisters. You know what, I don't know what kind of game you're playing. Still, the information you have goes beyond my regular record, which means you had me investigated. That shit ain't cool.

Tabby: You know what's not cool? Putting your hands on women and making a pattern out of it you sick fuck

Jaquan: You know what Tabby, I think you have had way too much to drink.

Tabby: No, I see clearly for the first time ever

Jaquan: Well, let me help you see a little clearer, I don't need this shit from you. I can explain what happened, but your attitude tells me you don't care what I say.

Tabby: Don't know what you could possibly say to change my mind about that.

Jaquan: You are so smart that you're dumb, Tabby. If you look over that record, you will see that the domestic violence on the record is the same charge from the original arrest. They would bring that charge back up every time I came back in front of the judge.

Tabby: All it takes is one time if you do that shit once, you'll do it again

Jaquan: I'm done with this conversation. Since you know so much do some more research and you'll see, I never put my hands on anyone. But ok. I don't really have time to be with someone like you anyway. I thought being with an older woman would be different. But you seem just as immature as these young girls out here. You're not healthy for me, anyway. You showed me your true colors.

Tabby: And what does that mean?

Jaquan: Look, I've been feeling really funny lately, and I know I ain't fucked nobody else. So, you tell me about that

Tabby: Excuse...

Jaquan: Save it, I'm out

And just like that, Jaquan stormed out of the house. That was our first argument, and I felt sick on the inside. Not only did he have domestic violence on his record, but he also accused me of having an STD. I thought about that for a moment, and the reality of the multiple dicks I've had over the past year came to mind. I didn't always use protection. As a matter of fact, the word condom didn't enter my vocabulary for most of those encounters. Maybe he was right. What if I had an STD? This was the last thing I needed to deal with, considering the marathon was only a couple of days away. I decided that I would deal with the backlash of everything in the morning.

During my morning run, I thought about the events of the night before. The day before. My conversation with Tara stung my nostrils. I took a deep breath in and out and sped up the tempo. I then thought about Jaquan. This whole thing still seemed a bit confusing, and I needed to sort it out. But I also thought about his response, and it was a little childish. Then he dared to call me immature. It made me wonder what I was really getting into. I guess it didn't matter anymore after last night.

I felt the pang again and picked up the pace. I couldn't get Jaquan off my mind. I had tried to call him several times, but the phone kept going to voicemail. He had blocked me from his phone. I went to social media to get a clue about what he was thinking but didn't see that he had posted anything in a few days. At least I wasn't blocked from that. It was clear that right now, he wanted nothing to do with me, and if I gave him an STD, I could understand that.

The verdict was in, no STD. I had a bacterial infection which could be caused by a few factors:

1. Sex with a new partner
2. A not so clean partner
3. Multiple partners

I wonder what my root cause was. I called Jaquan to give him the news, the phone went to voicemail. I sent him a message on Facebook. He looked at it and ignored it. It was over before it began, and I didn't feel good about it.

I tried to keep my mind occupied, as the marathon was less than 24 hours away. I wanted to get some rest, but I couldn't eat or sleep, and my mind wandered. This was the longest I had been without speaking with Jaquan since we met. I wondered if he was even thinking about me. I also asked myself why I had these thoughts about a man with a violent history, like his. I looked over his record again. This time I noticed what he was talking about. He would get pulled over for a traffic violation and be hauled in court for the previous domestic violence charge. He was right, and I couldn't see it in the beginning. I looked over the rest of his record. Minor drug charges and traffic violations. I felt so stupid. I tried calling again, straight to voicemail. Although I needed to see and talk to him, I had to let this run its course.

That evening was the longest that I experienced in a while. As I mentally prepared for the run the next day, I pampered myself to a soak in my oversized tub. The whole time in my bubble bath, I thought about the events over the past day. In less than 24 hours, I went from happy to sullen. Thoughts of Jaquan constantly consumed me, and I didn't know why. That man drove me crazy, so why was I miserable right now? I laid in the tub and tried to focus. I knew I had to have my head in the game for tomorrow. I thought about the race, and how accomplished I felt knocking something off my bucket list. Now, what's next?

Going to my newly acquired beach house in Atlanta seemed more and more appealing, especially considering the recent events. I made up my mind that after the race, I would spend a few weeks there figuring out my life and my business. Yea, I decided to start my own business. Exactly what I didn't know. I laid down and brainstormed the possibilities until I ended up dozing off.

The next morning, I felt a rush of adrenaline. It was the day that I had been preparing for over the last 6 months; my first marathon. I got myself together and made sure I had all my essentials; cellphone, wireless blue tooth, and fanny pack for running snacks I may need along the way. I was nervous but excited at the same time and headed there early to make sure that I didn't miss any of the action. As I was stretching to prepare for the run, I noticed that the local news outlets were there. I thought to myself that this must be a big deal but then bent over to finish my leg stretches. As I was working through the kinks in my body, I was unexpectedly interrupted by a camera guy who bumped into me and almost knocked me down.

Reporter: Oh my God, are you ok? Can you still run today?

Tabby: Yes, I'm fine.

Reporter: Actually, you're perfect. Sammy, get the camera rolling, will ya.

Tabby: Wait a minute!

Reporter: Thank you for watching WGRU. This is your local lady about town Liz Mcgee coming to you live from the Nantucket County Marathon. I have with me one of the contestants that we happen to bump into, what's your name

Tabby: Tabitha. Tabby Monroe

Reporter: Well, Ms. Monroe, how are you this fine morning? Are ya ready to go?

Tabby: As ready as I'll ever be. A little nervous, this is my first marathon.

Reporter: Your first marathon! How exciting! I tell ya what; let's keep an eye on Ms. Monroe as she runs her first race. We'll see ya at the finish line Tabby. Once again, this is your lady about town, Liz McGee, at WGRU.

That was interesting. Unexpected, and yet interesting. I finished my stretch and headed over to the start line to begin the race.

At the sound of the gunshot, we were off. I immediately tuned into my positive affirmations to get my run started. I had set a playlist on my YouTube channel based on the current pace I had accomplished during training. It was always the same; affirmations, the strangest secret, by Earl Nightingale, and rounded off with encouraging words from Abraham Hicks. Most people get motivated by positive, upbeat music. I, on the other hand, knew that I needed more to help me tune in. I laughed on the inside as I ran at what had become my life. I had gone from miserable housewife with a cushy corporate America job to a meditating flake who had taken up running. "I was a wealthy flake, though," I thought. As I listened to the affirmations, I focused on my breathing and picked up my pace for the next leg of the race.

About the halfway mark, I started thinking about the finish line. I visualized how it would feel to cross the finish line in record time for me. I would be overjoyed. I thought about that as I breathed in and out. A sense of accomplishment came over me. I had set out to do something positive, and I was doing it. I looked around me for a second. I took in all the scenery around me.

People were cheering us on along the road. I wondered if they were all friends and family of the runners. Then I thought about that for a second. All these people down here and no one would be there to greet me. I got sad for a moment. Although this was a good thing that I was accomplishing, I felt like I had no support system. My only true tie to this place was now gone. My best friend, Ebony. I thought about Ebony, our friendship, and our bond. I really missed her. I knew if she was here, then she would be right there at the finish line with a Margherita in hand.

As I rounded towards the finish, a rush of adrenaline hit me. I felt a surge of energy as I listened to the advice of Abraham Hicks about the power of asking. I took in the scenery once again. I could hear the people cheering. There were only 3 runners ahead of me, and I realized I was going to place in my very first marathon! I got excited and picked up the pace. I noticed the other runners picking up the pace also. At that moment, I found the energy to burst into a full sprint. I passed the other 3 runners in record speed and was in front. I looked back once. I saw the other 3 runners had begun to gain speed. I ran as fast as I could and didn't look back. I got to the finish line, and a bunch of bystanders ran to me in congratulations, all of whom I did not know. What the hell just happened?

It took me a second to realize I had won the race! Here I was, a newcomer to running and I won the whole fucking marathon, what are the odds? After the congratulations were over from strangers, I headed to the winner's circle. I looked over at the other participants. Each person had at least 3 people there to support them. My eyes began to water at the thought of leaving her alone. I looked up. Standing in the far distance, looking back at me was Jaquan. I smiled at him but could not read his face. I noticed he made no steps towards me, so I began walking in his direction. At about five paces, I was rudely interrupted by none other than the Lady about Town Liz herself.

Liz: This is your Lady about Town for WGUR coming to you live again from the Nantucket County Marathon! I'm here with the winner, and who also happens to be first-timer to the marathon world, none other than Tabitha Monroe. Tabby, tell me, how do you feel right now.......

The 5-minute interview started like that and was ended by a ripple of applause from bystanders, followed by several mini-interviews and business cards from news stations promising national interviews in the future. It was all surreal, but all very exciting at the same time. After the crowd cleared, I looked for Jaquan. He was gone. I felt sadness instantly. I didn't know what to expect. Well, yes, I did. In my mind, I expected the crowd to clear, and that he'd be on the other side of the crowd waiting for me. At least that's how it all played out in my mind anyway.

As I walked back to my car, I tried not to focus on the loneliness. I closed my eyes and took in the moment again; I took a deep breath, got happy. All this had happened for a reason, and my life was taking the shape it needed to, and from what I could see, it was getting pretty damn amazing! I had a few properties and half of account #8, which was more than enough money for one person to spend. I figured, at this point in my life, I could write my own ticket. If it wasn't in the cards for me to have a love to share with me at this time, then I would be ok with that. I would have to. I put on some trap music and headed home to rest secretly hoping Jaquan would make contact with me.

As I settled in for the evening, I prepared a bubble bath and a glass of wine. I still had not heard from Jaquan, and I was stilled a little bummed about it. I got on social media and checked his page. His last post was from the night before, where he posted a picture of his boys' night out. That picture had 100 likes already, and comments from desperate young women leaving heart and kitty cat emojis, which was the national symbol for "he can fuck if he wants to."

A wave of jealousy hit me as I saw he liked each comment. I tossed the phone on the couch and took a sip of wine, and picked it back up. I looked at the emojis again. I then looked at the women placing the comments. Some were cute, some were not. I thought about the possibility of him giving it to one of those girls, and I wanted to tear up something! I came to myself and went to my timeline. I took a picture of my medal, and several other pictures from the race and place them on my timeline. I was getting really good at this social media thing.

The rest of the evening was pretty uneventful. After my soak in the tub, I packed a bag in preparation to head to the beach house. Atlanta would be the prime spot to not only relax but to see what momentum I could catch with this victory I just had. Perhaps I could connect with some people of color there that would help steer me in the right direction. The thought alone made me excited for what lied ahead for me. I then talked briefly with Tara and had a lengthier conversation with Samantha. Both went well, and I knew that the thought of having no support was all in my mind.

I also received a call from Lady Liz herself, telling me they would air my interview during the Sunday afternoon show tomorrow. She congratulated me again, and I couldn't wait to see myself on television the next day. I decided to turn in early for the night. It had been a very long day. As a matter of fact, the last 48 hours had been extremely emotional. My body, mind, and soul really needed to rest. I decided to go with my better judgment and turn off all my social media notifications. I laid down for bed and rested peacefully for the first time in a long time.

The next day, I finished preparing for my drive to Atlanta. I didn't know how long I was staying, or even if I'd want to come back at all. Perhaps I could sell the big house. It had no value to me now. That mansion served as a constant memory of the hell I went through over the past 10 years. All I knew is that decision wasn't one that needed to be made right this second, and I was certain the answer would come to me while I was away. Right now, the most pressing thing on my agenda was to watch my interview on camera.

I tuned in a little after twelve. I wanted to make sure that I didn't miss my moment of fame. After several minutes of crime and mayhem, the local news switched gears and focused on the weather. The weatherman talked about a local front heading our way in the next six hours that would bring torrential downpours. I thought it would be best if I headed out in the next couple of hours to get ahead of the storm. I listened intently as the next story unfolded:

"In other news, Rico "Suave" Green was arrested on felony charges of fraud and scam. According to the police, Rico Suave, as he is known, has a history of dating women and getting them to finance his lifestyle. In the latest case, Rico Suave Green is being accused of preying on an elderly woman and scamming her out of $75,000. Mr. Green came to the alleged victim and offered handyman services. Shortly after that, a relationship ensued. The victim's family members were concerned about her due to the age difference in the relationship. After some digging, it was discovered that Mr. Green had helped himself to the victim's bank account. In addition, there is also another pending case in which a young lady is suing Mr. Green for a $5,000 loan that he never paid back. Mr. Green denies all the allegations. If convicted, Rico Suave Green could face up to 25 years in prison."

I couldn't believe my ears. Rico had scammed someone after me, and apparently had a deeper history than I imagined. Well, they say karma is a bitch. Rico better use that gift of gab to keep him honest in prison.

My story was up next. "In other local news, a Jackson County native-born and raised won the Mantucket Marathon with a speed of 2 hrs and 15 minutes setting a new record for that Mantucket Marathon"! How Exciting!

As I listened to the story, they made me feel like quite the hero. I watched myself on camera in amazement, as a part of me felt I was made for it. Perhaps I would take some of these people up on their speaking opportunities and national interviews, what did I have to lose? Lady Liz went on and on about what an accomplishment it was. And they featured me in a good light. I felt proud, and I looked down as the notifications on my phone began to go off. It was congratulatory text messages. A flurry of them. I was really feeling the love.

"And you know we like to always end our news segment on a

positive note, isn't that right, Carol? Why yes, Steve, what do you have for us? Carol, you would love this, it reeks of nothing but love and pure romance, and it's a local story. Well, do tell Steve. Local man claims his undying love for his long-time lover by renting out the tiffany's store."

I looked at the television in shock and disbelief. Could it be? Nah…

"Local corporate guru turned entrepreneur James Taylor proposed to his lifetime love yesterday in the Tiffany's on Sheffield and Clover blvd. According to sources, Mr. Taylor rented out the whole store for the day and allowed his bride to be to pick out any items in the store she wanted. That didn't come without a hefty price, though. Sources say the couple spent over 1.5 million dollars in the store that day, and he proposed to her from a helicopter on top of the store. Ah, how romantic.

Yes, it is Carol. I would love to see what happens with this couple. Well, I'm glad you mentioned it because you'll have your chance. The hot new reality show "A love like ours" has agreed to come to our town and feature this couple in the sext season of the show! They have even asked Celebrity Pastor Doug Chambers to be their spiritual advisor on this journey. How exciting, Steve! Yes, Carol. Very.

I turned off the television. Did I just see what I thought I did? What kind of shit was that? All I knew was, I REFUSED to watch that bullshit.

I heard an engine revving outside my condo. I looked through the window to see Jaquan on a red Harley Davidson Motorcycle. I was impressed. He looked sexy as fuck in his red fitted tee, and black Imperial jeans. My pussy was getting wet just looking out the window. I looked at myself in the mirror real quick to make sure that all the right places he liked would stand at attention. I went outside to greet Jaquan.

Tabby: Nice ride

Jaquan: Yea, something I picked up yesterday after the race. Congratulations, by the way, you did real good. I knew you could.

Tabby: Well thank you

Jaquan: You look pretty

I wanted to melt. Jaquan was never one to mince words. He always told me how sexy and beautiful I was, and to be honest, I had gotten used to that shit. I blushed, and he touched my face. I felt the electrical charge go through my body from his touch. But this wasn't sexual, it was intimate. I felt all of who he was in his touch, and I knew we were connected.

Jaquan: Why don't you take a ride with me? Go on a journey.

Tabby: Right now? To where?

Jaquan: Wherever. Who knows where life will take us. All I know is right now I wanna be with you.

Tabby: But where are we going?

Jaquan: I don't know, it's up to you to decide. Do you want to take this ride with me or not?

I knew exactly what he meant. He wanted to take love's journey. The unspoken didn't need to be said, and this time it was for real. I knew by the way that I felt. I also knew because I could feel his energy, and I knew that he could feel mine. A part of me was scared, but the deeper part of me was calling to him. I wanted him in every way; to be connected to him, to know him, and to love him. I wanted to take love's journey to see where we would end.

Tabby: Ok, I know a place we can go. I was already headed there anyway. Let me get my bag.

Jaquan: Nah baby, that's not necessary. Just hop on the back and let me guide you.

Tabby: But what about my things?

Jaquan: Don't worry, I got you.

Tabby: Jaquan, you don't even know where we're going and what we need.

Jaquan looks at me for a moment. He grabs my hand and draws me in for a kiss.

Jaquan: You're right, I don't know where we're going. But I know where we're headed. And I know that I NEED you in my life. I don't know what your plan was, but I want to walk with you and watch this plan unfold. So, are you gonna take this ride or not? No more questions.

I looked at Jaquan and smiled. I leaned in for a kiss, and he took the palms of his hands and placed them on both sides of my face. He gave me the most passionate kiss that took my breath away. He said:

Jaquan: I told you when I met you that some of us like to ride. The thing about the ride is that things won't always be smooth, but you have to make sure you're dedicated to the ride; to the destination where you're going. I may be young, but I'm ready for all of that. So, you hopping on or what?

I smiled and got on the back of that Harley Davidson. Before he handed me the helmet, he planted another hot kiss on my mouth, then on my cheeks, then forehead. I knew I could fall in love with this man. I put on the helmet, and my body melted into his as I prepared to take the ride of love's journey. As I took in his aroma, I breathed him in and out. The aroma of happy. That epiphany hit me; I was getting back to happy! As he drove in the near distance, I sunk into him and became one with my soulmate that I called happy. I realized that I was in the best place in my life I could be right now. I had found in him a bit of happiness that had superseded anything I had known before. I was getting back to my old self. Yes! I was getting back to happy, and I was somewhere in between almost happy and finally there......

THE END

ABOUT THE AUTHOR

Jaylonna Stevette is a writer, speaker, mentor, entertainer, and entrepreneur who went from a six-figure salary in corporate America to helping others do their life's work. Jaylonna has a bachelor's degree in Psychology and currently working on her MBA. As a spiritualist Jaylonna believes we have the greater power inside of us to change our circumstances dramatically. Jaylonna has been described by many as smart, fierce, sexy and in control. She is known as an executor; one who gets things done.

Born to a single parent of four, Jaylonna understands not only the plight of the single parent, but the many facets of life that being raised in that element brings. Jaylonna had a childhood that was filled with many memories that left a mark on her life and writing and entertainment was her way of creating a safe outlet to express her feelings. Jaylonna's stories are centralized in real life themes that the reader can relate to.

Jaylonna also has had a life-long passionate for those with Autism Spectrum Disorder, as there is a personal connection for her and the diagnosis. Her oldest son Aaron was diagnosed when the disorder was very uncommon. Jaylonna looks to give back in the form of charities and organizations that are passionate about autism and other developmental delays.

Jaylonna's writing style is unique; she likes to expand her writing and her works vary from various fiction genres to Self-help and personal testimonials. As a writer, Jaylonna can tap into diverse streams of her artistic talent to perfect her gift. Jaylonna is often looked at as a risk taker and her work can be seen in the following genres:

- Urban Erotica
- Poetry
- Comedy
- Religious fiction
- Autobiography/biographies
- Self-help
- Spiritual books and readings

Jaylonna began her writing career assisting a local playwright in Columbus, Ohio. In 2012, Jaylonna wrote and produced her first stage play, "The Lounge" which sold out the first weekend. The Lounge had a centralized message about domestic violence that that captivated its audience. In 2014, Jaylonna's play was accepted to the Atlanta Black Theater Festival and the DC Black Theater Festival. Jaylonna has also taken on various roles in the local film industry. In multiple films, Jaylonna served as an extra, Script Supervisor, Set Location Manager, and Unit Production Manager with Awalkonwater Entertainment.

A lot of Jaylonna's writing tends to tie in a central message at the end for her readers. Her writing has exceptional stories that will take you to the depth of your emotions. Jaylonna can add a special touch to her writing and comes down to the level of her readers and they appreciate that.

With a passion for health, Jaylonna has overcome extreme depression. Jaylonna fought her way out of a loveless marriage and shed 75 pounds as a result of finding out who she really was. In doing so, Jaylonna is able to empower women of all ages to be happy and to live the best version of their life that their heart desires. As a writer, speaker, entrepreneur, entertainer, and mentor, Jaylonna brings to the table a host of diverse experiences that she shares with her audience in complete transparency. Her following feels safe with her and Jaylonna's life experience and education combined has been used to help others on their life's journey to achieve greatness.

facebook.com/jaylonnastevette
twitter.com/JStevette
instagram.com/jaylonna_stevette

www.ingramcontent.com/pod-product-compliance
Lightning Source LLC
Chambersburg PA
CBHW070920190726
48292CB00004B/1038